M

Trespass

TRESPASS

Grace Dane Mazur

Graywolf Press
SAINT PAUL, MINNESOTA

Publication of this volume is made possible in part by a grant provided by the Minnesota State Arts Board, through an appropriation by the Minnesota State Legislature, a grant from the Wells Fargo Foundation Minnesota, and a grant from the National Endowment for the Arts. Significant support has also been provided by the Bush Foundation; the Lannan Foundation; Marshall Field's Project Imagine with support from the Target Foundation; the McKnight Foundation; and by other generous contributions from foundations, corporations, and individuals. To these organizations and individuals we offer our heartfelt thanks.

Published by Graywolf Press
2402 University Avenue, Suite 203
Saint Paul, Minnesota 55114
All rights reserved.

www.graywolfpress.org

Published in the United States of America
Printed in Canada

ISBN 1-55597-364-7

2 4 6 8 9 7 5 3 1
First Graywolf Printing, 2002

Library of Congress Control Number: 200196558

Cover design: VetoDesignUSA.com
Cover photograph: ©2002 PhotoDisc, Inc.

I am grateful to many people for their encouragement and for their help with matters of fact and matters of fiction.

My thanks to:

Barry Mazur, Zeke Mazur, Aniko Szatmari, Robert Boswell, Charles Baxter, Stratis Haviaras, Michele Rubin, Elaine Scarry, Pete Baker, Alison Moore, Mimi Herman, Lauren Yaffe, Sadi Ranson, Mark Polizzotti, Paula Panich, Brian Bouldrey, Sarah H. Baker, Heather Hamilton, Daphne Dor-Ner, Zvi Dor-Ner, Blandine Ripert, Nora Stenson, Marian Goldsmith, Ed Howe, Benjamin C. Baker, Tony Millham, Capi Corrales, Ann Georgi, and Angie Warner.

For Barry, Zeke, and Licsi

Trespass

Chapter One

SOMETIMES WE DO THINGS that are not us. But once we do such a thing it becomes and defines us. From that time onward, looking into the fires of darkness, we acknowledge it. Although we may recognize these eruptions even as we are doing them, such consciousness often fails to stop us; driven by passion or possession or divine inspiration, we continue, and only afterwards, exhausted, ponder what has happened.

Maggie Gifford thought the noise that afternoon was just a stray breeze having its way with an unsecured cellar door. The wind had come from the southwest all week, bringing with it the buzzing green heat of the meadows and the smell of the sea. Gusts would burst in the front door, swirl around the kitchen, and trail out through the garden. In spite of the breeze, that mid-June Sunday was relentlessly hot; Maggie's husband, Hugh, had just set off for a week on his boat. Their house was fairly secluded and distant from the county road, and Maggie wasn't wearing anything. As she went to see about the thumping in the basement, she paused in the hallway to feel the warm draft on her bare skin.

Maggie was a tall lanky redhead, with a gorgeous skew to her face. For her nose had been broken in childhood and it remained both important and a bit off center, making her look as though she were tilting her head like a bird, to get a better view of you.

The sun streamed in from the upstairs-hall window catching the single streak of gray in her dark red hair that she wore up in a twist against the heat. With her deep-set eyes, the left one slightly larger, she had that smooth auburn complexion which is rare in New England but often seen in beautiful women of the Mediterranean countries.

The air feathered over her, stirring and soothing and full of questions. She turned slowly and gave her naked back to it, then opened the cellar door to see about the noise.

At the bottom of the cellar stairs she stopped. "What?" she said. "What the hell?"

A naked man was sitting in one of the laundry sinks.

Maggie flinched, startled, but did not move.

They looked at each other.

Later she was not able to explain why she did not yell out or simply run up the stairs and away from him. She knew that was what was called for, but she refused. Instead she stayed put, holding onto a supporting column, glaring at him, angry at the invasion and the ruin of the peacefulness of the summer afternoon.

A scream was coming and she tried to divert it into a cough but it came out as a sputter and a sneeze. She put her hand over her mouth and nose. Crotch and breasts now gave their own instinctive calls for cover. Again she refused. She wondered if she could outwit the absurdity of the situation by choosing a different posture, by avoiding the well-known classical pose of undraped modesty, but she wasn't sure what to do.

Maggie made her arms drop down to her sides. It was her house. She was in place, *he* was out of place. Let *him* cover himself. She sneezed again.

"Bless you," the man said.

She shook her head as if that would clear him away. She glanced at him again. She was sure she had never seen him before. Clearly he had not been there long enough to do much bathing, his face was smudged with dirt though water dripped from his beard, and he seemed all angles and flesh, with his knees up to his chin and his arms bent. Murky water hid his genitals.

The stranger gave her a disarming smile. "Caught in the act," he said. He tried awkwardly to stand, as though he wanted to greet her, or to leave.

"Don't get up," she said, too quickly. Maggie wondered if the man knew that, except for them, the house was empty, that her husband was away. Her cousin Jake would be coming over for supper, but that wasn't for hours yet. Having decided not to try to cover her nakedness with her hands, she cast about for words. "I heard you down here. But I thought it was the wind." She paused to catch her breath, then said, "The breeze gets curious in the afternoon, opening the doors and then slamming them again."

"Tentacles," the man said.

Maggie jumped slightly. "What did you say?" A strand of her hair came loose and fell to her shoulders. Perhaps Jake would wander over early. He often did. But she wasn't sure she wanted to be observed in this situation, this odd geometry.

"I like to think the wind has tentacles," the man explained.

Maggie looked at him more closely and asked, "Do I know you?" She knew that this was the important thing, not whether she was looking at him, or he at her. The man appeared familiar and without menace. But still the cymbals clanged in her ears, reminding her of her nakedness.

"I don't think so."

"What?" she said.

"I don't think you know me."

Maggie fought back a smile. She wondered if the man could see the humor here. "Look," she said suddenly. "Wouldn't you rather bathe in the tub upstairs?" Oh, God, why had she said that? She was in for it now.

"I don't use bathtubs," he said.

"Oh," she said, relieved and puzzled. "Why not?"

"I'd rather not talk about it."

"Oh. I see." She was lying. She didn't see.

Maggie did know that whenever the dailiness of life had lulled her into thinking that she knew all of its habits, things would erupt in unforeseen configurations. She was not afraid of this man, but it flustered her that his small conversational rudeness—the abruptness of his refusal to explain about bathtubs—seemed to have given him the upper hand. No matter, he was starkers and an intruder and folded into her own laundry tub, and even though she was naked and fifty years old and alone in the house, she was strong and she knew how to kick, and besides, there was a long-handled shovel leaning on the wall right behind her. Another strand of auburn hair had come undone; she tried to tuck it back, then unpinned her hair entirely and shook it about until her neck and shoulders were covered. Then she coiled it all up again and pinned it into place. She stood up tall and full of ligaments, resting her hand on one of the low beams overhead, a shaft of dusty sunlight catching her narrow face. She peered at him and decided not to ask him who he was; that would be too easy and, in the end, not very revealing.

The man now grinned at her as though they were in collusion. "You wouldn't have any Scotch, would you?" he said.

This grin of his was premature, Maggie thought. She was so surprised and grateful, however, for his suggestion of a drink, that she almost forgave him for it. She wondered why he didn't feel as tentative as she did, inching her way into the peculiarity of this visit. She realized then that she had decided to go through with it, whatever *it* was, and follow wherever it would lead, a decision at once comforting and terrifying. Still, she would be happier if he were behaving in a more helpless manner, vulnerable and folded up in a strange sink— but she decided to let him have his little victories. She was saving up. "Scotch whisky? she replied. "I suppose I might. Are you asking me to get you some?"

"God, yes. Most humbly." Again the radiant smile of a man who charms women too easily and pretends to be unaware. She had known that type of man and look, and presumed that past exposure meant current protection. She held back her own smile until she had turned her back to him and was climbing the stairs to the kitchen.

Alone in front of the liquor cabinet she shivered and asked herself what was going on. She thought of her husband but knew that this was between her and her visitor. She filled a glass with water from the tap and gulped it, then looked in the broom closet and considered an apron, but that was ludicrous. A raincoat from the front-hall closet was a possibility, but that, too, had a silly aspect, and with either one it would be clear she had lost. For at some point, she didn't know when, it had become a contest of wills. Besides, to dress at this point would lack a certain fairness. She poured two glasses of Scotch. Before going downstairs she threw a dish towel over her shoulder; it had a border of green frogs. It didn't cover her; she didn't feel clothed, just amuletted.

They drank slowly, careful to watch each other's faces. He was so dirty she wondered where he had been. He smelled of earth and sweat and some sort of machine oil.

"Shall I scrub your back?" she said.

"I can think of worse things," he said.

Immediately she asked herself if she had really made such a bizarre offer. She had always hoped her body would give out before her mind. Her position of standing uncovered, except for a dish towel on her left shoulder, several feet away from this man's unclothed presence now seemed a haven of safety compared to the act of bathing him. She wondered if there was anyone in the world who would understand what she was about to do. But she had made the offer and it had been accepted.

The room smelled of iron-scented steam, of dank and shaded underground space, of unwashed male. Maggie rinsed a sponge under the hot tap of the second sink then rubbed it on a bar of olive-colored soap. As she lathered his back, he lowered his head onto his knees, holding his half-empty glass out to the side. Her long bony body, summer-darkened around the lighter shadow of bathing suit, hovered over his broader, folded one. His back and neck were tanned, his legs and knees pale above the graying water. She could feel his back through the sponge as she scrubbed—shoulder blades, vertebrae. She filled a tin cup from both taps and poured it down his spine to rinse off the gray-green foam. As she soaped his neck she tried to remember when she had last bathed someone. Each of her four children, decades earlier. This was different, though, this undeserved intimacy. When she rinsed his neck, his hair got wet. Black, streaked with gray, it needed cutting.

"Hair?" she asked.

"Might as well," he said. "While we're at it."

It wasn't just the oddness of the situation; it was more that she didn't know what had caused her to burrow into such subservience.

Was it subservience at all, or had she just been daring herself? Besides, bathing oneself in a laundry tub must be so awkward. She put the bar of soap on his head and worked up a foam.

"Lean back," she said. She rinsed his head into the other sink. "There. I'll just go up and get you a towel."

Upstairs, taking a large white towel from the linen closet she pictured him wrapped up in it; she was eager to have him covered up and dressed and out of her house and away, returning her cleft afternoon to her so that she could weave it back together.

But when she returned to the basement he was gone. Wet tracks led across the cement floor, footprints and splash marks. The door to the outside stood wide open. Had he run off naked into the woods, carrying his clothes wadded into a bundle? There in the laundry sink, the gray scummy water drained slowly. His empty glass hung on the hot-water tap, tilted upside down. She sniffed it: he hadn't rinsed it out.

At the cellar door, the thick towel intended for her visitor now draped over her, Maggie looked out into the shimmering daylight, wondering what she had done. She could not see anyone. Branches swayed, leaves glinted, flecks of pollen drifted—as though all of nature conspired to obscure her view.

Chapter Two

THAT EVENING, JAKE BEECHER WALKED along the river on the way to Maggie Gifford's house for dinner. He took the marsh route on purpose, so that he wouldn't be tempted to run to her place. He was full of the urgency of love. The fact of his love for Maggie pierced his life. It had come in waves ever since he could remember, and this summer it was stronger and sharper than he could bear.

Maggie and Jake were first cousins and had spent their summers together as children on their grandparents' farm. This was on the Cranford River in southeastern Massachusetts, between New Bedford and Fall River. Now they lived on the adjacent properties made from that farm, and Maggie had grandchildren and Jake was a middle-aged remittance man and fly-by-night minister. And they still told each other just about everything that was in their hearts—with the crucial exception that Jake had never told her of his love. He wasn't sure, exactly, what had made him decide that it was *now time*. Perhaps it was the confluence of his fiftieth birthday the week before and Maggie's husband setting off in the morning on a sailing trip, but suddenly hesitation seemed a mortal luxury, and silence not discretion but coyness.

Now Jake forced himself to walk slowly along the margin of the river, carrying his bottle of wine.

⌣·

Jake was a man of the edges and shallows, the swampy places where the marshes are sliced by gutters, those thin canals made by the government during the Depression to drain the salt grass and discourage mosquitoes. Few people love the shallows: farmers prefer dry fields far inland, while offshore fishermen follow the deep blue whale paths out at sea. But Jake leaned toward this rich shifting boundary, which had freed itself from definition as earth or water. Here he could jump his kayak over a sunken log, or pole his way through the reeds by the sweet reeking fertile mud of the shore, among blue crabs, quahogs, egrets, and in the fierce company of swans.

Along these margins, too, Jake had a few seasonal pursuits that brought in a bit of money, like the kayak and canoe rental that he operated in a boat shack at the edge of his land, and a small patch of cannabis, covered by scrub oak and fertilized by guano, that he cultivated out on a small rocky island that he owned in the middle of the Cranford River.

But his only year-round lucrative hook into the world of ordinary finance was his position as a remittance man; that is, his parents paid him a small quarterly salary to stay out of Newport, Rhode Island, where they lived. This was also his only contact with his parents— except for the yearly phone call at Christmastime. Jake did abide by the agreement, and kept away from Newport, except when his friend, Sally, would beg him to have dinner with her in a seedy part of town: a meal, a few drinks, a spin around the Viking Tower, and they were gone.

Jake's work as a minister only rarely helped his finances. He did not feel that he was a holy man and he called himself "fly-by-night," though he was really "mail-order." He had became a minister only because a friend had asked him long ago if he would perform her wedding. She didn't want the cops to do it, she said, meaning the powers of the State, and she didn't want the holies. Jake told her he wouldn't do "Jesus," and he wouldn't do "Obey." She gave him the address of a place in California that offered to transform him, for $19.50, into a minister, legal in all states.

Jake knew for that first wedding he needed more information about how the ceremony should go, so he took a bath, trimmed his beard, filled his truck with gas, and drove up to Boston. A friend at Harvard loaned him an ID card so he could browse the Divinity School library. Jake was unprepared for the icons by the doorway, the bronze heads of saints and holy scholars on the walls. Gandhi shocked him, looming from a painting in the stairwell, large as life. Jake felt like an impostor and waited for the sculpted heads to laugh, for Gandhi to raise his bony arm from the canvas and point a skinny finger. As Jake gathered books on Christian and Jewish rituals, Greek and Roman ceremonies, the anthropology of weddings, his legs seemed to twitch and he was afraid he would start to bellow or dance. He wished he had brought Maggie's husband, Hugh, along with him. Jake had always been afraid of librarians and here there were saints lurking in the bookstacks; the floors made of thick green glass glowed like icebergs, illuminated from below.

～.

Although he had cobbled together a fine wedding ceremony for his friend, Jake never found a sect he felt close to. His mail-order religious organization, *The Church of Universal Light*, was a dubious California Protestant outfit that sent him advertisements offering three doctoral degrees for the price of two—complete with diplomas suitable for framing. The cult Jake finally devised for himself had only two rules: no celibacy, no followers. People kept coming to see him, though— even when they didn't need a ritual performed—and some of them would actually pay him for listening to their stories—by bringing food, or broken stereos, or rusty old tools for his garden work.

～.

Jake's true calling was in his gardens; there was the one place where the fertility of his mind resulted in the glory of matter. He had always been a gardener—even his very short career at Harvard College had been devoted to botany. So, while his visitors told him what was con- voluting them, he weeded and prodded the soil, letting it tell him dark secrets as he inhaled that sweet green oxygen-loaded air given off by the leaves.

He planted moon gardens with white flowers that glowed in the nighttime, and a blue garden, which seemed to disappear except at midday. He dug a pool, heaping the edges with rocks to trap the sun, and there he grew flowers from the tropics of the Amazon, gaudy and strident, raucous as parrots. He grew cucumbers and tomatoes and zucchini over tall trellises where one could walk inside and pluck the dangling fruits.

And each year, for his cousin Maggie's birthday, he constructed a secret room in the forest for her delight.

～·

Aside from gardens, Jake's private sect had no tenets, only observances. Early each morning he would go down to salute the river. There he studied the slip and thrust of the tide. He would look for the great blue heron and listen to the swoop of the gristled fabric of its wings as it flapped away beyond the promontory. Suddenly green things proclaimed the light. Dogs barked welcome to the sun as it rushed onto the far shore. Then Jake would walk home to make his breakfast.

In the evenings he went back down to the river to put it to bed. You might not know that this was his observance if you saw him. You might just say to yourself: *What's he up to, the scruffy bearded guy, standing there—too long—by the river?* How long would he stand there? Long enough to be present, to face it, to stay. Long enough for the mind to settle and its parts to unlock. Habit has a strange way of turning into ritual.

～·

Jake's being a minister bothered some of his friends, and sometimes, in private, gulping with shyness, they would ask him if he prayed. He would respond by asking them what they meant by prayer: Christians kneel briefly, Buddhists kneel for days, Jews stand and sway, Moslems prostrate themselves. Yogis seem to go through all of the above when they salute the sun. Jake was pretty sure he did not pray. The only time he knelt was in the garden, and the happiness that settled on him then came from the smell of earth mold and from breathing in the oxygen given off by the plants as they went about their photosynthetic business. This was the delirium of matter, he thought. Alone at the beach, sometimes he danced a little. But there had to be no one else around to catch sight of a disheveled middle-aged man hopping at the edge of the water—awkward and humiliating.

For Jake, the dimensions of silent prayer were Entreaty, Gratitude, Awe. "Please." "Thank you." "Oh." He would tell his embarrassed friends that even the most devout atheists get into situations of beggared crisis where they say to themselves, or to some undefined other: "No. Don't let it happen. Make it OK." We chant this to ourselves. Where do we learn it? In infancy. It is something we would call from the crib, holding onto the bars, knocking the headboard rhythmically against the wall.

Jake's friend, Sally, who had spent some years teaching English in Japan, told him that one of the first words she learned in Japanese was *Itadakimasu,* which is said before taking the first mouthful of a meal. Roughly translated, it means, "I partake"—in the sense of gratitude, rather than "here goes" and doesn't imply or invoke a God. It is a useful thing, this form of Godless grace, and sometimes Jake found himself mind-muttering it before certain meals, or on the verge of grand happenings, when he was swamped with gratefulness or overcome with being.

But mostly Jake was an idolater. He worshipped the created thing rather than the creator. Light. He couldn't help a sharp intake of breath at sunset, or an awestruck concentration at the grays and greens and sands of Horseneck Beach when the mist rolls in over the Knubble, that elephantlike outcropping of rock at the harbor mouth.

These things he called prayer were a diminishing progression: from the short supplications, to a single word of gratitude, to a gasp of wonder. Perhaps you don't need more than an exhalation to make a prayer, as long as some time-taking hesitation is there, allowing focus or recognition. Remember, though, that not every gasp is a prayer. Some are simply for stubbing your toe on the way to the bathroom in the middle of the night. Some are for when you didn't see a visitor waiting quietly in the shadow by the kitchen door.

～･

The ancient Greeks described a condition known as Noon Panic. Think of walking along a meadow in the middle of the day. It is summer. Cicadas are drilling. Amber-colored grasshoppers spurt from the weeds as you step. The sky is intense beyond sapphire or lapis. All noises drop away into silence. A quiver runs up your spine until the back of your neck prickles and your hair stands on end. Gasping, you look at your watch: exactly noon. Hidden in the nearby brambles someone is spying on you, laughing. That old goat-faced god of fields and woods and flocks, of pastoral orgies and stampede mischief. That cloven-hoofed maker of skittishness and startle.

Noon panic occurs at that moment when shadows are reduced to nonbeing and the light floods us, dazzling all our senses. The real reason, then, for our terror is that the soul of the universe is suddenly visible. This is what blinds us and makes our hair stand on end. This is what makes desert wanderers erect a sheet on poles, so they do not have to gaze on it. At the equator, when the sun is overhead, the traveler looks down into a well at his peril.

⌣·

That June evening Jake tried to force himself to walk slowly with his bottle of red wine for his cousin. But soon he was jumping the little canals and loping over the spongy salt grass. Finally he climbed the log steps up from the river. The air had cooled a bit and the meadow grass brushed against his legs, damp and fragrant.

"Maggie! Where are you?" Jake called out as he neared the house. "Oh, Maggins. There is so much I have . . ."

But Maggie rushed out of the house and didn't let him finish. "Oh, I'm so glad you're here," she said. She gave him a hug that felt far too gentle. "Come in. Oh, God, I need you. Something so strange has happened. You have to listen to me." She stopped to catch her breath, and Jake understood that his own message would have to wait.

Sometimes sexual desire can be a blackness in which our animal selves—bestial spirits—slither over and around one another, until the light of rationality comes to rout them, leaving us poor souls for a while with nothing but persistent and maddening afterimages.

Jake blinked several times to clear his vision, then put his hand on Maggie's shoulder to calm her—and to steady himself—and they went inside. There, at the kitchen table, drinking the red wine he had brought in celebration, Maggie's excitement about her visitor burned away, for that evening at least, any possible mention of Jake's love and his desire. In a fever, she told him of the man in the cellar and asked him what it could possibly mean.

Jake Beecher had experienced noon panic all his life. However, as Maggie recounted to him the story of the man in the laundry sink, a new form of chronopathy set in, and Jake began to panic every hour. Whenever the minute hand pointed due north.

It is like the moment before you hear the fire-engine siren, or the time between the cuts of the blades of a helicopter. That pulse of pressure preceding something grave. A state of soul shudder for a few moments and then it leaves you. A sigh escapes, a lopsided grin.

For most of that strange summer, Jake did not know how to avoid the onset of his hourly fright. When he stood watching the dawn sweep over the river, or when he bent over his garden, or when he rode the afternoon waves at Horseneck Beach—even then the shuddery time could come and he would be raked by longing.

Chapter Three

THE TERM LOVE TRIANGLE, though evocative and useful, is probably incorrect and only those who are inside complex configurations are so limited in perspective that things seem three-sided to them. But from the outside, the patterns of love are often seen to more closely resemble the interlocking mosaic-tiling patterns of the great Moorish palaces and mosques, with their interwoven stars and crosses and diamonds.

While Maggie had a French or Italian air about her, her husband Hugh was tall and thin and New England. Sweet-souled, angular-bodied, he loved Maggie and his books and his boat. They were a close couple, even during the events of that summer, and although the farmhouse they lived in had many rooms and ells and nooks, they tended to gravitate toward each other during the day, despite the varied projects that occupied them. Through the day they would call to each other in that chirping song of unfinished sentences, in the haiku of long intimacy.

Early in their marriage, Hugh had taught history at a private school in Providence, but when Maggie's parents died there was enough money for him to leave teaching and become the historian of the town of Cranford, a hopelessly unsalaried position. But he loved history, no matter how small, and was perpetually writing up his notes for the historical society about minor religious cults in Southern New England. He also bought a decrepit secondhand bookstore at the edge of town. He had always collected books—obscure, sometimes perverse—and had turned the ground floor of their old cow barn into a library, installing pine shelves from floor to ceiling and then steel tracks around the top for his wheeled library ladder to hook onto.

When he wasn't sailing, Hugh would go on gathering expeditions to yard sales, country auctions, or to the town dump, which he called "The Gift Shop." And when he brought the books home he would scrub them with soap to remove the mildew; then he would lay them out on the grass to let them dry. The odor never went away completely, and his library always had a scent of old mustiness combined with remembered hygiene. After he had completed lugging in and washing a new carload of books he would go to Maggie, who would drop whatever she was doing so that she could rub his shoulders.

In deepest winter Hugh and Maggie would go on long walks in the woods, often lasting for hours. Sometimes Jake would walk with Hugh, when Maggie was busy; he enjoyed Hugh's company, and considered him one of his closest friends. The fact of Jake's perpetual longing for Hugh's wife had long inhabited a different part of Jake's brain and only rarely emerged to induce a painful shimmer of jealousy while the two men were together.

When winter was over, as soon as water and air had softened and warmed a bit, Hugh would sail his wooden boat, a 28-foot Hinckley, weaving in and out along the coast and over to the islands. The boat was Hugh's territory; he loved to be alone on it, which was fine because Maggie almost never sailed with him, not liking the smell of the cabin, and not submitting to the orders necessary to be good crew. Although she didn't, as a rule, go sailing, every Sunday Maggie would explore the local rivers by kayak or canoe. She would go with Jake and with friends or whichever of her children happened to be visiting. She often said that her deciding not to go sailing with Hugh was what kept them so happy with each other. They never fought, there was nothing to fight about, though they often wove teasing into their love.

When Maggie joked with Hugh about the amount of time he spent scavenging at the town landfill, he would tease her back about her clothes. She really didn't dress so terribly—it was just that things had to look old or broken-in before she would wear them. Hugh accused her of aging her new clothes, like wine, hanging them for years in the back of the closet before she would put them on. Then, too, he called her his beloved spider lady, as she was always working with threads or yarns, knitting sweaters, or constructing sculptures out of cloth. Hugh complained that when she was working on a large piece, she would not listen to him or respond; he joked that she had spiraled out of herself and into the object she was working on, and said she mustn't forget where she was and sew herself into her embroidery. "How will I get you out again?" he would ask her, laughing.

Chapter Four

THE DAY AFTER HER STRANGE VISITOR, Maggie was puzzled and jumpy. She found herself missing Hugh intensely and wishing he would telephone so that she could tell him what had happened. She wanted to know why that man had been bathing in her basement. Who was he, and what did he look like with clothes on? How did he carry himself when he wasn't folded into a soapstone tub?

The following day, Maggie called her friends and asked them for lunch, thinking she might find, in their gossip, mention of her visitor. When they left, she spent an hour walking up and down the the main street of Cranford, hoping to run across him.

Finally she went to see Jake. She found him weeding his stand of oriental poppies.

"Do you think it's just that I don't recognize him?"

"Who?" Jake said, stalling for time, waiting for sweet rationality to descend on him. His love for Maggie made him want to help her through this, but it also cut him with bitterness. He had been fine when Maggie had told him about her adventure, even though it had meant not announcing his own love for her. But later that night, when he had taken himself home, he found himself burning and raw. If Maggie was to be bathing any naked man besides her husband, well, wasn't *he* next? Didn't his years of patient adoration count for anything? He felt demoted and crushed and vowed to himself that he would never bring up the subject of the stranger in order to increase the chances of Maggie's forgetting all about him. Jake had been unable to sleep, wondering what would become of them all.

"Oh, stop. Look, I've only seen him naked," Maggie said. "He could be anybody."

"Are you terribly sure that he isn't just a figment of your decaying imagination?" he asked, smiling to try to show that it was a joke. But then he went on. "These are the wanton desperate hopes of middle age. Naked men don't just materialize like that. Naked women don't bathe them."

"Oh, but they do," she said. "I did."

"You never told me what he looks like," Jake said, growing redfaced with the effort of staying calm and sweet. Where was the woman, he wondered, who would trespass nude in his basement? He didn't think women did that sort of thing.

"Well, he had a beard. And greenish eyes. But I can't describe him really; I don't know his stance. With Hugh or you, for example, if you are walking toward me from miles down the beach, even when you are made tiny by distance, I know it's you. You have a sort of rooted way of walking. And Hugh is sort of twisty. I don't have words for it, but I recognize you both. But with this guy, I don't know how he stands or walks."

"What does he sound like?"

"From here, or Westport, or Tiverton. Southeastern Mass. or coastal Rhode Island. But then, he didn't say very much."

"And you? Did you talk much?" Jake regretted the way these words sounded, prurient and bitter, and hoped Maggie wouldn't notice. He dug with his trowel, hitting a stone.

"Hardly at all. It didn't seem to be called for."

Jake kept quiet. He wondered if perhaps it would have been safer if they had talked more, done less. Or put some clothes on, for Christ's sake. Why couldn't she have done that?

"Jake?"

"Mmmn?" The stone was larger than he had thought.

"Do you think there is something I could have done to get him to talk, or to stay a while longer? Why did he run away?"

Jake put down his trowel, on top of the pile of weeds he had unearthed. He stood up slowly, brushing off the knees of his jeans, then rubbing the small of his back with his fists.

"Oh, God, I'm stiff. Why did he leave, your man? Oh, I don't know. Come, let's walk a bit." He rubbed his hands on his shirttail and then put a hand lightly on Maggie's shoulder to direct her to the part of his garden that he wanted to show her.

The following day, when Maggie came home from her errands and searches, her kitchen looked cleaner, or dirtier, or differently arranged. It was like the time that Hugh had shaved his beard and what she noticed was only a smudge of dirt on his cheek, not the absence of the hair that once covered it.

The bulletin board over the kitchen phone caught her eye just as the phone rang. It was Hugh, calling from Martha's Vineyard. She was bursting to tell him her story and to have him laugh about it with her. She realized, though, as he told her about his sail and the beauty of his anchorage the night before, that she couldn't bring up the subject of bathing someone who had appeared without clothing or introduction in their basement. She blushed, even though there was no one to see her.

"Hugh? Did you take that one? I've just noticed it. What a nice picture."

"What, dear? What are you talking about?"

"Well, it's a snapshot of a blue heron standing in the marsh and I don't remember ever seeing it before. It's here on the bulletin board in the kitchen." She unpinned the photo and held it up to the light and described it to him.

"Nope," he said. "Couldn't be mine I'm afraid. Haven't taken a picture since the children came last summer. Must be one of yours?"

"Right," she said. "Perhaps I just forgot."

But it wasn't right. She didn't forget photographs she had taken. They talked for a few more minutes and she smiled to hear him, but there was some mantling feeling that she had been looking forward to, which always came when she talked to Hugh, that was missing this time.

"Call me, my love," she said. "Call me soon."

Moments later when she reached over the sink for a pan to fry up some onions, she realized that her smallest skillet was missing. She remembered hanging it there in the morning.

Maggie began to inspect the kitchen. She found herself tiptoeing and silently opening drawers and cabinets, as though her body had already made the decision not to tell anyone that things were out of place; as though she didn't want to alert anyone, even though no one was there. Besides, almost nothing was missing: a stick of butter, two red-skinned potatoes, an onion, and the old spatula with the nicked blade. She knew that Hugh had not taken them, as they had all been there after he had left on his boat.

She felt one of those flickering private joys that bring on the ghost of a smile: if things were gone, then her visitor had been back to take them. He had left the photograph of the heron in exchange.

~·

The property of Hugh and Maggie Gifford was the land adjacent to Jake Beecher's, the other half of their grandfather Beecher's farm. Now both places were used for pasture and for cornfields, with cows and corn belonging, by arcane contracts and legal arrangements, to a local farmer.

It had been a week. As Maggie walked down the half-mile driveway to check her mailbox, she wondered if there would be some message from her bathing visitor, or if she would spot him in the undergrowth. Above, the trees arched summer-heavy branches into an infinite doorway of dappled light and shadow. It was a morning full of doorways: the sagging iron gate at the cow meadow; at every small field a stile—each one a whimsical construct of tree trunks and slender logs, put there in order to sieve cows from humans. But such stiles all depend on the mood of the animals, their tameness or placidity. Any reasonable cow with a mind to it could smash through the thin logs, the sapling gates.

There was no mail. As Maggie walked back to the house, clouds purpled over the cornfield; a pair of gulls caught a salient of light and appeared to glow from within.

~·

She wondered where Hugh was. The midmorning flies were thick on her typewriter but her flyswatter was floppy and swaybacked and it

would no longer kill properly. Generally she wrote letters, occasionally poems. They weren't deep poems; she refused to get all meta-
physical, as she told Jake, though sometimes they seemed to flip out
of the plane where she had meant them to be and into some other
place, against her will and without her participation. Her poems were
of daily life, and she wanted them to stay that way: about potholes in
the driveway, about a head of lettuce brought by a friend when the
woodchuck had gnawed her own lettuces down to pale innocent
stubble. They would disagree, Maggie and Jake, about the tight mental clamps she put on her poems. He thought her poems were rather
like her gardens, hobbled by guilt or functionality. Their discussions
about poetry were like a cat's cradle of arguments, with new and
complex figures arising out of old and simple moves. That day she
was working on a poem about the town dump and the way Hugh collected things there.

> Plucking books and veiled hats
> out of garbage
> dumpsters full of folded cardboard
> he steps delicately over discarded
> truck tires serpenting
> up through clay and smells,
> hiding heads and tails
> while oily fumes make midday fever
> in ashcans choked with green glass
> curated by those solemn charlatans,
> seagulls, proud
> of their dominion

But the words were sticking in her mind like cobwebs, ungraspable
but gluey with too many connections: they wouldn't be guided and
they wouldn't let go. Finally she left the poem, which shamed her,
and went out to the garden to gather lettuce for her lunch, and to
plant some more.

Maggie never showed her writing to her daughter, Gillian, because Gillian was a poet and took such things too seriously. But her
other daughter, Connie, was lean and sweet and had a mind like a

whippet. Connie would race through these badly written lines and ask her mother charitably where her brain had been, and then they would laugh. All four children were due to arrive in a few days, with their spouses and their children. The place would be full. Hugh would be back.

When Maggie came in from the garden with a basket full of salad greens, there was her visitor, sitting calmly at the round kitchen table, as though he had been invited. He stood to greet her. She was still dazzled by the sunlight of the garden and it took some moments for her to see him clearly. He wore a cobalt blue shirt, jeans, old running shoes.

"Bath time already?" Maggie said. She didn't want to show how pleased she was to see him, but knew she was uncontrollably smiling.

"Actually, I was hoping it was lunchtime," he said. "Don't you wonder where I've been?"

"Are you being chased?" she asked. "You disappeared."

"I know," he said. "I do that." He gave a sheepish grin. "No. I don't think anyone is after me. Look, for all you know I have a day job in Fall River or even Providence, and just come here on weekends."

It was true; the last time had also been a weekend.

"Ah," she said. "For all I know they're looking for you in seven states, none of them contiguous."

"Why would they be looking for me?"

She didn't know how to reply; the real answer was that *she* had been looking for him.

"Are you hungry?" she asked.

"You know what I really yearn for?" he said. "I really yearn for soup. Do you happen to have any?" As a matter of fact, she said, she did have a sort of minestrone that Hugh had made before he left. She took it from the freezer, then turned to look at him. His hair looked neater; he'd gotten a haircut. "Do you . . ." she hesitated, suspecting that he didn't like direct questions. "Do you come up from the river? Or do you come in from the road?"

He shrugged and gestured with his hands in a way that could have meant anything.

She saw it wasn't going to be simple. While the soup was heating she made toast, a green salad.

"I said 'soup'," he said, serving himself. "Not a whole meal." Luckily, he smiled.

"Of course you did," she said, brushing the air and his statement with her wooden spoon. "But I wanted greens and toast as well, they are correct with soup. You can suit yourself." She set the table with white plates, earthenware bowls.

She watched him eat. He probably snored. What? Where had that thought come from? "Do you snore much?" she asked.

"No one has ever accused me," he said, casting her one of his looks, as though he understood her, an expression she found at first calming and then bothering.

"I suppose you have a name?" she said. This felt even more hazardous. Perhaps the time for names had passed.

He said, "Aren't you asking things in the wrong order?"

She shrugged, poured them each some iced tea from the blue glass pitcher.

He stood up:

"John."

Maggie looked at him, relieved at the ordinariness.

"Hiram."

She watched his face; there was no reason for him to make this up. He looked slightly sheepish. She wondered why he even told her this one.

"Stuart."

She eyed him and wondered if he was nearing the end. Family naming had always been a mystery to her.

"Grenville," he said.

"Well, then," Maggie said. "Is that all?"

He put out his hand.

She shook it. "How do you do, John Hiram Stuart Grenville. Couldn't you have a normal name? What do your friends call you?"

"Stu," he said. "Or Grenville."

"Now, you are supposed to ask me my name," she said, pointing her teaspoon at him.

"I suppose I should. But I would be very surprised if you weren't Margaret Beecher Gifford."

At this she cocked her head; she looked at him and refused to ask how he knew.

He looked at his watch. "I've got to be off," he said. "Thank you for the lunch. And the company." He slipped out the garden door and was gone. Again she wondered if she had omitted to say that crucial thing which would have made him stay, or allowed him to linger.

⌣·

That afternoon she searched the farm. She peered into lean-tos, hutches, outbuildings; there were so many places where Grenville could be staying. Each of them had been used by her children and then her grandchildren, as clubhouses, hideouts, love nests. At the edge of the west meadow the woodpile looked larger, more orderly. She wasn't sure. In front of the wineberries the grass looked trampled, as though a large animal had slept there. She couldn't tell. She was hunting for spoor. She caught the door of the old outhouse swinging slightly, as though someone had just left. It could have been the wind. She didn't know if he was in hiding from the world or simply from her; how could she find him unless she knew? She hated being at the mercy of his appearances.

Chapter Five

HUGH GIFFORD CAME HOME THAT EVENING, sunburned and happy from his sail. Maggie hadn't made dinner and suggested they go out to the local restaurant. She had been too jittery and weak to cook, although she didn't put it that way to Hugh. She was bashful now about not having told him about bathing Grenville when they spoke over the phone, and she was planning to tell him over dinner about that and the more recent visitation at lunch today. Hugh would help her figure it all out, she thought; he would appreciate its strangeness and perhaps defuse it.

"You ready, dear?"

"Yes, I'm ready, are you?"

"Shall we go?"

"Let's."

From the front door to the car along the narrow stone path between the shrubs, he would go first. Or she would go first. Always within a pace or two, within seconds of each other. Maggie had once said to Jake that this was what marriage was—among other things: it was timing. The constant aligning of two beings so they were always ready at the same time.

Jake had avoided getting married. He worried about such parallel arrangements for himself, and wondered what such simultaneity did to Maggie and to Hugh. Perhaps it wasn't permanent: when Hugh was off on his boat, Maggie's own tempo drifted—she got up earlier, went to bed later, if at all. Perhaps her timing was more like his own, Jake thought, than like Hugh's.

⌣·

Maggie had thought she would tell Hugh of her visitor and her odd reaction to him as soon as they got to The Fluke, but it was crowded with people they knew and they stopped and chatted before sitting down.

In the end, the restaurant was not private enough for Maggie to tell Hugh about bathing a stranger. She would wait and tell him after dinner. He would like it. He often brought home stories of his encounters with the boatyard girls, those young women who hang around the marina offering to help scrape and paint boats in exchange for company or money or almost anything. He would also meet sailors and sailing couples picnicking on uninhabited islands; families wanting to share their pickles or root beer or some other food he had not known he was missing.

Jake was at The Fluke, too, with Sally, his sometime girlfriend. They were together that night, but arguing about their future, and thus would soon be apart. In those days Jake could rarely see Sally's charms, and whenever he could, it was only because they had fought and she had left him. Unlike Maggie and Hugh, Sally and Jake never teased and always fought. What Sally loved in Jake were his obsessions with gardens and with the edges of rivers. His observances. She saw in him some brilliant core that others never glimpsed, seeing only a man on the margins. Jake was puzzled by Sally's love, and curious that she would think him worthy of attention. Often, however, his desire for his cousin Maggie set up such a clangor in his brain that he forgot how to focus on Sally.

Sally was a car salesman. That is, she owned a Volvo dealership. When Jake first met her, ten years earlier, she had been twenty-seven. Having just returned from teaching English in Asia, she was a graduate student in Providence, at the Rhode Island School of Design. And when she wasn't working on her thesis on ephemeral art— performance art, fireworks, and such—she did odd things with trees. She would make recordings of poetry, and put the tapes in boom boxes, high up in trees on the campus of Brown University and at RISD. At twilight she would turn them all on by remote control. By the time it got dark, groups of people could be found, standing at the base of an oak or a maple, looking, intent and listening, up into the branches. Only when you were next to the trunk could you hear it: the tree talking, reciting poetry in what seemed to be the tree's own voice. Clusters of listeners would wander through the night, from tree to tree, to hear different poems. To come upon a tree reciting poetry seemed magical and a bit frightening.

Sally was happy as a graduate student until her parents did an absurd thing: her father ran off—with her mother. They had both turned seventy. They had been good for too long, they explained, and now they wanted to see the country and settle in the Southwest. They sold their house, purchased a criminally ugly recreational vehicle, and signed over the Volvo dealership to Sally.

The night she had first heard about it, she complained to Jake. "What do I know about internal combustion?" She sputtered tears. "Women don't sell cars." They were having supper, as always, at The Fluke. The only other restaurant in town served Jell-O salad with little marshmallows and they were too young to go there.

Jake argued that selling cars wouldn't be so bad. Sally didn't have to be like other car dealers; she could invent it as she went along. She could bring performance art into the showroom. Actually Jake didn't understand performance art and they often argued about it. He would tell her that he just couldn't get interested in people who chose to dress themselves all in lightbulbs. He was puzzled rather than thrilled by the people who powdered their bodies white and then hung themselves naked from high office buildings. "Look," she would tell him. "Watch it now, because you'll never see it again."

But when she heard what her parents had done, she wept to Jake, and they argued about cars. "Would you do it?" she asked. "Would you sell automobiles for a living?"

She did have a point, Jake thought, but he countered, saying, "I'd make such a lousy salesman. Car people don't have organically grown and fertilized beards, like mine. I'm too messy. In order to sell new cars you have to be kempt. You are better at that."

Sally wept. She poked her ice cream with her fork, mashing it into her strawberry-rhubarb pie. "I know I'm a spoiled piece of shit not to want it. That makes it even worse. Millions of starving people would be happy to have their own car business, but it feels like a boulder rolling down onto my life."

Jake gentled a bit and pointed out that Volvos sell themselves—she wouldn't have to know anything, she could stock up on *Consumer Reports* and other car magazines and let her customers do the reading. She should view it as a way to pay for school. "Just think," he said. "A salary!" They didn't know many people with salaries. Around their part of Cranford it was, as Jake's grandfather always said, mostly barter and disability, eke and scramble.

When Sally took over Roger Williams Volvo, all the salesmen quit, except for Alfonso, who was gay. She kept him on and promoted him to manager. In turn, he made her jettison her faded jeans and T-shirts and took her shopping for tailored clothes, gray suits with subtle patterns. He went with her to the hairdresser where her long spiky yellow hair was cut and swooped onto the other side. When Alfonso was through with her she looked like a blond seal—sleek, mammalian, knowing.

It turned out, of course, that women preferred to buy a car from another female. When it became known that no one at Roger Williams ever said: "Now I'm going to be frank with you," the women flocked to her. They came from all over Rhode Island and eastern Massachusetts in order not to have to listen to men hawking sales pitch flavored with new-car smell. These women thumbed through the car magazines in the showroom, then they slowly wrote out large checks and drove away with deliberation.

⌣·

After Sally finished her degree she got a job teaching ephemeral art in the evenings. She still worked at the dealership in the daytime. Sally and Jake couldn't manage to stay together for more than four days without one of them stalking off, but even when they weren't living together, as long as they weren't actively fighting she would come to Jake's house every Saturday night and cook dinner. She was now thirty-seven and avid for babies.

That June night at The Fluke, Maggie and Hugh had come in just as Sally was whispering to Jake, crooning questions of biology and time. Then she turned to Hugh and Maggie and said, "Aren't they good, babies? Shouldn't we have one?"

"Jake would make a wonderful father," Maggie burst out. Hugh was about to speak, but Jake excused himself, saying he had to go to the men's room. Actually, he had to use his bronchodilator. He never used his spray in public, even when he knew he was probably turning purple, and especially not when it might appear that he was using it as a form of argument. For he had no real reason to be against babies and settling down except that talking about such subjects left him wheezing, without courage, unable to breathe.

The men's bathroom at The Fluke contained his favorite mirror: the salt winds and damp fogs had tarnished it to a dark and speckled tin; if he stood correctly it hid his prematurely white eyebrow, the left one, in a patch of mottled brown glass.

～·

After leaving the restaurant, Hugh and Maggie drove to East Beach where they could see the hovering island forms of Cuttyhunk; Penikese, the old leper-colony island; and, between, in the far haze, Martha's Vineyard.

They got out of the car and walked over the shingle to the sand. "You know . . ." Maggie started. But then Hugh hugged her, saying, "God, Maggins, I missed you!" And it wasn't the right time.

The sun was setting and the bay was a sheet of quicksilver orange. The trailer homes of the summer people were silhouetted in the light, their metallic hulks transformed into dark mystery. "The afternoon of the day you left," she started again, "I thought the wind . . ." But an incoming wave raced up the sand toward them and they jumped back laughing. They hurried along the beach ahead of the curling water. They stopped and talked to old Nat Morrill, fishing at the water's edge, standing in that taut motionless dance with his line, waiting for bluefish.

On the road back, with its five-mile lesson in stone walls and its demonstration of river meanders, the rise of earth's shadow and the call of the first stars kept them both silent.

At home as Maggie navigated the narrow path in the growing

darkness with Hugh just behind her, the yew tree felt suddenly taller, darker, protective and unknowable; the junipers, when she brushed against them, prickling and fragrant. The moment had passed for telling. She would wait until morning.

Later, "Are you coming to bed, dear?"

All that timing. That yoke of marriage and its loving but necessary coinciding. You would think that after so many years together it wouldn't chafe anymore, that the knots and splinters of their individual wills would have been planed and sanded. Perhaps. But it was also as though the grooves had gotten deeper. It was more difficult, as she got older, to be nice, Maggie said, and easier to be smart. She lectured her children, snapped at her grandchildren, found she had no patience when the young ones chose surliness or silence. Her children, and the older ones of the flock of grandchildren, claimed she had always been sharp—too sharp—but they meant something else, tongue, not brain. When Hugh would return from one of his trips, though, Maggie would hover over him, doting like a bride. Jake would watch her doing this, sometimes, and it looked to him as though Maggie wanted to inhale Hugh. Then it would seem to Jake that Maggie was a glorious presence.

Maggie didn't tell Hugh about her visitor the next morning, either. As time went by, it became increasingly impossible to mention, for then the length of her silence would have to be explained as well. The next afternoon she glimpsed a new shadow behind the toolshed—but it might have been a cloud, or the sumac perturbed by a shift in the wind.

⌣·

Often it is the male of our species who grows the kitchen garden, if he gardens at all, while the female allows herself to play with beauty. In Jake and Maggie this was reversed, and Maggie's gardens were practical things, kitchen gardens, with occasional spots of color— sharp yellow marigolds to keep the rabbits out, nasturtiums to protect the tomatoes. They would argue about her need to grow things one could eat. When Jake would claim that perennial borders were really sculptures that gave texture to time, Maggie would reply that he was too abstract. She had children and grandchildren to feed all summer. The most she could manage were banks of daylilies against the stone walls and an occasional stand of yucca.

Maggie worked with yarns, threads, cloth. She was one of those filamentous people who are happiest when they are weaving things together, sewing, any sort of work with colored strands between their fingers. Here, unlike her gardens, things did not always need a function. Sometimes she would knit impossibilities, bottle-shaped objects with no inside or outside, things dimly remembered from an older cousin of hers who had dabbled in geometry.

One day Jake was comparing the pattern of the stitches in a dark green sweater Maggie was knitting to the spacing of lettuces in her early summer kitchen garden. He was trying to tell her that the same music of rows was there in both the knitting and the garden—the motor-music, he called it, of repetition and the variations. But Maggie kept not understanding and asking him what he meant.

They were sitting outside after lunch. Hugh was dozing in the hammock, Maggie sat beside him in an Adirondack chair, and Jake sat cross-legged on the grass, digging up dandelions with his jackknife.

"But what are you talking about?" Maggie said.

He was talking about love. Whenever Jake talked to Maggie he was talking about that, no matter what he happened to be saying. "Look," Jake said, finally. "Think of knitting, or waves, or the shingling of a house: isn't it the small irregularities that are really attractive?"

Maggie did something with her needles and tugged more yarn toward her from the green ball. "Am I a particularly clumsy knitter? Is that what you're getting at?"

"No. That isn't what I meant at all." Then he had to convince her that he wasn't criticizing her. He tried to explain how stitches, shingles, clapboards—all of them had an allowance of variation that we could see if we looked really closely. And the presence of this not-really-perceived variation was what pleases. But if the variations were too great, if one could see them at first *glance,* then the work would seem clumsy, childish, primitive. Jake thought he was being clear, but his conversations with Maggie sometimes got tangled with his desire.

"Jake," Maggie looked up from her needles. "Where do you find these thoughts? Where do you keep them when you're thinking about ordinary things?"

"These *are* the ordinary things," Jake said. "Think of your poems. Patterns are like rhyme. Without jags it can lead you very quickly into doggerel." He stopped talking and dug around the base of of a weed. Finally he said, "Look. It's really a question of aluminum siding." Jake knew Maggie hated aluminum siding, and that she would see his point. Since he had clinched the argument, he got up and offered to make them all something cold to drink.

"I'm not sure," she said, when Jake returned with iced tea. "I don't think there should be a philosophy of knitting, or of shingling, or of lettuces and beans. Perhaps they just are."

Maggie would ask Jake later if he thought that Grenville had come to tell her something. Both she and Jake had inherited from their grandfather an unnatural ability to listen. People always wanted to tell them things: they would show up at her door, or at Jake's, uninvited, simply wanting a listener, never noticing how little was said in return. Jake would keep quiet, give his full attention, then spend weeks or months constructing a story to account for some small puzzlement in what was told, trying to make sense—for himself—of some twist or omission. Jake was the only person Maggie confided in, except for Hugh, and she sometimes said that she was afraid to burden Hugh with some of the odder parts of her mind. She loved him too much to worry him.

Maggie would take her visitors into the kitchen; Jake would bring his into the garden so he could pull weeds, as he had not learned how to be still. The tellers would touch their scars and say, "Now this one . . ." every scratch reminding them of some escape, some piece of private history, as though each mark on the body acts as a springboard into that dark pool of stories that makes the soul. Bruises are more important than we suspect. When Maggie's grandchildren came to visit, the youngest ones always showed her the newest wound since last time. Then she would rub it with a bit of their spit or her own. Cats do this, monkeys; it must go all the way back.

When Jake sat in his garden and listened to visitors, he could sometimes hear the low moaning of a lighthouse over on Martha's

Vineyard, a handful of miles across the bay. In a south wind the sound of that old foghorn comes right up the Cranford River, weaving its lonely warning into the bass line of whatever story is being told.

∿·

Restlessness was taking hold of Maggie like muscle cramp. She would get up in the middle of the night and sit by the screened window in the kitchen, knitting. Then she would drop her needles into her lap and look out at the night through the moth-laden screens. She drank a slow Scotch or two, wanting to call out to the darkness.

What could she do except keep silent? The act of bathing a stranger seemed important and foreign and absurd. Meaning kept hovering over everything. She felt a distraction coming on. Committing the great sin of hurrying the seasons, perhaps the greatest sin—misusing time—she began to wish for midsummer to pass, for hurricane season to come, full of desperations and warm pelting rains, followed by exhausted calm.

Chapter Six

AFTER BREAKFAST ONE MORNING Maggie sat on the living-room couch with all her sewing baskets around her feet on the floor. She was holding a needle up to the light to thread it when she noticed Grenville standing in the doorway watching her.

"Oh," she said. "It's you. Would you like coffee? Breakfast? What time is it?" She knew what time it was, but she was startled—for once she hadn't been thinking about Grenville, and there he was, even though it was Thursday. She wondered if he knew that Hugh had left with the changing tide the evening before. "Coffee?" she repeated.

"In a minute," he said. "First tell me what you're doing." He gestured toward the cloth form reclining next to her. "What on earth is it?"

"Oh, this?" Maggie said. She looked at the figure as though she were surprised to find it beside her. "I make things." She waved her hand in the air to lead his attention elsewhere. "It's a mermaid, sort of."

Grenville came closer.

Maggie reached for her eggplant-shaped pincushion and stuck her needle into it.

"Could you stand her up for me?" he asked.

"No," Maggie said. "I don't think so." She got up from the couch. "Mermaids don't really stand up, you know."

"What I meant was, could you hold her up—so that I can see her full size?"

"I suppose, if you really . . ." She let her voice trail off.

The figure she was making was a woman, hefty and bulging where Maggie was all dips and hollows. This cloth woman took up most of the couch, and one arm draped itself over the seat cushions, its long fingers pointing straight ahead. Maggie bent down, put her hands under the arms of the mermaid, and lifted so that the velvet tail fins just touched the gray wooden floor. The tail was smooth and dark green, the scales outlined with yellow stitching. The cloth head lolled above Maggie's own, the clear silk face with its penciled features resting on top of Maggie's red hair.

"Are those breasts?" Grenville pointed at the torso, which already had five mounds on it, and scalloped pencil lines indicating the future positions of many more.

"Well, they're actually shoulder pads. My daughters save them for me from their blouses and jackets. But yes, they are meant to be breasts."

"Why does she need so many?"

Maggie lowered the mermaid to the couch and smoothed the flesh-colored torso. She explained that the creature was supposed to be a cross between an ordinary New Bedford mermaid and the ancient Middle Eastern fertility goddess Diana, who had so many breasts that they looked rather like the kernels on a cob of corn. This was the largest sculpted figure Maggie had ever made, except for the elephant that she had constructed for her children when they were little. The elephant now slumped in a half-sitting position in a corner of the barn, its chicken-wire skeleton poking through the papier-mâché.

Maggie had never shown this mermaid to anyone who wasn't part of the family, and she felt mind-hobbled with embarrassment. Hugh liked her sculptures and was amused by them. Even Jake did not make her feel defensive about them; they just were. She sat down, now, beside the mermaid and held onto its arm. Then she worried that Grenville would want to touch it as well, to fondle its incomplete parts, and the idea of such touching became unbearable and obscene.

She got up. "Why don't we go into the kitchen?" she said. "It's time for my breakfast." This was a lie, but she was panicky. "And you look like you could use some as well." She started for the door, hoping that Grenville would follow her without talking about the mermaid anymore.

As Maggie fiddled with the coffeepot, Grenville said, "Why does he leave you alone so often, your husband?"

"What do you mean?" She didn't turn around.

"He's always off sailing. That leaves room for me."

"For you to what?"

Grenville made no answer. Maggie put blueberry muffins and coffee on the table. Changing the subject, he said, "She's very large, your woman, she's bigger than life-size."

"What is life-size for a mermaid?"

"You know what I mean," he said.

"I didn't really intend it."

"What, exactly?"

"I didn't have in mind that she would be so large—I made the pattern quite small—the size of a small harbor seal, but when it came time to cut out the green velvet for the tail, I had bought far too much so I just kept making it bigger. Then, of course, the rest had to follow."

"There are so few heroic sculptures of women," he said. "They must bring a lot."

"Bring?"

"You do sell them?"

"Not really. Not at all."

"What do you do it for, then?"

Maggie tilted her head and looked at him.

"Function," he said. "What is it that makes you spend so much time on them?"

Maggie got up from the table and cleared her plate and coffee cup, letting them clatter as she stacked them beside the sink.

"What is their use? Larger-than-life dollies for lonely mariners?"

She ran water over the dishes.

He got up and flashed her one of his smiles. "Now I've gone and annoyed you," he said. "When you've been so awfully nice to me."

And then he was gone again, as smoothly as he had come.

She wanted to call after him, *Wait. Not annoyed: bothered.* What had upset her was not his irony, but that she didn't know the answer. None of her family or friends had ever asked why she sewed or wove. They were too close, they had always seen her do it. She had never asked, or told, herself why. She wanted him back, here in her kitchen, to have him ask his questions again.

~·

The wind had lowered to a gentle air, a looming stillness of the sort called *inclinable to calm*. It was Friday and Maggie was preparing for the mid-July visit of the whole Gifford clan. She wore her usual housecleaning costume: an old pink T-shirt and cutoff jeans. She opened all the windows in the barn and then tried to air the guest rooms in the main house and in the ells. In each room she poked at cobwebs with a broom, leaving a few spiders to clear the air of flies. Beneath every south-facing window lay a fly graveyard. She swept, pulled up the screens, and scattered the crisp black carcasses out into the sunlight. She put clean sheets and blankets at the foot of each bed.

Downstairs, too, she swept. The wind had stopped, for a moment, its willful carrying of the outside world into the house. Sand, spores, seeds, bits of seashells, insect parts, and unknown organisms—a vast collection if you were to look at it under a magnifying glass, but that would start the kind of infinite regression that would have captured her when she was a girl. When her parents would tell her to sweep her room, she would start and then she would stop in order to study the wind drift under a glass, drawing it with a hard pencil, painting the drawings, finally asking her father for his insect books so she could identify whose leg parts, wings, antennae she had captured.

The children were coming, the spouses, the grandchildren. Maggie had to be nudging time; she would only sweep once today, though she knew that when the wind was up it only took ten minutes for a visible amount of dune-scatter to show in her kitchen, as though the air currents were trying to carry the beach—layer by diaphanous layer—over the twisting river to her house.

Maggie loved these summer visits, song and squeal, chatter and confusion, until, of course, she couldn't stand them. The four Gifford offspring, their three current loves, and the six grandchildren shimmered in and out of her definition of herself like some optical illusion. Until they arrived she was nervy and love-anxious. And after all fifteen of them had been living together on the farm for a couple of days, there would finally be too many bodies, too many socks, too many sounds. At that point Hugh would disappear to his boat, and Maggie would go over to Jake's house. He would settle her in the back room with a book and a drink. After a bit she would come and find him and they would talk quietly, almost in whispers. She would ask Jake what he was reading, or writing, for he was always jotting something down, trying to make sense of the stories people told him by writing his own versions and then putting them in a box under his bed. Nothing would ever to happen to these writings, they were not intended for publication or posterity. Rather it was Jake's way of allowing himself to stop thinking about things, once he had figured people's stories out enough to write them down, had committed them to the plane of the paper. As Jake and Maggie talked they would make their way through his gardens and invariably she would end up by chiding him for not having found a wife. At this point Jake would try to keep from having what Maggie called his wild-eyed look as he laughed with her about this.

While Maggie was visiting Jake, her brood would be making dinner. She had long ago trained them to take over all the cooking and cleaning during the summer visit; otherwise, she told them, she would run off and never come home.

When it became evening, Jake and Maggie would walk slowly through the pasture and the woods to her house, and then he would stay and eat with everyone, outside on the grass under the old trees. Jake's presence calmed Maggie and he was glad to be included in the large family gathering.

One such night the previous summer, the Giffords had had an extra houseguest, a historian from Toronto, who, over dinner, kept defending Canada against perceived, but invisible, attacks. He had never met Jake, and asked him what he did for a living. It was clear he thought that Jake was being elusive when he recounted the scatter-shot list of his activities.

"Are you perhaps a cat burglar?" He was joking, but only just.

"Oh, no," Hugh interjected. "Jake here is a remittance man. His family lives over in Newport, Rhode Island."

When they stopped laughing and Jake got them to explain the

term "remittance man," Hugh told him that his parents hadn't invented the scheme of paying him to stay away from home—the British used to do it all the time: to send a quarterly remittance or salary to their wastrels, drunkards, or simply their younger, and thus noninheriting, sons, usually on condition that they go away from Britain and settle in Canada or Australia or even the United States. Hugh and his Canadian guest explained that most of the British remittance men left home between the late 1800s and the end of the First World War, and that significant parts of Australia and Canada were settled this way.

Jake was glad, during that dinner, with all the grandchildren present, that the Giffords' guest had not asked what had caused his parents to desire his removal so vehemently. Schoolboy pranks get less interesting as we get older and more thoughtful, even as they get wrapped in a metallic gauze of nostalgia. And then, too, Jake's final misdemeanor hadn't really been a prank.

Jake's girlfriend, Sally, had been there also that night, and as a female car salesman she wanted to know if women had ever been remittance men. Hugh thought for a moment and replied that the closest thing he could think of were the young women who were sent from their wealthy American families to Paris because they were too artistic, too literary, or too interested, romantically and sexually, in other women.

"It's good for society to have such steam valves," Hugh finally said. "To be able to send the young men to the colonies or the women to Paris. You can think of the remittances as a form of tax or dues—paid by a society too hidebound and stagnant to embrace its most original citizens."

Sweet old Hugh: Jake as a young man had embarrassed his own family beyond bearing, and Hugh could still find a way to talk about it with generosity and reason. Jake was flooded with gratitude; he was often beset with fondness for the very man who kept him from having what he wanted. Jake's thirst for Maggie was the motor of his days, the whirring propeller of his nights. He did not think to cure himself of this.

That Friday of the leaning calm Jake went over to ask Maggie and Hugh to come to supper at his place, since he knew she would be cleaning all day. He found her on her way to the boat shed, and she accepted the invitation. Then she said,

"How are things with Sally?"

"She's gone all smooth now, in those gray suits." Jake tried to explain that Sally's salary made him uneasy.

"Because she earns more than you?"

"It makes her want babies."

"What's wrong with that?"

"They wreck gardens," Jake said, sweeping his arm about. "And sex."

"Oh, Jake. Grow up."

As he left her to go home, Jake promised he was working on the wife problem.

⌣·

Maggie continued on into the mossy gloom of the shed where, among dilapidated sailing dinghies and kayaks, she looked for a brick to wedge against an upstairs door that insisted on tapping the wall whenever there was the slightest puff of air. The bricks were usually stacked in the corner by the stack of sash weights, the iron bars that act as counterweights for double-hung windows. Hugh had salvaged them from a neighbor's house. The bricks were there but the sash weights were missing. She wondered briefly where they had gone to. No matter. She chose a brick, brushed the spiders off.

As she walked back from the shed, Maggie noticed that poison ivy had migrated from the edge of the forest into the grass. Until she got rid of it, until everything was in place, there would be no work on any of her sewing projects. Instead, she would be obsessed with order. She was in a cleaning storm.

⌣·

The poison ivy had crept everywhere, just under the loamy surface of the garden, thin as veins. Sliding her fingers through the dirt—she wore long black rubber gloves—she plucked at it, deceptively tender so it wouldn't break before she had enough to pull on. Narrow strands that seemed to have no beginning and no end; their main cord was rooted so securely that she had to lean her weight against it until it gave up its grasp on the earth with a disturbing ripping sound. Tiny hairs still clutched bits of dirt.

She bent and coiled the roots into circles; the leaves were still spring green. "Hugh," she called, waving a thick braid of poison ivy at him as he wandered, thinking about something, down the path. "Hugh. Do you think I should make a bouquet? Or a Christmas wreath?"

"What say, dear?"

"Nothing. Joking. Look at all this."

"Shall I help you? Are you sure it's right to clean so before the children come? As soon as they've been here a day or two, the whole place will look like a summer camp for the very unfortunate. Shouldn't you rather be messing things up?"

Of course Hugh was right. But visit jitters often led to an ordering instinct that was stronger than reason. Besides, the first glance of the place was important: it would form the frame of the whole summer for them. She threw the ripped-out plants onto a sheet of plastic to dry out and die. She wished there was some better way of murdering them, but you only burn poison ivy once in your lifetime. Sweat trickled into her eyes, down her neck. It felt as though the vines were creeping around the cuffs of her black rubber gloves and up the sleeves of her shirt and into her armpits. Whenever she yanked too suddenly, the vines sprang back toward her, reaching for her eyes and mouth.

◞·

On Sunday Maggie woke up with a blistery rash covering her arms and one side of her face. Hugh asked if he should stay home with her, but she told him to go off on his boat, that she would actually be happier if no one saw her looking like a leper.

After he left, the midmorning heat intensified her itching until it seemed to buzz in collusion with the ironic cackle of katydids and the metallic burr of cicadas. She didn't know which was worse, the insane sadistic tickling, or the private humiliation of having skin that bubbled and wept. At midday she fled the house, hurried across the west meadow, and descended to the marsh.

The river, when it gets near both Jake's and the Giffords' houses, is still tidal estuary and at low tide the water seeps from the mud flats to the channel in trickles. Maggie walked on the boardwalk over the marsh grass, loose boards clacking as she passed. As she stepped into the riverbed it gave with an urgent suck, pulling her sneakers down into the soft blackness. On its surface the mud was hot from the sun, but below was strange and cool. Only when she had submerged to her knees did her feet find bottom. A small stab of retrospective fright: *What if the bottom hadn't been there?* She bent down and scooped up the black muck, patting it on her face, arms, shoulders. The south wind dried it to a tight shell of clay.

Dark yellow sulfur smells, sharp blue of salt, and the flat sweet fragrance of sea grasses. Gulls wheeled above her asking if she would miraculously produce fish. An egret stalked the marsh, pretending it wasn't worried. A motorboat droned, then idled in the distance. Salt grass danced in the heat-glazed air. Moonsuck pulled at the channel water, luring it out to sea. Above, an osprey's sharp whistle.

Maggie edged out to deeper water, but swimming was not easy: the crawl became a flailing in the feathery ooze; the breast stroke felt like the wallow of an old frog. She did it anyway. The slurry cooled her skin, gave it other things to think about.

"Shall I throw you a rope?"

It was Grenville, yelling at her. He was barefoot, wearing shorts and a gray T-shirt.

"Shall I leap in and save you? Are you drowning?"

Startled by his sudden shouts, Maggie rose from the swirling mud and shook her head. Black droplets scattered.

"Are you contagious?" he asked.

"Yes," she said. "Actually, I suppose I am. But only if you rub up against me."

"I'll wait for that, then," he said. "You look horrible."

"Thank you. And how are you?"

"Dirty, as usual. Though nothing compared to you. And a bit hungry. I don't suppose you have anything to eat."

"Do I look as though I were starving as well as scrofulous?" She stretched her arms out, then hoped he wouldn't take this gesture as a sign of her wild pleasure at seeing him.

"No more than usual. Is it scrofula, then?"

"No, ass. Have you never seen poison ivy?"

"Not personified. Not as a goddess."

"If you want some food, you'd better come and cook for both of us. I shall put something over my face if you'd prefer."

"I would, actually." he said. "Definitely."

Outside the kitchen door, Grenville stood and watched while Maggie hosed herself off. "Look," she said, to stop his gaze. "Can you pick some lettuce? Over there." She pointed. He looked briefly, then resumed watching the way her white tank top, streaked with black mud, clung to her body. She told him to pick some tomatoes and cucumbers as well, and carrots if he knew how to pull them properly. She went in, trailing muddy water on the gray-painted wooden floor.

⌣·

At the back of Maggie's closet was a black hat with a veil. It was a crazed, proud thing of layered velvet, with a white silk rose pinned to the side. Hugh had found it at the town dump, its cardboard hatbox still tied with silk laces, the name of a long-defunct Boston hat shop in flowing gold cursive on the top. He had taken it home as a present for her, thinking vaguely of costume parties—which no one seemed to have anymore—or funerals, which were getting more frequent.

Having showered off the mud, Maggie itched again. In the morning she had called Jake and asked him to bring her some calamine lotion, as she felt too hideous to show herself in town. But she had told him not to bother coming till late afternoon. Now she took some aspirin and then put on the velvet hat. She looked in the mirror. When she pulled the veil down she found she could breathe perfectly well but it was warmer that way and hard not to giggle. She kept mistaking the patterns in the lace for flies.

Walking into the kitchen she said, "Is this better, then?"

"I have always liked black lace on my women."

She ignored the implications. "Where have you been keeping yourself?"

"Around and about. Mostly about. Did you miss me?"

"Miss you? I don't know you enough to miss you. I've only seen you twice. Three times. I know nothing about you. I know your name, finally, but not your business or what you're doing here." Her ignorance about him frustrated her and made her angry. She was afraid that she had blurted out too much.

"Right now, I'm making us something to eat. You can eat, can't you?"

"Depends on what I'm offered."

He had washed the greens, slightly, and was chopping cucumbers. She didn't like it when others used her knives. They blunted the edges and then left the knives and the wooden chopping board soaking in dishwater, hastening rot. Grenville was chopping incorrectly; he wasn't ruining the knife so much as making the wrong slices from each vegetable he attacked; now he was giving the carrots a half-twist between each stroke. She kept silent, thinking, *If he cooks, he cooks. I will sit and wait and soon he will be gone. And then I will want him back.*

"Do you itch?"

"Horribly," she said. She set the table with straw mats, white earthenware plates. Then, as though it didn't matter—as though it came in the middle of some other thought—she said, "How did you know my name?"

"No mystery, really," he said, comforting but not explaining. He carried the salad bowl to the table. Then, "Real estate. For years I've worked in real estate. I know every property around here between the interstate and the sea. I know who belongs to which land."

As Grenville told her his peculiar ideas about what kind of people should own which pieces of land, Maggie began to wonder if he thought that the function of a real estate *agent* was like that of a federal narcotics *agent:* to prevent, rather than facilitate, any sale of land or houses. When the wrong kind of people came along, he guided them away from those properties with statements like, "Of course, I myself would not buy this place because of the retaining wall there.

D'you see how it's leaning? Why, with global warming the river will carry it away in a year or two." Or: "The last time they had the engineers in here, well, they just threw up their hands . . . it's not technically wetlands, and once it even passed a perc test, but the seepage is something wicked. Anything you build here will just get sucked under in a couple of years." Then, if his clients were city people, he walked them past dark holes in scree-covered slopes and talked of the eastern coyote's habits: "Now, no one thinks that the coyote goes after *children* . . ."

Grenville loved land almost as much as he loved the river and the coast. He knew which meadows would catch the sun and turn it into sweet corn, which protected valleys would grow the most aromatic grapes. He had seen enough houses built into hillsides to know who would always need a dehumidifier throbbing away in the basement. Having watched the dance of the pilings along the river he could predict which docks would be next to collapse. He knew which cabins had been built with cinder blocks containing cockroach egg cases and would have to be demolished and rebuilt. He loved knowing all this, he told Maggie. It was selling that he hated. Tract houses he could part with, ranch homes, sloppy jobs, filthy houses whose owners had kept too many parakeets or long-haired cats. But the peculiar and personal houses, the solid and beautiful ones, these became harder for him to part with. Of course it didn't work; the market went so low that everything was multiply listed, and if he didn't sell a place one of the other agents would. He found he could break even if he sold one or two houses a season. Swales and dales, seeps and fields, they were his, and in his off-hours, before he drove home to Tiverton and his wife, Denise, he used to wander the properties he handled, exploring the neighboring lands as well, carrying a book on mushrooms, or a bird guide and field glasses, to show that his explorations, if not legitimate, were harmless.

⌣.

When Grenville had finished explaining to her his mode of real estate, Maggie took off her veiled hat and began to braid her damp auburn hair. "Ah," she said. "I see. But what do you do now?"

"It's not too clear, is it?" he replied. "I'm not sure what you could say I do."

"What do you live off of, then? Is that a better way of asking it?" She put the hat back on, pulling the veil down.

"Actually, this is a bit difficult for me. You see, I'm not against telling you," he paused while she looked at him.

At this point she was sure it was drugs. She said nothing.

"But you won't understand it," he said. "You won't like me. And you won't be able to bear it."

"Try me," she said.

"Patience," he said. "I will." He got up and walked toward the sink, then turned to face her. "You see, I went to spend the weekend on a friend's sailboat, near here, over in Westport Harbor. I wanted to see what it felt like."

"What *what* felt like?"

"Just to step out of things for a moment. To be where no one knew where I was. But then," he stopped talking, walked to the window and looked out. "I stayed. Then I found I couldn't get myself to step back into my life. My friend finally needed his boat, so I left it. Mainly I've been borrowing places."

"Places? What kind?"

"Unused fishing boats, sailboats. Houses for sale, cabins, shacks. When you're in real estate you acquire a large collection of keys."

"What does your wife think?"

"Lost, stolen, strayed." He shrugged.

"Did you ever do this vagrant thing before?"

"God, no. It's not the kind of thing I'd do."

"But you could still go back—you could find some sort of explanation."

"I could. Perhaps. It's been two months. She will have changed. I am a different person."

"But does she know you're alive?" Maggie pushed her chair back and got up from the table. Her food was untouched. "You left a perfectly good life to take up that of a water rat? That's the dumbest thing I've ever heard of." She paced across the room to the far windows. "How can you be so low-souled in the way you talk about this—so flippant and adolescent? What you say is too bizarre. People just don't become homeless that way." She paused, too angry to go on. She breathed deeply. Then, "It's the saddest thing I've ever heard."

"I'm not homeless," he said. "I have more homes than anyone you know. I just don't have the home I used to have. Look, this isn't easy to talk about. You're not even trying to listen."

Maggie was stung by this and stayed quiet for a while. Then, more gently, "Does it bother you?"

"Not going home? I don't know. No. Not yet."

"You have to explain it—at least to me, at least to yourself."

"I'm trying, really I am. I'm just not sure I can."

"Are you normally cruel?"

"I don't think so. I was a perfect friend, perfect, well, good, husband for ten years. I could have stayed forever."

"This is ridiculous. Your walking away makes the world seem so fragile, you make it seem unbuffered, as though any little tap could shatter everything." She knocked with her wedding ring against one of the small panes in the window behind her, its white paint peeling off the sash. She half expected the glass to craze and collapse, but though it shifted in its frame, it stayed whole. "How cruel to make her grieve for you so early," she said. "While you are—I am supposing— still grief-worthy."

"Men die earlier, anyway," he said. "She is not too old to find some- one," he said, adding, "She's a doctor. A good one."

"This is wrong; these ideas are stupid and cruel. You are wanton. Loss is everywhere. We don't have to manufacture loss: it rains down on us. Where have you been that you feel this way?"

"Haven't you ever wanted to step out?" he asked, softly, watching her face. "Haven't you ever felt you wanted to be out of reach of the vast and sticky cobweb of answering machines?"

"That, I wouldn't know," she said, a bit stiffly. "My telephone is virgin." She gestured at her unmachined phone. "Look," she said. "People don't just fade out of a marriage. I mean, I suppose, they might dim emotionally, but they don't disappear. Are you sure your wife wasn't, as they say, screwing around? Are you sure you weren't?"

"Of course, I could say she was. That would make you feel better, wouldn't it? It would give me a reason for slipping overboard. Everyone understands hurt male pride. Possessiveness. Jealousy. But no, that was not it."

"So you want me to believe that you left for a day or two and it became forever?"

"I don't know anything about forever. I know that I like it here," he swept his arm to include the meadows, the outbuildings, the river. "I also know that I can't explain it. That's one reason I haven't gone back: I've been looking for a way to explain it. Aside from my being simply cruel. Which I did not think I was."

"Well, you haven't convinced *me*. As far as I can see it's pretty beastly."

"I know." He went to the table and sat down. "I know," he repeated. "I can't explain it to you, but I can show you. And if I could show you, perhaps I could figure out how to show her." He toyed with his knife. "When this business on your skin clears up, let me take you somewhere . . . on a very small voyage. Just to show you the mood."

"Not possible," she said. "I have a husband. I have four children, their spouses and lovers, and their six children coming to visit for the summer."

"Yes," he said. "But your husband is always going off sailing. Besides, when they are all here, all that family of yours, you'll need to get away. It must get to you at some point, having so many of them here, doesn't it?"

"Perhaps. But then I visit my cousin Jake, down the road."

"Just once," he said. "When I see your husband go off on his boat, I'll give you a call and ask if you're ready."

～·

That evening Maggie told Jake more of Grenville's story. Jake had brought over the calamine lotion along with a bottle of white wine for her and a couple of beers for himself. Jake had avoided asking Maggie for a physical description of Grenville, although she had originally told him of green eyes and a beard, and now he began to construct a picture that grew more distinct as the summer went on.

He suspected Grenville was tall and muscular, for Maggie to be so taken with him, also tanned and somehow, in spite of his nomadic living, his beard would be still black and neatly trimmed. Even his name was athletic, Jake thought, with his three given names *John Hiram Stuart* like the running start needed to execute the broad jump of the final *Grenville*. Jake felt his own name rooted and squat in comparison. His growing jealousy delineated Grenville's every muscle, and where Jake's eyebrows, for example, were unruly and unmatched, the one having turned white a few years earlier and the other still brown, he was sure Grenville's brows lay flat, both still black, perhaps ironic.

Chapter Seven

IT WAS NOW THE MIDDLE OF JULY and the forest was advancing toward the gardens; the brambles threw their canes farther into the meadow, enlarging that border space which hides and feeds animals of all sizes.

On Tuesday the younger generation of Giffords finally arrived: Connie, the strawberry-blond smart one, came first. Maggie loved her most, talked with her, fought with her, trusted her.

Tony, the next oldest, still lived in Cranford with his two children; he worked at the vineyard over in Westport. Although he rarely spoke about it, Tony felt that his siblings and their spouses were interlopers when they came for their summer visit. He kept to the edge of things when they appeared, sometimes going home to his place for the night, and during the days, going over to Jake's place after work, or wandering along the five brooks that cut through the old Ezekiel Beecher farm, cleaning out debris of sticks and leaves so the water could flow freely in the stony beds. Tony's wife, confused and suicidal after giving birth to their son—whom she named Osprey—had run off with a man who drove one of the trucks for the local gravel quarry. The rest of the family all thought it was good riddance. In contrast to his ex-wife, Tony had always been solid, uncannily anchored, someone you would go to for advice, even when he was an adolescent.

Gillian, the poet, was the third of the Gifford offspring, and in her the deep-set eyes of Maggie's side of the family had become troublingly dark and haunting. None of Gillian's poetry books were well known, yet. Jake thought her work was brilliant: tangled and contrary and erotic, though he knew he was incapable of judging it.

Personally, he distrusted her, and kept his distance when he could. Gillian was always leaning against a tree, bent over a book, or writing her own difficult and ambiguous lines, black hair coiling over her face as she avoided, during the day, whichever male friend she had brought along to keep her company at night.

Although Philip, the youngest, didn't read as much as Gillian, it was he who had inherited Hugh's covering of book dust, and he loved and talked and breathed books.

Each summer Maggie watched the shifting loves and loyalties of her brood: one of them would not be speaking to her, while another would be her champion, a third would be having the marital horrors, and the fourth buoyant in an upwelling of peacefulness. They grew and bloomed and gave birth and shrank until she longed to command them: *Stay still now. Realize that this is happiness.* Once, Jake had tried to convince her that she should think of her children as gardens, as imaginings and processes, rather than as static beings. But then she would ask him: what were they proceeding toward—except lives having been lived? All she could do, she said, was hold the strings of their lives and try to braid them into some noble and felicitous knot.

With Maggie's children came the grandchildren, all six of them with impossible names. As the family increased, Jake wanted to make sure to remember their begats, so he drew a rough family tree and tacked it in the little pantry off his kitchen:

Margaret Beecher Gifford — — — — — Hugh Gifford

Connie—David	Tony	Gillian~(——)	Philip—Celia
Turko 11	Storm 11		Milo 1
Clay 7	Osprey 8		
Blue 5			

Maggie mocked Jake for having to make this, and then for keeping it tacked up on the wall, but he knew he avoided many more blunders by having it there. Before they came each summer, Jake added a year to the grandchildren's ages, and rubbed out the name of Gillian's previous consort.

As soon as they all arrived, Hugh would always try to get his grandchildren to help him clear walking paths in the woods; sometimes the oldest cousins, Turko and Storm, would work with him. Turko was Connie's red-blond eleven-year-old boy. His real name was Turkmenistan—though Connie had never told Hugh or Maggie why she named him that. Sometimes the music of a name is enough. Tony's girl, the dark-haired, wiry Storm, was also eleven; she was always in blond Turko's company.

"The jungle should always stay behind the wall," Hugh would tell them, when they chose to follow him. "But often there isn't any wall," he would add, with lanky truthfulness. "We've got to get the burrs and prickers and thorns out of the paths—and our real enemy, of course, is damned *multiflora*." He gave them each a pair of red-handled clippers, and taught them to cut the invading rose to the ground.

When Maggie had inherited her part of the farm, she and Hugh had moved there from Providence, and they had both come with romantic ideas about wildness. All of the forests surrounding the pastures and cornfields on the seventy acres were overgrown and they liked it that way, though they tried to carve narrow walking paths through the scrub. Where the meadow licked the lawn they planted their kitchen gardens and, closer to the house, the geometrically formal herb garden. During the years and years of children they left most of the forest alone. Later, Hugh began to look to the forest seriously. After he cleared patches of tangled multiflora, orange Turk's-cap lilies suddenly appeared. Clearly, that was a *sign*, he thought.

Now, during the summers, the grandchildren helped him fight the thorn bushes. But their attention was divided and often they helped Jake construct his hidden room in the woods for Maggie's birthday. Each year Jake needed to insert something planted, something thought-out, into the wild disorder of the forest. Perhaps it was done as an offering—certainly to Maggie but also to some hidden sylvan presence. Or perhaps it was just male spraying, lifting his leg to mark that he had once passed along this way.

Jake would work on these secret places all summer long, with Tony and sometimes with the children. Then in the second week of August, Jake would tell Hugh where it was, and early in the morning on Maggie's birthday Hugh would lead her there; if the day was fair he would bring a thermos of coffee and some sweet rolls and they would eat their breakfast in the new space that Jake had made.

The eleven-year-old cousins, Turko and Storm, were fascinated by these clearings. The first one had been a simple wooden bench made from a large split tree trunk sitting on smaller half-rounds. The following year Jake planted a flowering shad bush beside a table of black slate. The slab of slate he had found at Botelho's rock yard, over in South Dartmouth. Four slices of a thick maple tree served as stools around the stone table. One summer Tony and Jake transplanted moss to make a patch big enough for two people to sit on. They surrounded it with a stand of toad lilies. It was hard to persuade the moss to grow where they put it, but finally they learned to dig very deeply under any piece they were transporting and to give it a drink of manure tea and buttermilk. Each September the toad lilies would suddenly show their purple-speckled blooms, like small ferocious orchids.

Another year, Jake had found a stand of birch trees about to be bulldozed for a development. Tony went with him, with his chain saw, and together they cut them and brought them home in Jake's pickup truck, a chocolate-colored Nissan that made up for its looks by having the sweetest disposition in Cranford. With the birch logs Jake constructed a pewlike bench, with startlingly tall back and sides, and this seat defined a new "room," sudden and chalk white in the middle of the bracken.

Once, Jake simply implied a space with a brass ship's bell hanging from a branch above an iron lantern that he had placed on a stone. He liked the thought of the lantern's candle glowing in the middle of the woods, reflecting the eyes of night seekers.

Each spring Jake was anxious until he had decided what form that summer's room would take. Each spring he was sure he could not invent a new room, that the forest was full, that he would not be able to think of anything worthy. It had to be both like and unlike the rest of the forest, a rustling chamber, uncanny and familiar. Sometimes it was necessary to plan a year in advance: one fall he tried to transplant the mysterious tall white funguslike Indian pipes, to make a circle around an oak tree for the following year, but they shriveled and blackened and never came back. At the last minute he attached an old wooden gate between two sugar maples. There was no path nearby, and the gate seemed to open from everywhere onto everything.

⌣·

Sally rarely helped Jake with these constructions. Not because she wasn't interested—she was a grand and peculiar gardener—but because she had to be at work, either at her Volvo salesroom or teaching her class in the history of ephemeral art at RISD. Whenever Jake showed his latest forest room to her, she would wonder about people walking there a hundred years later. What would they think? How would they explain these alterations and arrangements out in the nowhere tangle?

This summer it was Turko and Storm who went with Jake to Sylvan's Nursery down on Horseneck Road. As they got out of the truck, Jake told them he wanted to build a room walled by evergreen trees. They looked at him solemnly, Turko's reddish hair glinting in the sun.

Storm twisted her bracelet made of braided string. "Not juniper, I hope," she said. "Juniper sucks."

Jake agreed with her, and they trailed along the rows of evergreens until they found *Thuja occidentalis 'Smaragd,'* the emerald green cedar, with its slightly humorous needles like small vertical fans. They went to back to the nursery office and ordered two dozen.

Later, in the forest, they found the perfect spot. Hidden and flat, it was far from any of the other rooms Jake had made, and not on any of the paths. They paced it out. They laid string and argued about the dimensions. Finally they realized that it was so far from any of the brooks traversing the property that it would be impossible to water any new plantings. They rolled up the string. Turko found a better place, near a brook. Again they paced, and the string, now matted with bits of leaf and dirt, was unrolled again and pegged into place.

Each year these hidden arrangements had become more complicated. Jake wondered if it was mad, rather than simply peculiar, what he was doing, when he returned to the forest with the two children and all the shovels. And yet—wouldn't it be sly and surprising to come upon a green room in these woods?

They raked the leaves from their rectangle to indicate the floor of the proposed house. Again they marked it off with strings and stakes, making sure that the corners were properly angled. It felt very small. Jake's school of planting said that you should dig a hole whose diameter is three times that of the bagged and burlapped tree, and that in exchange for this generosity you don't have to enrich the dirt with compost or manure. They had measured the rootballs of the trees in the nursery. Their room would be walled by five trees on the short sides, seven on the long.

It had rained a lot in the past days and the leaf mold felt soft in that layered deceptive way it has, sweet-smelling and easy. Jake had refused Tony's offer to bring his minitractor and dig twenty-four immediate holes for him. This was a present for Maggie and Jake wanted to do it with his arms and his back, not with a machine. So, he told Tony to join them later, without his tractor.

The children and Jake had three shovels, and they started digging at the corners of the future room. The first three holes were simple, an occasional meandering root needed to be snapped, but nothing more. When Jake had almost finished the hole at the fourth corner his shovel clanged on something. Rocks always appear at the point where you have almost achieved depth, or breadth, and you step back and wonder if the roots would really be too cramped if you just left the obstruction in place and pleaded with the new tree to grow around it.

Storm came over to inspect. "Treasure?" she said. "Hidden and forgotten?" She clawed at the dirt with her hands. "There were Indians here; what if we found a skeleton?" Her skinny arms were dusky with a fringe of forest dirt. She was still at the age where the body is dominated by fingers, wrists, elbows. She pulled a red elastic tie out of her jeans pocket, twisted her black curls through it until they were in a tight knot at the back of her neck.

Turko said, "What if we found not just one, but a whole gang of them, so it wasn't just a dead person, but a burial ground? Then what? Aren't there rules?"

"If it's an Indian burial ground," Jake said, resting for a moment against his shovel, "you're not supposed to touch it. I think you're supposed to tell the local tribe."

"How do we tell if they're Indians, if they're just skeletons?" Storm asked.

Turko looked up from his shovel, brushed his orange hair back from his forehead. "Because they put arrowheads in the eyes," he said, with jabbing gestures toward his own face.

Jake told them that he often found arrowheads when he dug for new gardens, but he had never heard of them in eye sockets.

"Suppose they're not Indian," Storm persisted. "Couldn't we dig them up and then you do your minister business and give them a burial somewhere else?"

Jake said he would probably want to plant the trees somewhere else if they found a slew of bodies. He had only performed two funerals in his career as minister; they were for the recently dead, and even so he had found the ritual awkward. He didn't think he had the language to rebury a conclave of skeletal remains in a lonely forest.

"I suppose I could," he said. "But I don't think it would feel right."

Storm and Turko watched Jake attack what seemed less and less like a rock. He was panting and fuming by the time he rolled it out of the hole. It wasn't a rock, but a metal box. The children whooped. The box was painted red, rusted. It was heavy and as Jake shook it, something shifted and thudded inside. He handed the box to Turko so he could whack open the rusted lock. The whole box looked absurdly small compared to the effort it had taken to get it out of the earth. As Turko pulled the lock off, the back hinges flaked apart and the whole top came off.

The contents of their red metal treasure box were so banal that they increased the mystery: wrapped up in a pair of denim farmer jeans were three milky glass water bottles, with the legend: *Drink More, Drink Pure.* Turko spread the jeans out on the ground. They discussed whether it was somebody's garbage or somebody's secret. It didn't seem to be treasure.

The children never hit on any rocks, but three holes later Jake hit another one, so large he needed his iron bar and mallet to gouge around and under in order to see how far it extended. No matter where he tapped, the rock was always deeper.

With pickax, crowbar, and iron bar the three of them pried out the monstrous rock and rolled it out of the way. Jake sat on it, to show that it was vanquished. He wondered if they would really be able to do all twenty-four holes. His back was now speaking to him in jagged colors. If it went into spasm, he wouldn't be able to move and he would have to send the children to find Tony. Then they would all have to put Jake into the wheelbarrow and roll him home. Or Tony could bring his minitractor after all and put him in its tow cart. It was getting harder to get enough air into his lungs. The forest bent over him, closing in and leaving him breathless. They had to get it all done today: it was Thursday and the trees were being delivered the next morning. Connie had agreed to take Maggie off somewhere so she wouldn't see the truck from the nursery. Jake willed Tony to come sooner rather than later.

⌣·

"It's way too deep," said Storm, measuring the latest excavation with her arm. "We'll have to fill in some." Then, without pausing, she changed the subject: "Maggie says that even though your eyebrows are piebald, you have very gorgeous ears. What is 'piebald,' anyway?"

Jake was puzzled by the way his left eyebrow had turned white before the right one and he always hoped that other people did not notice it. He was embarrassed by Storm's mention of it but his raucous heart danced at the last part of her comment. He gave a furtive touch to his right ear. It felt very finely formed. The left one, too. He needed to hear more. "What?" he said, as though surprised. "My ears?"

"Just kidding," she said.

Sometimes Jake yearned for middle-aged hypocrisy. Or fine middle-aged vision. He heaved himself up from the rock. It was very low. They would each dig another hole or two and then have lunch. Perhaps Maggie really had said his ears were lovely and Storm had decided to withhold that information. "Never get old and hairy, OK?" Jake said to the kids. "They say clean and strong and wise is better. Let's dig."

Tony joined them in the middle of the afternoon, and with his help they finished shoveling all the holes. The kids gave a series of loud sweaty cheers and began to throw dirt up in the air.

◦

Sally was at Jake's house when they got back; she had wanted to make dinner for him after the digging, and she joined them all on the porch. Jake took some pain tablets, the kids had Cokes, the grown-ups had beer. Jake's back was so loud that nothing anyone said seemed to make sense. Sally looked lovable in her gray T-shirt, though her blond hair was still salesroom-smooth. Jake tried to pull it up into its old spikes, but it wouldn't stay. He wanted to nuzzle her but he was waiting for the pills to take effect and for Tony and the kids to leave.

Afterward, Jake showered until the walls of the bathroom sweated. When he came into the kitchen, Sally had lit candles and their glimmer reflected from the windows over the sink and beside the table. She was cooking bluefish with mustard and garlic, from the smell of it, and he knew the rest of the meal would be relentlessly, di-dactically healthy, the unspoken lesson being that if he would just learn to eat narrowly, arcanely, all would be well. This made him feel resentful—he was one of the two men he knew over forty with no overhang; Hugh was the other. Still, Jake was delighted to have any kind of meal cooked for him and he wondered how soon Sally would let him wrap himself around her and why he was always so set against her plans for his future when everything smelled so good.

They were drinking the white wine Sally had brought. "Why am I doing this?" Jake asked her. "What makes me do these things?" He knew he was getting into dramatic, tortured-artist mode, tugging at his beard and hair. His back still hurt. The bill for the trees would consume most of the July remittance from his parents in Newport.

"Actually," Sally answered, "I had a question about that."

"About what gets into me?"

"No, about the rooms—how private is this one? How private are all your rooms in the woods? Because, if they are private, then I won't even ask you."

"Ask me, or tell me?" Jake's instinct was to back off from her question, but they had both gotten in too far. They couldn't just leave it.

"No," she said. "Not tell. Ask."

"They're not at all private, then," he said. "First of all, the whole family knows about them. Turko and Storm helped me on this one and they've worked on many of the others, so has Tony. The rooms are outside where everyone can see them. The woods are private property, but my constructions are just there."

"Well, I wanted to know if it would be OK for me to bring my RISD class there—they're all artists or art historians. They wouldn't damage it in any way; they're sweethearts really."

"Your class? In our woods?" Oh, God, but she was smart, his Sally. She was so much smarter than he was that it often it took his breath away. Such a reasonable request, just a question of pedagogical generosity. What she had hit on was the boundary between private and intimate, and she knew it and Jake knew it and he couldn't let it stand.

"Your class is on ephemeral art," he said. "My rooms will be there after all your students and their students are dead."

"Oh, come on, it's not just short-lived stuff; it's also installations. It's not only fireworks—it's the whole transmitted history of fireworks, from the ancient Chinese, for example. You know that."

She certainly made it sound reasonable.

Jake was panicky, desperate; sweat seeped under his beard and flares went off inside his ears. It was a defilement that she was proposing, in order to find out the nature of his attachments.

The brass ship's clock in Jake's kitchen chose that moment to strike the hour.

Jake waited until the clock had finished striking. "Why don't you run garden-club tours?" he said, standing up and pushing his chair into the table. "Call the Cranford Art Association and invite the watercolorists there to paint and picnic. Sell pictures to *Horticulture* or *Garden Design*. Sell pictures of yourself in bed with all your sweethearted ephemeral students," he added. "But leave me and my things out of it."

Sally did leave him, right then, without having eaten her bluefish or her wheatberry salad. She packed up her things. She had gotten good at that. He had given her too much practice.

⤙·

The next morning was cool and misty. The newly delivered emerald cedars stood behind Jake's house in two long lines, roots wrapped in burlap. They looked ready to burst into motion, heavy-footed dancers about to begin their crazed reel.

Tony and the children lifted the trees into Jake's brown pickup, and they wheedled the truck as far into the forest as it could go; then they trundled them the rest of the way by wheelbarrow.

When all the trees were planted, Jake took a long piece of garden hose and showed Storm and Turko how to submerge it in the stream to get it to siphon, since he didn't have a pump. He tightened the brass nozzle on the near end once they got it flowing. He had been unable to sleep that night, after fighting with Sally, and it was three in the morning when he thought of siphoning water rather than carrying it in buckets to the new plantings. It pleased him, to have figured this out, but it didn't soothe the burn of his stupidity with Sally.

⤙·

The next day, while they watered the cedars, Jake asked Storm what they should do with the floor of the room. Forest litter? Moss? Dirt?

"What do you want to go on in this place?" Storm asked.

Jake tried not to leer.

"How comfortable do you want it to be?" she asked. "We could bring pine needles from the grove."

What *did* he want to use it for? He imagined himself there with Sally, who, being gone, seemed ever more desirable. But he also imagined Maggie there with him. It was impossible not to. He would lie with Maggie in his arms until the moon fell from the heavens.

Before answering Storm, Jake paused to disentangle his sleeve from a bramble. "I want it to delight Maggie—and Hugh." He tried, but could not say it without a slight hesitation in the middle.

The whole time they were making that green room, and watering the trees, mixed with Jake's excitement was the horrible suspicion

that he was working on something that would increase Maggie's happiness in her life with Hugh, and that this happiness would exclude
him. He felt this way often, and when he did, one of his foul black
moods would descend. Then he would go and sit in his own garden
and pray for damnation and pull up weeds.

Chapter Eight

PADDLING ON THE RIVERS around Cranford is usually a tame and homely sport, especially in the middle parts, where you always know where you are and what to do. Upriver, though—when it all of a sudden goes quiet and dark and the other boats have vanished and the river presents tributaries and offshoots—a green and gloomy silence descends and you suddenly wonder who you are and why. Farther downstream, where the branches of the river join to form the harbor and the harbor meets the ocean—there the sea fog can roll in and everything that was familiar becomes uncanny; the foghorn sounds and you lose your bearings and the moaning call seems to come from all directions at once.

Except for Hugh's, all the boats of the Gifford and Beecher clan were brightly colored. The wooden canoes were painted: one yellow and two green, and the plastic kayaks came in primary hues. Hugh didn't like plastic or fiberglass boats, and had made for himself a kayak of varnished wood. The others called it "the mandolin." When they were all down by the ocean, in among the marshes, and the afternoon fog billowed in around them, Hugh's boat was the first to disappear and Jake was grateful for the Crayola colors of the rest of the flotilla. Maggie made Hugh carry a boatswain's whistle against the fog. Whenever Hugh would say that all the other boats reminded him of Tupperware floating in the kitchen sink amidst orange peels and apple cores, Jake would say that one day he would make a sinewy craft out of skins and hides and bones of reindeer or whale. "I'll shellac it," Jake promised, "with polar-bear grease."

It was a Sunday in July. Jake and the Giffords were exploring upriver on the Paskamansett, five of them in kayaks, and seven in canoes. Tony Gifford preferred to stay home when all his siblings were out on the river; he would watch over the children who were too young to go with the others, and he took care of the kayak and canoe business while Jake was gone, renting out whatever was left that would still float.

Early in the morning Jake had made his lunch, always with chocolate and also a few extra sandwiches—peanut butter and bacon and that rarer pleasure: peanut butter and sardines—that someone would need late in the afternoon if they had beached their boats and penetrated too far into a stranger's land, if the brambles and poison ivy had been too dense for all the scraped knees and tired arms.

It was a strange trip that Sunday. Hugh was with them, which was unusual, and Sally was not, as she was still not speaking to Jake since their argument about her class and the forest rooms, three days earlier. The air had been full of portents when they had put in: it wasn't threatening rain, exactly, but the ospreys were upset about something and wheeling overhead. A male swan dive-bombed Jake's kayak for coming too close to a nest in the cattails.

Maggie always went with Jake on Sunday expeditions, even if no one else did. Even if Hugh was away and she was hoping for a visit from Grenville, she would go out on the river. Connie and her husband, David, had their seven-year-old boy, Clay, with them and they were all giggling in the yellow canoe, and Jake felt left out by their closeness and Sally's distance and Maggie's unattainability. He wished he had someone that he could chatter away with. But then, he was not exactly a chatterer. Philip Gifford and his wife, Celia, alone with each other in the green canoe, smiling and silent, their baby Milo back at the house with Tony. Tony's Storm and Connie's Turko, Jake's favorites, shared the small green canoe. Gillian and her boyfriend, Paul, had been sniping at each other all weekend; they each took a kayak and kept as far from the other as possible. Paul wouldn't look at anybody, and Gillian's eyes were dark and smudgy. Even when she was reciting a seemingly innocent Emily Dickinson poem about a bird coming down the walk, Gillian had the kind of eyes you didn't want to look into for too long or else you felt you'd acquiesced, you'd acknowledged desire.

~·

Duckweed covered the river surface so that each paddle stroke left a whirlpool in the bright green particles; then, behind you, your trail closed in again. When you looked back—careful not to capsize—to see if you could capture in the green layer any trace of yourself, or of where you had come from, it was as though the green mass wanted to deny that you had passed through. Still you kept hunting for some change that you had made in the configuration of things. Perhaps that swirl there was due to you, that scar in the surface skin. The water beneath thrilled rich and warm and black.

~·

It was exactly noon when they got to the stretch of river that goes under the highway. Jake felt as though he were a paper bag floating down a culvert into a sewer; the cars overhead roared with menace and he thought as he came out the other end of the watery tunnel that if the people in them could see him they would throw something, or shoot at him, or their rogue vehicles would leave the road entirely and they would follow him into the riverbed, full of the nameless venom of strangers.

Noon passed and his panic subsided; the water lapped quiet again, deserted and peaceful.

White water lilies with pointed petals like lotuses surrounded them, along with the fragrant sweet-pepper bush—whose Latin name, *Clethra*, never fails to sound like a dark mixture of anatomical parts. In the shadowy places cardinal flowers shot up their surprising crimson flags like glorious and startling secrets.

They passed under a disused railroad bridge, all brownstone and iron, which called back at them with an echoing clangor as they spoke to one another. As they left civilization Hugh was far ahead and Maggie had disappeared down one of the small side channels. Jake felt itchy not knowing where she was, so he went after her, but when he finally found her he had to back out: the stream was too narrow for both of them at one time. Then they paddled in tandem, Maggie and Jake, and she talked softly of Grenville, how he had not appeared at her house this Saturday, when Hugh was sailing—but she had found him in the marsh, standing in the shallows.

"I hope you don't mind," Grenville had said, when he saw Maggie coming toward him. "I thought I'd catch some blue crab, so I borrowed the net hanging in the boat shed, and the pail."

"And Hugh's wading boots," Maggie said.

"Well, yes. One gets so waterlogged otherwise." He made a quick dart with the net, twisting it to trap the scissoring crab, and flipping it over into the bucket where it joined two other crabs knocking against the sides.

"How will you cook them?" she asked.

"In that thing," he said, pointing to a contraption of nested tin cans sitting on a bed of charcoal. "It steams them."

"In river water?"

"It gets boiled in the process," he said. "It's a tasty broth, quite nourishing."

She couldn't tell if he was joking. "Do you need anything else?" she asked.

"Well, if you wanted to, you could leave me some potatoes and a lemon. Oh, and some butter. The rest I can pretty much gather for myself."

When she asked where she should leave them, he pointed to a space under the boardwalk, above the tide line.

"And is that all?" She was joking.

"Well—if you had an extra bottle of Tabasco."

She had only dared stay with him a few minutes longer. The addition of the Tabasco sauce frightened her.

As Maggie recounted this conversation to Jake, her voice was full of strangled longing, and Jake pictured Grenville wearing Hugh's green waders—striding dark and immensely tall, and charming all the women.

⌣·

Hugh led them down a side branch into an old mill pond. The mill itself was no longer standing, but its stones lay tumbled like bodies, its foundations home to wild blackberry and fern. At the edge of the pond three boys stood in the water in their undershorts. Beside them bobbed an aluminum canoe. As Hugh and Jake arrived, one of the boys looked up, having just hidden something under his clothes in the canoe. Beer cans dotted the shoreline, submerged in the pond water. Empties lay in the aluminum boat scattered around a glass jar of sluggish minnows. There was something not right about these boys. They appeared to have stalled in the most unattractive ditch of pubescence: their bodies too large for their brains, yet too small to be drinking; their faces were too furtive for midday. Hugh asked them about a larger pond that he thought should be nearby. They looked at him but didn't focus and appeared sheepish at being addressed in their underwear.

Finally the tallest one looked straight at Hugh. "You interested in swimming?" he asked.

The other two boys laughed.

"Well, if you're going upriver, maybe you won't be too interested anymore."

"Yeah, maybe," the smallest one chimed in.

"Yeah, not too much," said the middle one, who was fat.

"Maybe you'll feel more like fishing," explained the tall one.

"Sure, fishing," echoed the smallest. The fat boy laughed.

Hugh and Jake turned around, spooked by the boys and their underpants and their tuneless laughter.

⌣·

At times they were all within sight of one another. Then the river meanders would tighten, or side channels would beckon, and soon no other boat would be visible. The river closed in on them, tree branches interlocking overhead. Exposed roots grappled the banks and fingered their way into the water. The air was gray and the surface of the river an olive mirror. Jake stopped paddling to unbutton his shirt. Hugh was still far ahead, but the others passed him. Maggie was looking serious; Connie and David were telling Clay a story about crocodiles; Paul, in his blue kayak, was still furious at Gillian; Philip and Celia were chattering about what things cannot be said in language; Turko and Storm were off in an eleven-year-old world of their own.

Jake came upon Gillian a bit later. She had pulled her kayak up onto the riverbank. She was standing, talking to a man who sat leaning against a sapling, with his back to the river. She bent down to scratch her ankle, her black hair tumbling out of its pins. Jake could see into her blouse, to where the tan of her neck gave way to a fragile-seeming whiteness of her breasts, but it wasn't Jake she was leaning over for.

"I'm Gillian Gifford," she announced to the man, looking up at him, still scratching. She had on her come-and-get-me look. "What are you doing here?"

Then she looked up and saw Jake floating by. She asked him to tell the others she was stopping there, as her boat was too long to make the increasingly sharp and narrow turns and she had to keep backing up.

It wasn't until Jake had gone around the next turning that he realized that the man with his back to him was probably Grenville; it made sense for him to have inserted himself even into their Sunday river trip. He hadn't been able to get a good look at Grenville, who was like a cat disappearing around the corner, a mote, a floater. He would be Jake's *delirium tremens* totem, if Jake drank a lot more than he actually did. Grenville had captured the soul of Maggie, and now he haunted the riverbanks of Jake's Sunday observances. Jake wanted to beach his boat and go up on the riverbank to get a good look. He had seen the man's blue shirt, and knew that he would be long and insinuating and dark-bearded. Grenville would find Gillian irresistible, Jake suspected, especially once she started reciting poems to him. Perhaps Maggie would finally realize how awful Grenville was, if he did take up with Gillian. But Jake also wanted to grab Gillian from the riverbank and let her have his own boat; he was sure he could handle hers, even as the river got narrower and the turns tighter.

They continued upriver; the trees clutched more tightly at each other until finally the undergrowth was so thick that the only way they could proceed was by slither and pull: lying down, they forced their boats through the curtain of twigs by pulling on the branches. At the same time they had to shield faces and vital parts with their hands. It was always a leap of faith that there was in fact any river left on the far side of such spiked and branchy gateways.

The river opened up a bit, deep now and cool, with a meadow on one side, trees and ferns on the other. Feeling scraped and hot, Jake beached his kayak, pulled off his shirt, and waded in for a swim. The water was clear, showing the leaves matted on the bottom. The others would soon catch up, he thought, and lying on his back he swam around the next bend, kicking slowly and happily, thinking how glorious summer was. He stopped kicking and floated dreamily looking up at sky and leaves, until his head bumped against a furry piece of shore. He redirected himself, kicking lazily. Then, because the shore had felt much too soft, he turned over.

A large brown eye gazed at him unblinking. Black and white fur surrounded it, submerged. A Holstein calf. Drowned and yet standing upright, only the top of its head and that one eye out of the water.

Jake flailed back to his boat. He took a coil of line from the compartment behind the seat. Maggie arrived just as he was setting out toward the cow again. "Is it nice?" she called. "Shall I come in?"

"No, don't," Jake said. "Follow me in your boat, I need your help."

They roped the calf around its forelegs and belly and pulled it up onto the bank. It used all of their combined strength to do it. Jake was afraid that if it were really dead, it might come apart on them, but it wasn't bloated and didn't smell. It hadn't attracted flies or fish, yet. Together, they lifted it by its hind legs to drain the water out of its lungs. Then Jake sat on the animal's side for a moment, then got up, sat and got up, hoping that he could work its internal bellows before his own knees gave out, and knowing that he could not bring himself to perform mouth-to-mouth respiration on a wet cow.

"Those boys must have done this," Maggie said as Jake continued with strange-looking knee bends. "That was why they were snickering so. What little shits."

Jake nodded and squatted once more as the cow twitched and turned to face him; finally it vomited on his leg, covering him with half-digested milk, tinged green with bits of grass, not yet rumenous. Jake lurched up and tumbled himself into the river. Maggie loosened the rope and the cow scrambled to find footing. Then it slowly walked away.

"Here," Maggie said, tossing Jake the rope. "Rinse this off, too. You've some green stuff in your beard." She got into her boat and backed away from shore. Jake scrubbed the cow vomit off his face and legs.

"That was quite lovely, what you did," Maggie said. "Those knee bends. I never would have thought of that."

Glowing from her compliment and from the exertion, Jake swam back around the curve to where he had left his kayak. The others were already there, perched on the sandy bank, unwrapping their lunch things. Maggie told them what had happened with the sodden Holstein. Jake explained that Gillian had decided to stop back at the narrows.

Maggie sensed that Jake was holding something back, and she began to question him, asking, "But whatever did she want to stop for?"

Jake explained about the length of her boat and the tightness of the turns.

"What about lunch? Shouldn't one of us go back and take her something?" Maggie asked.

Jake told her that Gillian had said she had her picnic with her. Again Maggie gave him a look, as though perhaps he wasn't telling something.

"She's got her writing book with her," Jake said. "And one of her fine-tipped pens."

⌣·

It had been Jake's idea, originally, to drop everything on Sundays in order to explore the rivers around Cranford. Such voyages seemed to put his own yearnings and scratchings after progress in perspective. It told him things could wait for a day: his own gardens could grow without him; Maggie's cloth mermaid could sit alone on the living-room couch, gesturing its pointy fingers at the shaft of sunlight drifting across the floor; Sally's fireworks could simply hang on hold. It was a time to get out of himself and look at the otherness of things, Jake thought. Spirit scrubbing, he called it. Cleaning the mind-slate. He still had to fight off his hourly skittishness about the passing of time. They would all die and what had they got to show for themselves? That they ate dark chocolate on the river? You eat a single square of black sweetness alone under the arching willows, when all the other boats have disappeared and all you can hear is a faraway humming, the distant buzz of a farmer sawing a tree at the edge of his field. You sit alone for a moment and the water is quiet; looking down you see the reflection of intricate branchwork and sky superimposed on the golden leaf mold of the stream bed and you wonder what could be grander than eating chocolate on the river. Witnessing the play of light on the river while you eat that chocolate.

Chapter Nine

MARGARET BEECHER GIFFORD had never been devious, but over the course of the summer Jake watched with increasing uneasiness as she turned secretive; she would ask him questions about foxes, moles, and others who tunneled the earth or made their dens in walls or hedges. She continued to hide the man who was living somewhere on the margins of her property and except for Jake, no one was supposed to know about this apparition: not her husband nor her four children and their mates, nor the six grandchildren. Grenville, whom Jake pictured now as dressed in a pale linen suit, with a neatly clipped black beard and perhaps with a gold necklace in addition to the gold watch Jake was sure he wore, had apparently moved to a more distant shack now that all the Gifford family was staying on the farm; he never showed up in the Gifford's kitchen anymore, and Maggie haunted the marshes and the forests in hopes of finding him.

Early the following week, as Jake crouched in his kitchen garden tying zucchini plants to the bamboo trellis to convince them to climb, Maggie stood running her hands over the giant flower heads of ornamental garlic now gone to seed.

"I am not in love with John Hiram Stuart Grenville," she announced. "His name is too long, for one thing." She brushed away a bee. "For another, he is charming but he is never nice. But I do like the questions he asks."

"Like what?"

She told about his questioning her motives for sewing the mermaid. *Look*, Jake kept himself from saying, *I could ask you that. But I didn't think I had to. You sew because you sew. That's what you do. I garden. And fuck things up with Sally. And want you.*

"I'm not in love with him. I'm still in love with Hugh. Hugh is wondrous."

Well, that is awfully convenient. Jake moved over to the tomato plants and tied them to the uprights of the trellis.

"Grenville fascinates but doesn't satisfy," she said.

Early Girl. Brandywine. Yellow Pear. Green Zebra. "Why do you let him live on your land?"

"I don't exactly 'allow' it; I'm not even certain that he does. I just assume he does, but we've never discussed it." Maggie tucked a strand of red hair behind her ear. She felt as protective of Grenville as if he were a fugitive, she said, and as secretive about his living on her farm as if she were clandestinely in love. Now, during her family's visit, she was afraid that one of her grandchildren would stumble upon his lair and she hoped that he had retreated upriver, or down. Jake's property, while large, had a number of sheds, but they were used all the time, so Grenville wouldn't be there.

Jake began thinning the *moula,* a large white daikon radish from Nepal, whose seeds a French woman had once given him. He put the sprouts in a corner of his basket.

"Do you think he'll come back when they've all gone home? You know, I really want you to meet him: I think you two would get along."

Jake put some moula leaves in his mouth so that he could appear to be chewing and tasting and thinking and wouldn't have to answer. He stood up and rubbed the small of his back with his fists, as though that and the chewing of the peppery leaves were all he could manage at one time.

"I'm sure you'll like each other."

Jake was sure they would despise each other. *Nightshade, water hemlock, oleander.* He crouched by the salad greens to thin the katsuma and the pak choi.

"Would you come with me when I go looking for him?"

The mizuna with its still tiny feathery leaves demanded all Jake's attention.

"Are you listening?" She came over and put a hand on his shoulder. "Would you come?"

"Where?"

"To the river. To meet him."

"I'm really pretty busy." *What do I need with some black-bearded archaic hero-type walking my marshes.*

Not in love, she repeated—what she felt for Grenville was more in the nature of a disease, she explained. Like a hump or a limp. Something she could try to mask in public, but when she was alone, or with Jake, it surfaced and she could not get away from it. She wanted a word for what she felt. Not just to pigeonhole him and forget him, though that in itself would be a relief, but when she had a word for something she could use it as a cipher and move it around the game board of her mind. Without a word, there was nothing to contain it, to make it draw in its tentacles so she could maneuver it, take it in the house, drag it upstairs.

"This Grenville," Jake said, looking up at her. "Do you think that he's your familiar?"

"He is," she said, smiling with relief. "My familiar."

Or incubus, Jake thought. He wondered whether his mail-order ministry licensed him to perform exorcisms. He plucked some leaves of giant red mustard and ate them. The taste was so strong it made him hiccup. His eyes watered. He plucked some more and chewed them thoughtfully.

Grenville was not, Maggie said, strictly speaking, a fugitive. He had left his normal life and wife, but was in hiding rather than flight. She paused. "He is out of his *ordinary*."

"Ordinary what?"

"Oh, come on."

"You know, it's going to get legally pretty sticky: tax returns. He'll have to do something about his marriage, won't he?"

The irony of Jake being the one to talk about civil responsibility was not lost on Maggie. She snorted with that great crooked nose of hers. She laughed.

"We've never talked about any of this stuff," she said. "He tends to keep away from the lumber of the practical."

Jake wondered if that was Grenville's phrase, the lumber of the practical.

"It's as though he's taking a private vacation. He did say that it was possible that his wife had alerted the police, but he didn't really think they could do anything to him. One isn't legally obliged to go home."

～

Later that same afternoon, Maggie was in such a convolution over Grenville that she decided to seek out his wife, Denise. Grenville had hardly talked about Denise except to say that she was more a reason for him to stay at home than to leave: she was a doctor; she was smart and much too good for him. Now that Maggie saw Grenville so rarely, she felt greedy and anxious about him and wanted to know more. She needed another view and thought Denise might be the key.

Maggie searched through the local newspapers, the parish weeklies, the watershed association newsletter, to see if Denise was on any committee she could join, so that their meeting would appear gradual and natural rather than elaborate and contrived. She was ready to perform some calamity at Denise's door: a nosebleed, a twisted ankle, crashing her car into a telephone pole; but Jake warned her that if such a thing didn't work the first time—if Denise was not in or didn't want to talk—the laws of coincidence would seem to prohibit a second emergency on the same doorstep. Finally, an old clipboard hanging in Maggie's pantry caught Jake's attention. Not the stacked sheets of neatly penciled gardening notes, but the board itself spoke of ringing, with impunity, the doorbells of strangers. Clipboards make one immediately legitimate. Jake suggested to Maggie that she could type up a survey and ask Denise Grenville if she would answer the questions. Her answers would show what kind of a woman she was and what had caused her husband to wander away from her hearth: whether it had been some ordinary sexual blunder or, as Grenville claimed, a perverse inspiration.

～

If wooden bat-houses were available at no charge at town hall, would you put one up?

Maggie didn't know where the questions came from. They slipped into her mind as she worked on her cloth sculpture, stitching the embroidery of scales on the mermaid's tail. When she picked sugar snap peas or lettuce, more questions bubbled up; she wished that the summer visit of her brood was over already. All year she looked forward to these summers together; she loved watching their familial dance. One of them was always exultant or in trouble, but it was a different one each time, as though there was some rotation of distress or glory. Now she wanted to sweep them all away, to clear her brain for tracking Grenville.

What is your opinion of the osprey situation: (Desperate/Improving/ Under control?)

They always wanted to know, her children, what she was working on, what she was thinking about, what she was reading. She had to account for herself. Usually some part of her mind was occupied in tracking their lives, figuring and worrying and trying not to interfere. Her brain now felt crowded.

Do you prefer wooden sailboats or fiberglass?

Have you ever mulched your garden with cocoa bean shells? With coffee grounds? Buckwheat hulls?

She would wake up needing a pencil, questions having sprouted in her sleeping mind. She found she was unexpectedly nosy. She liked to ask things. She would find out who Grenville was by discovering the wife he had left behind. It was midweek, usually a hollow time, the longest between his visits. But now that her house and barn were full he seemed to have gone away entirely; the festoons of his visits had gone slack, fallen. She went to bed at night hoping she didn't mumble questions in her sleep.

How would you describe yourself: (Desperate/Improving/Under control?)

Of course, it was suspicious that there was no apparent purpose to her survey. It reminded her of the marketing questions one is asked to answer camouflaged under the guise of "registering" a newly purchased appliance. She wondered if she could pull it off. She knew she was prying yet she felt no shame. She was surprised at herself.

How many different computers have you owned?

How often do you go to a restaurant for lunch? Dinner?

Are you single/married/separated/divorced?

If you are separated, would you like to be reunited with your spouse?

She began to wonder about the very nature of questioning. Bits began to slip out, in spite of her vigilance.

One evening, as the midsummer sunlight slipped through the fern-like boughs of the locust trees, she sat at the edge of the herb garden, weeding, and cutting rosemary and oregano. Connie was grilling eggplants and potatoes. Tony had made the grills years before out of oil drums that he had sliced in half with Jake's acetylene torch. Maggie had been afraid that the remnants of oil in the drum would blow up, but the cleaving had been uneventful and the drums soon burned clean.

Connie called to her mother through the cooking smoke. "Maggins, what are you thinking of at this precise moment?"

Maggie looked up. Connie's gray eyes held her gaze, while, in the brush at the edge of the field, where so many animals shelter, something moved: the cat, perhaps, or a woodchuck.

What is the likelihood that you and your spouse will be reunited?

"What is the likelihood," Maggie began. "What is the likelihood that Milo with his sky-blue angel eyes will eat all those carrots in the blue bowl?" Why did all her grandchildren have such names: Turko, Clay, and Blue; Milo; Osprey and Storm? Nouns, adjectives, animals, and places; not names. As each new grandchild was born she listened to the given name and was wise enough to say only, "Ah." Sometimes it made her feel queasy and disoriented, and she wondered what had become of the old names, the ordinary ones. But mostly she felt glad to be a part of it all, even one generation removed. Turko and Storm were her favorites, perhaps because at eleven they were the oldest. Blue, Osprey: they would give future historians and genealogists something to puzzle over. "Come here, Milo," Maggie called to her youngest grandson. "You can help me find snails."

Milo crawled on fat baby legs over the grass toward her. Was it some other child playing a game off there by the stone wall? Maggie was too preoccupied with her questions to look.

Connie brushed her red-blond hair out of her eyes, leaving a charcoal smudge on her forehead. She said, "I meant before, actually. Before Milo went for the carrots, what were you thinking of?"

"What."

Connie repeated her question.

Maggie said, "That's right, Milo: give the snails to Grandma and she will cut them with her trowel."

Milo squalled, grabbing for the implement of snail death.

"Oh. Would you rather we throw them over the wall? We can do that. Look." She flung two yellow snails over the tumbled stone wall. She turned to Connie. "Sorry dear, but I meant *what* in answer to your question. I was thinking about what *what* means."

By the stone wall, the bandy-legged animal lurked.

"What?"

"What."

Her son Philip looked over at her quizzically. Dark-eyed and dark-browed, he was her youngest. He and his Celia had just started their own publishing house in order to bring out obscure and deserving books. Celia wore long skirts all summer long, even here on the farm; she had gentled Philip, yet she would speak fiercely to Maggie about poetry, trying to make her write more.

Philip said, "Is Milo in your way, Maggins? What is it about the nature of 'what' that interests you?" In his late twenties, Philip had finally outgrown his scorn for her. It could return, Maggie felt, at any time.

"Look, Milo." Maggie hoped to change the subject. "Here's one with only one stripe. An orange snail! How rare."

How much time each day do you spend in the garden?

Maggie realized that what had begun as a lark and as a scam had now grabbed hold of her. She wondered how often confidence tricksters found themselves lost in their own contortions of reality. She wanted to stop thinking about Grenville and questions and Grenville's abandoned wife. Hugh was off getting ice cream for dinner. She wished he were back. Flames and grease smoke flared up from the grills as olive oil dripped from the eggplants.

"Isn't *what* a sort of questioning grunt-word?" said Celia. "Why are you thinking about questions? Why now?" Celia's skirt today was purple, Indian, gathered. She had just come out of the barn where she and Philip and Milo stayed in the converted living space on the second floor. A large kitchen had been put in and much of the summer cooking for the extended family was done there. Gillian and her friend Paul occupied two small rooms on the ground floor, just off of Hugh's vast library.

As Celia had left the barn, carrying the dinner salad in a wooden bowl, the screen door clapped shut, but the animal in the tall grass at the meadow's edge did not startle or run.

Maggie stood up to watch her daughter Gillian strolling over the meadow, back from her afternoon walk. Gillian had been staying longer in the marsh each evening although Maggie had tried to convince her to walk elsewhere this summer, not along the river's edge, thinking that if Grenville were still around she particularly didn't want Gillian to encounter him. Gillian was slinky, she was foxy, she was always in the middle of somebody's divorce. Gillian could vortex love down into blackest want. Gillian hadn't told Maggie much about her new consort, Paul, who was off with Hugh getting dessert—but then, Gillian's truths were often personal and relative. They were based, Maggie knew, on arranging objective reality to paint some imperative and burning explanation. This summer Maggie had begun her own veerings away from the truth, and as part of them she took Gillian for walks anywhere but along the marsh; they had gone to the bird sanctuary, the Poor Farm, the mushroom-filled woods of the old Boy Scout grounds, hoping to get her daughter to haunt these places rather than the edge of the river—but Gillian persisted in traipsing through the marsh grass by the water, coming back so mysteriously radiant and secretive that Maggie feared the worst.

Now Gillian was walking back across the field with Connie's husband, David. It wasn't as though they were holding hands but they were walking in step even though Gillian in her green rubber boots had a shorter stride than David and should have had to skip to keep up with him. As they came close, Gillian was saying, "He has to look back, don't you see? How could the hero not look? And then, of course, he loses her. Everything sweet has disappeared from his life and music is born from his grief."

Something about the pair of them worried Maggie. It was as though they needed to be pried apart. Maggie wanted to take David and put him beside his Connie at the grill, and say, "You two tall strawberry blond ones play together now like good children." "Davie," she called. She couldn't stop herself. "Perhaps you could take over the grilling. Here's some herbs to throw on top of the eggplants." In wanting to keep track of them all, Maggie got so involved and she became terribly sure that only she could keep her children on the right track. Hugh was more trusting, or more complacent: he said they were grown and that was that.

Oregano and rosemary now crackled on the eggplants and scented the air. David took the fork and poked each foil-wrapped potato until it gave a hiss. Earlier that afternoon he and his brother-in-law Tony had gone to catch the fish for dinner. As usual, it was only Tony who caught anything, though they stood side by side in the waves, wearing rubber waders up to their armpits, next to Hugh's friend, old Nat Morrill, the chef, who counseled them: "Think like a fish, Davie. Think like a fish." It always worked for Tony, but not for David. They both liked to go to the beach in the late afternoon though, when the bathers had left and only Morrill was there, with his yellow knapsack; then the bluefish would be running in the riptide between the rocky promontory that formed the other side of the river's mouth and the nearby sandy shore.

Still slightly jealous of Tony's luck at fishing, David began tossing small sticks at the hammock where Tony lay dozing. "Hey, Tony, should we bring the fish from the kitchen? Is it time yet?" Tony startled wildly, then sat up in the hammock, dangling his legs over the side. If David hadn't woken him, he told them all later, he never would have seen the raccoon who now stumbled drunkenly beside the stone wall, strings of drool hanging from its jaw as it walloped toward the mulberry tree by the house. There the animal paused, climbed the trunk, paused again, traversed the main branch and crawled up the shingled roof. Then it scrabbled up the bricks of the chimney and disappeared inside.

"Holy shit," Tony said. "Is anybody watching? A raccoon just climbed down the chimney. Mom? Dave? How many kids are in the house? Man, he looks so ill. Hey. Let's get something, tools from the shed."

Maggie sprang from her chair and reached the garden shed before her sons. Even now she didn't want anyone looking in a shed before she did. "Here," she said. "I'll get them for you." She swung open the door and reached into the chalk-smelling cobwebby darkness. She grabbed the machete and the pitchfork. "Be careful," she said. "Is it really sick? Get all the children out; I'll call the police. Wait: Milo's out here with us; Clay and Blue went in the car with Hugh and Gillian's Paul to the ice-cream place. But that leaves, Oh, God, who does it leave? Turko," she counted on her fingers. "And Osprey and Storm." A momentary rush of irrelevant pride that she could keep track of all those names. She grabbed a hoe and followed them to the house.

"But why do we have to?"

"Can we see him?"

"But they're so cute; why do we have to go outside?"

"We could make him better."

"Why do you have that knife-thing? Are you gonna hack him?"

Tony and David shooed the children outside, telling them to go to the wooden box where the balls and bats were kept, and to play on the grass until dinner. Then Tony, with the machete, and David, with the pitchfork, began stalking through the house.

"Kitchen," Tony said. They checked the fireplace there, and then the one in the dining room. Nothing. They tiptoed upstairs, trying to locate the rustling noise they could hear behind the walls. Maggie stood by the front door, listening. Finally a crash of dishes brought her running to the kitchen. With her hoe raised in front of her, she opened the swinging pantry door. The raccoon crouched on a high shelf in front of a tall stack of white dinner plates. These plates were old porcelain, white with gold rim, they had come from Grandfather Beecher, and Maggie was fond of them, though they were so formal she never used them. The animal had already swept all the cups and saucers off the shelf and was now flinging the plates, hooking his claws around the edge and sweeping his foreleg out to the side. Raccoons had come in the house before, but they either drank sedately from the toilets or went for the trash pails. As Maggie stood there, this one seemed not to notice her but continued sliding one plate at a time off the pile, to crash on the shards already on the pantry floor.

"Hey. Cut that out." Maggie swung her hoe, but it was as though the raccoon could tell she didn't really mean it, and it just bounced off his side. This made her mad—suddenly, she *did* mean it—she tightened her grip on the wooden handle; she pointed the tip of the blade at him and flailed. It caught him this time, gashing his side, hooking him, and the continuation of her swing brought him off the top shelf to the floor beside her. The furred body thudded on the crockery. He was too close.

Maggie climbed up onto the wooden counter in case he was winded rather than dead. There she stood, her hoe poised. The raccoon caught his breath, rolled onto his belly, crouched on all fours, then raised himself on his hind legs to look up at her. Woman and animal, they stared at each other. He looked crazed, she thought, wild and wrong. Rabid. They were both quiet now. Still. Everything had stopped. She couldn't tell if she was still breathing. Or if he was. She didn't dare call out. The wooden handle of the hoe felt sweaty in her grip. She could feel the grain. She would need to oil the handle this fall. The blade probably needed sharpening, but where was the file, the mill bastard? In the shed.

The raccoon was bleeding; blood pulsed out of his side. Rolling drunkenly he walked toward her. She focused her grip on the handle. The animal screamed in that unusual haunting whoop it saves for fighting or mating. She swung and beat his head. Anger flowed into her. The more she hit him, the more she wanted to. She savaged his body. The blade caught in flesh and fur and she had to coax it out, holding with one hand onto the cupboard shelf so she wouldn't lose her balance. She turned the hoe so the haft would hit him, not the blade. She preferred to knock him senseless rather than to chop him up. Between blows she held to the cupboard to catch her breath. The evening had been so calm before. The light in the garden.

"Hey, Mom. Hold on a moment. Mom?" Tony edged into the pantry stepping on the broken crockery now splattered with blood. The raccoon stirred, tried to pull its legs into a crouch. Tony cut neatly with his machete, whack, thump, Tail, legs, head: beast became meat.

"Tony. Tone?" David stood at the door. "He's pretty much done for, now, don't you think?"

Tony lowered his machete. He wiped his face with his free hand. He placed the bloody knife like an offering at Maggie's feet. Then he held out his arms to his mother and lifted her down.

Maggie looked at the small wood-paneled room: blood, teacups, fur, flesh. "Amazing," she said. "What a mess an old woman can make if you leave her alone with an animal and a few dishes." She stood her hoe in the corner. "Lock the front door," she said. "Don't let anyone in until we've cleaned up. Don't let the children see this."

Maggie put the crockery in doubled paper bags and found trash bags for the animal parts. She took rubber gloves from under the kitchen sink. "I guess we should save the head for County Health."

They washed the walls and cupboards and floor with Mr. Clean. They threw their gloves into the trash, and double-bagged it. They washed their hands and arms in the kitchen sink with more Mr. Clean.

Tony and David insisted Maggie take the first shower. Before she did so, she leaned out the bedroom window and called to Connie, "Everything's fine now. We're just going to wash up. We'll be out in a minute." Maggie could see from Connie's expression that she should have washed before showing herself. A quick glance in the mirror revealed her, wild-haired and blood-streaked.

Maggie was exhausted. But somehow it was a solace, the whole raccoon business, for during those moments of carnage she had been entirely at one with Tony and her son-in-law, David. She had been absorbed and now that single-mindedness cheered her, even though the task had been killing an animal. This was the first time all summer that her mind had not been half elsewhere, yearning, looking for Grenville. The sudden purity of focus had been a startling relief.

Hugh drove up just as Maggie came outside. "Black raspberry," he said smiling. "And chocolate and vanilla, OK?"

She told him about the devastation of the raccoon. "We saved the head. He looked pretty sick to me."

Hugh put the bag of ice cream on the grass and took his wife in his arms.

He was still holding her when the police drove up. Two officers jumped from the patrol car, guns drawn.

"Excuse me sir. Where's your animal?"

Hugh kept hugging Maggie, and gestured to Tony and David who were coming out of the house. They explained. Tony said, "Actually, gentlemen, you could put your guns away. The raccoon is very dead now." They followed him into the house, guns still drawn.

Turko had run over to Jake's house as soon as he and the other children had been sent outside. He and Jake arrived in time to see the two policemen come out of the house, the younger one carrying a green plastic bag, holding it gingerly, away from his body.

Storm ran up to Maggie and Hugh. "We want to know what happened and where the raccoon is and besides, when is supper?"

Maggie disengaged herself from Hugh and bent down to hug Storm. She held the girl's shoulders. "Come inside with me," she said. "We'll put the ice cream in the freezer and I'll put my tongue around some Scotch and I'll tell you everything that's happened, OK?"

Soon the fish was grilled. Eggplants and zucchini filled the stoneware platters, potatoes in foil sat in a blackened roasting pan. As the others served themselves, Maggie sat back in her old green chair. She sipped her drink and watched them. She wanted this sort of hot, excited calm to settle in like weather over her tribe.

The suspended daylight of the summer evening bounded softly over the fields, inhabited the lettuces in the kitchen garden, and glowed in the young white grapes hanging from the old wooden trellis. The light was constant and recurrent and dependable and astonishing. We think the rule is tranquillity. But, in fact, the rule is tranquillity-with-disruptions. Disruptions are part of the pattern, like the rocks in the stream around which eddies form.

Chapter Ten

"WHY DIDN'T YOU TELL ME you were going?" Jake said.

"I thought you would stop me," Maggie said, breathless and laughing. "I thought you would talk me out of it." It was late on a Sunday afternoon. Maggie, sunburned, wild red hair escaping from under her hat, had gone straight to Jake's house after sailing with Grenville.

That Sunday was the first time Maggie had ever missed one of Jake's Sunday excursions. Perhaps because of this, the river had been spiteful, with the late-July sun whipping the wind against canoes and kayaks no matter which direction Jake chose. Buoyancy no longer seemed to him a wild humorous miracle. A pair of sunken rocks had finally grabbed his paddle and split the blade off. He poled his way home in a stinker of a mood, and found Maggie pacing in his moss garden.

"Oh, Jake," Maggie said now. "Would you hold onto me? I need to settle down before I go home."

He held her. He would have done it forever. She smelled of the sea. He took her hat off; her hair was all matted with bits of seaweed, so he combed it with his fingers. Then he walked her through the shade by the rock pool, and into the sun, past the lavender and rosemary. He kept one arm around her waist and could feel that she was still racing.

At first Maggie had dismissed Grenville's invitation as nonsense, but she began ruminating on a remark that he had made about her seeming so self-congratulatory of a life that was quiet and safe and dull, so that when he finally telephoned—after he had watched Hugh set off for Block Island—Maggie accepted. She told the rest of the family she was going to visit a friend in Wareham and drove to meet Grenville at the boatyard.

"You know," she said to Jake. "I got to worrying about whether I had always been too prudent. I wanted to see whether I could experience this jumping out of one's normal life that he was talking about."

"But look what it did to him," Jake said. "It ruined him. He can't go back." He had been holding her around the waist, but now he let go and stepped away from her because he had begun shaking and didn't want Maggie to feel it. Maggie was supposed to come to Jake— if ever she stepped out of her life—not to some vagabond.

"He doesn't know how to go back," she said. "He thought maybe I could teach him, if once he got me to understand what he'd done. But then . . ."

She stopped, and Jake knew she didn't want him to go back, because then she would lose him. Jake didn't want to lose her. He gave her a hug; he wanted her to stay—in his arms, in his garden. He wanted to call down a lightning bolt to strike them both, to turn them into trees if necessary, and keep them there.

"What did it do to you?" Jake asked, releasing his hold again. "Did it capture you? Did he give you whatever it was that he had?" Meaning, are you contaminated now?

Maggie stopped walking and turned to face him.

"It was so strange," she said. "You have always been trying to explain something about light. And then, yes, I forgot Hugh, I forgot the children, I forgot the farm . . ."

Jake hugged her again, right at that moment, holding his cheek against hers, so that she could not utter his name on her list of forgotten things.

"But you came back," he said. He could only inhale jagged edges of air now, and he tried to keep the gasping out of his voice.

"He wasn't out to kidnap me," she laughed. "He just wanted to show me that one can step out. And I really did see it, you know. I don't know whether it was being with him, or watching the light, but I did see something."

As Maggie spoke, it occurred to Jake that perhaps intoxicants and controlled substances were safer ways of doing this—of stepping out, of seeing things. He didn't tell her these thoughts, he wanted her to continue. Stories can shatter if you break in.

Maggie said, "I will never call you a psychopathic luminist again. Remember when we used to argue about it, about your devotion to light?"

Jake put his broad hand on her shoulder and they continued walking.

Maggie and Grenville had sailed over to Cuttyhunk, arriving at sunset. They ate dinner at the single restaurant on the island—fish chowder and salad and ice cream—and then walked to the top of the island. There, in the ruins of the old lookout tower they lay down to look at the sky, which was flagrant with stars, overwhelming and brilliant. "Almost attack stars," she said. "Out of all proportion."

They found their way down to the beach in the darkness and rowed the dinghy back to the boat. They sat in the cockpit, drinking Scotch and watching the stars, until it was time to go to sleep.

Did you sleep with him? Jake didn't dare ask. He could see them: Maggie—tall and naked, her dark red hair unbound, her legs and arms wrapped around Grenville. He was taller, dark and sinewy with that short clipped black beard. He probably, Jake thought, kept his gold watch on, even as they coiled around each other, and all the numerals glowed.

Maggie and Jake wandered through the blue garden. For once he didn't pull at the deadheads of the balloon flowers. He couldn't see properly, for the air had started to shimmer: bees and midges were effervescing from the midnight purple salvia and the clear sky veronica; the afternoon light was buzzing into separate particles. Jake was afraid he was going to black out.

There, with Grenville, at their mooring in Cuttyhunk, Maggie had heard the noise of the clams, those clonking underwater castanets. Such an eerie sound, she said, which one could not hear above deck, only below. She asked Jake if they called to one another, the clams; she knew clams didn't have ears.

"Maybe," Jake said, "they send out pressure waves and then they travel toward each other's pulsing until they are close enough for whatever sort of sexual congress clams indulge in. I'm making this up," he admitted.

But did you indulge?

Sea, wind, halyards, and the sound of clams. Maggie told him she hadn't been able to sleep. She was in the main cabin, the dining-room settee, which converted to a double bed.

Oh, double: did you double?

She couldn't sleep because the light from the stars was too strong, and the noise of the clams too clattering. She could see the Milky Way through the hatchway. During the night she became aware of the many sounds of water: against the hull; plashing against the prow of the dinghy; jostling in the drains. Who would have thought that water could have so many voices: tickling, slopping. One sound as the hull slaps down on the water and another sound as the wave crashes into the hull. "Do you think it depends on whether there's a greater or lesser volume of water: when it's the wave, it's smaller, so it just makes a slapping sound; while when it's the hull thumping down on the water, there's all the ocean's depth beneath—is that it?"

Jake didn't answer. He just wondered:

Who was thumping? Who was humping? What were your joining noises?

Maggie said there were also other noises: the blue flag talked all night: *flap-slide-flap-slide,* while the ensign just said: *flut flut flut.* As dawn came she went out on deck and watched Grenville sleep. Now Venus was in the cup of the finely slivered moon. Even before the sun rose over the hillside, five houses on the island caught the early fire of first light in their windows and they looked to be exploding with it, in silence. The sleeper beside her turned over in his sleep to escape the light. Already a patch of radiance behind the dark hill. A motorboat grumbled out toward sea. And there it was, the yellow-white fireball. She couldn't look. She had to.

Jake was beset with wanting to ask Maggie if she and Grenville had had sex, and here she was telling him the important thing, that she had finally noticed the light. But had that anatomical joining occurred? He felt suddenly how odd it was that the force that drove him so—lust—was of such little real importance. Such a dumb motor. They were animals, all of them. He despaired.

Maggie and Jake turned through the grape arbor to walk into the wilder garden. The muscats hung down in full green clusters with just a hint of the warmer yellow tones to come.

"Tell me something," Jake finally said.

Maggie smiled as though she knew what was coming. She disengaged herself from his arm and looked at him. "What is it you want to know?"

Although Jake always told her of his adventures, he had never had to ask about her own. He touched her shoulder. "What you haven't told me," he started. "What you haven't mentioned, is the sexual atmosphere. Did you sleep with him, for example?"

Did the bastard lay a hand on you? Did you lay a hand on him?

"What do you think?"

"Well, on the one hand, how could you not have?"

She smiled. "And on the other?"

This was tortuous. The cymbals were clashing too loudly in his ears. Jake wanted to drop to his knees and put his arms around Maggie's legs, and beg her not to have become lovers with Grenville. "And on the other hand," he said, "I don't think, from what you've told me, that sex was what this trip was about. It seemed to be following some other path entirely." He tried to lighten his tone. His hope was showing, his jealousy and his desire.

"I said just now, that Grenville had slept on deck. But that wasn't really true," Maggie began. "I don't know why I lied to you. I'm not used to telling these things. I'm not used to having anything to tell. Though, you, of all people, are the only one I could say such things to. Anyway, after we rowed back to our boat in the darkness the air was still warm. We decided to swim. There didn't seem much point in getting into bathing suits, so we swam naked. Then we climbed back onto the boat and wrapped ourselves in towels. We sat on deck, drinking and watching the night. I don't know what he'd been planning. In my mind, I guess it had never been out of the question. Though that wasn't why I went on the trip with him. I'm not making much sense, I know."

"No, no, you are. You're fine," Jake said. He could barely walk, his heart so intent, his prurience so heavy. He was thick-legged with desire. "Go on. What was it like?"

"What was it like? You're asking me to describe how sex was with Grenville? He had been so elusive. I never knew when he would visit me at the farm, and then, when he did, he would disappear without warning and without reason. Now, I had him in a place where he couldn't get away. I was nervous and I wanted him."

"So?" Jake tried not to sound petulant. He tried to sound comforting, eliciting, pastoral. Oh, Jake, he told himself, you humbug.

"This isn't upsetting you, is it? We don't need to talk about it."

"If it were, would I be asking you?" Jake was jealous and he was also a blue-black liar. As soon as she left he would go shoot himself. Perhaps shoot Grenville first. The tall, tanned, black-bearded bastard who had taken his innocent cousin onto his white boat and enslaved her. He could have at least taken his watch off. "Please, go on," Jake said.

"There we were, drinking Scotch, getting warm again after swimming, and I really wanted to sleep with him. I mean, I was completely overcome. Whisky does that to me, but also Grenville does that to me. As we were sitting there, I turned my back to him, so I could lean against him a bit. He began to rub the back of my neck, until, well, I relaxed into him. We went downstairs."

"And?" Jake couldn't stop interrupting with what he knew were meaningless interrogations. Why couldn't he just keep quiet and let her tell it at her own pace? He was afraid she would trail away and just leave the rest of the story to his own imagination.

"And—" Maggie stopped walking and looked at Jake. "We fucked like bunnies." She gave a wicked laugh. She knew how unlike her it was for her to say that.

"Not like humans?" Jake said, hopefully.

"Oh, that too."

"What was the mood, then?"

"During or after?"

"Both."

"Well, during, it was sweet and urgent, and then sweet and slow.

And after, well, it was sweet and exhausted. I had never seen him that way. When he visits me he is usually, well, savage. As though he is out to batter me down. Conversationally, I mean. I like that, but it leaves me never knowing where I am."

"And did you 'know where you were' after screwing?" He hadn't meant to say it that way. Nor had he meant to sound bitter. It had welled out of him.

"At first I thought I did. I thought his tenderness was not just of the moment."

"But he turned rotten again?"

"No, he stayed gentle, extremely gentle, for the whole rest of the trip." She paused. "You should meet him, you know. You would really understand things then. Don't you think it's time? Would you come with me the next time I go to see him?"

"A bit of ring-around-a-rosy in sweet old Cranford?" Jake said. "I'm not sure I'm quite ready for that."

"Come on, Jake. Cut it out. You know that wasn't what I meant. What is this whole riptide here? Why are you being so awful, actually?"

"Oh, Mags. I'm sorry. I didn't mean that. All this worries me; it seems so unlike you. I just don't think you should do anything sudden. I don't know. Give me a hug."

Maggie turned to him and hugged him and all his jealousy and his desire and he held her and the fury of her excitement.

"Promise me one thing," Jake said.

She pulled back and looked at him.

"Promise me that you won't go telling anybody about this."

"Like Hugh?"

"Hugh," he said. "Wait on it. Wait until you're sure you understand what's going on."

Chapter Eleven

IT WAS HUGH WHO BROUGHT ABOUT the next meeting between Jake and Sally. Hugh was fond of Sally and was always trying to smooth things out between her and Jake. Jake wondered sometimes if Hugh also wanted to keep him happily entangled so that he would not have the time to be troublesome on other fronts.

When Hugh and Sally arrived at Jake's house the following Saturday, they were both full of some secret mischief. Jake had been working on his new toolshed with Tony, putting a window in, while Tony's younger brother Philip was sitting near them on a stump, amiably trying to get them to see the importance of some medieval poet whose work he was bringing out in a new edition. The closeness between Tony and his brother Philip was charming and odd, as Tony was dyslexic and not at all literary, and Philip's passion, aside from his wife, Celia of the long skirts, was devoted to the thin books that they published together. Age hardly separated the brothers at all, and that summer they hovered on either side of thirty. Like Tony, Philip sometimes needed to flee from the confusion of siblings and spouses and cousins at the Gifford house, and though he was useless with a hammer and dangerous with a power drill, Jake and Tony would let him help carry boards, or hold them in place while measurements were being taken. Philip's preferred tool was the spirit level; there he was positively gifted. When he wasn't determining their horizontals and verticals he sat nearby and chatted to them.

In the midst of all the hammering, Hugh and Sally appeared with their plots and smiles and bags of groceries. When things were good between her and Jake, Sally would cook dinner at his house on

Saturdays and sometimes she would bring lunch as well. Jake hadn't seen her for more than two weeks, since the bluefish dinner when she had left so abruptly. Although he had called her the next morning to try to right things, and repeated his calls on the following days, they never got further than the question of the possible future uses of that strange forest room Jake had made of emerald cedars.

"But why not?" she would say. "My students are not animals. They won't gore your trees or trample them down."

"But why?" Jake countered. "I don't want them in my room."

So that Saturday Jake was surprised to see her and he was pleased that Hugh had brought her. Jake needed someone to nudge his life: he was feeling abandoned by Maggie's increased entanglement with Grenville, and by his own inability to be good to Sally. He had thought he would have to imagine some new penance to make up with her, and he knew he wasn't very good at inventing such things, yet here she was, offering to make sandwiches for everybody. Jake had been planning to get meatball submarines from the pizza shop in town, and knew that Sally would have brought what he called sprouty-hairy green things with cheese from sprouty-hairy goats or other nonstandard animals, but he could always go and get the submarines later, in the middle of the afternoon, when he and Tony and Philip would need more sustenance.

She looked very fine, his Sally: the noon sun glinted off her blond hair, which was shagged today rather than seal-smooth, and her yellow T-shirt had a grooved, corduroylike texture that he could almost feel in his fingertips. As they sat on the grass with their goaty sandwiches, starving and grateful and about to partake, Sally was gleeful about something and Hugh, too, had the gloating look of impending news on his narrow craggy face.

"Let's tell them, Hugh," Sally said finally.

Hugh slowly rolled up the sleeves of his green plaid shirt and began telling another chapter of his researches into old cults in coastal Massachusetts. He had just found references to a sect over in South Dartmouth where the members had lived together on an island in the Slocum River in a commune started just after the Second World War. Each weekday they would row to the mainland in wooden dories, and go to day jobs in New Bedford. The women worked in bakeries and factories, and the men were hired by day to work as stevedores on the docks. Then at dusk, an old white REO school bus with a blue cross on the front would pick them up and bring them back to the riverbank and they would row home to the island. Their leader, who named himself after an Indian chief, believed in the transubstantiation of souls, bread and wine, and held services that alternated total silence with long and rambling sermons and then singing by the whole congregation. The congregation finally split, as such groups generally do, this one over the question of whether music scores should be allowed in the choir, and the schismatics, against written music, took off in the early 1950s and moved to an island off the coast of Delaware. "This part of Massachusetts," Hugh finally said, "always seems to have more odd religions than anywhere else." He grinned at Jake. "No offense, Jake. I mean 'historically speaking.'"

Jake always felt strange when Hugh made remarks like that, because he didn't consider himself a real minister. Jake didn't understand how or why anyone would ever start a cult. With his nineteen-dollar license he felt more like a Justice of the Peace without portfolio, a Notary Public without stamp.

Sally poured iced tea. "The thing I'd really like to see," she said, "is their church, or what remains of it."

"Well, exactly," said Hugh. He explained that in spite of those long Quaker silences during their Sunday worship, the church was lit by stained-glass windows, and the walls were lined with mirrors. "Infinite reflections of the corporeal self to remind them of the infinitude of the human soul."

"It must have been," Sally paused, as though visualizing the church, "well . . . like being inside a kaleidoscope."

"What's keeping us?" Jake looked over at Tony and Philip, then asked Hugh, "Do you know where it is?"

Sally looked pleased to bursting. Hugh took a hand-drawn map out of his pocket. "I made a sketch for you." He explained that he couldn't go along with them as he had a load of books to pick up.

Tony and Philip had already promised to help Hugh. Tony looked at Jake. "Look, you and Sally go," he said. "If it's good, you can take us all back there."

。～.

Sally and Jake put in at the landing on Gaffney Road, below Russell's Mills in South Dartmouth, and let the outgoing tide take them down the Slocum. The estuary stretched out wide and shallow, their pair of kayaks like blue pods on an expanse of pewter. The sky spread over them the warm gray haze of early August and the tide was so low that they had to skim rather than paddle. Even so, each stroke worried the black sulfurous mud that lay just under the clay-colored river bottom. Blue crabs swam their awkward sidestroke showing their underbellies of ghostly pearl.

Hugh's map was almost impossible to read: when your eyes are only a couple of feet above water level, each stand of rushes becomes an island, and distant inlets are invisible. But after landing and searching a couple of minor hummocks, Jake and Sally found what looked like the proper place, with decaying iron bollards guarding the shore like forgotten sentries. They beached their kayaks and paced the shoreline where wrack of sea grass lay bleached and dried, cushioning the stones. They soon found steps, and beside them a passageway leading to a cellar. Capernaum Island was small—it took them only twenty minutes to walk around it.

The sun lowered in the sky, heavy and bouncing. On the ground glitter lay in hollows formed by beach rocks, colored slivers here and there in the grass, or pocketed in the dried seaweed. Pack rats or other rodents had probably scattered it. Jake stepped silently as though the bits of broken glass were marvelous.

The orange glow of the heavy sun spread over sky and water until they were a single shade, no boundaries, nothing showing except a flock of cormorants, silhouetted black against the sun, perched on the ridge line of a rock, wings hoisted out to dry, heads to the wind.

Sally found a path through the brambles. Jake followed. Old orange daylilies and stunted lilacs long past bloom: sure signs of earlier habitation. A group of collapsed cabins formed a circle around the edge of the island, their planks rotting into sweet compost, chimneys and fireplaces a tumble of stones and mortar. As they walked through a village of ghosts, Sally reached for Jake's hand. On top of the only hill, scrub oak surrounded a clearing. The four cornerstones, slabs of granite, were easy to find. No timbers, not a toothpick; instead mirrors lay everywhere. There was something a little weird: the silvered bits were strewn on top of the ground, yet they should have been buried under forty years of wind drift and poison ivy and blowing sand. It was as though birds or the prevailing winds had been dusting them. Jake bent down to pick up some bits of mirror glass and slip them into his pocket. It seemed sacrilege to walk there so they made their way on tiptoe. Underfoot, the glass crunched and broke and reflected the warm glow of the sky at that particular moment, sparks of the orange late-afternoon sun. Finally they stopped moving and just stood there. It was like standing on the afternoon sky.

Chapter Twelve

MAGGIE'S DAUGHTER GILLIAN APPEARED at Jake's door the next Saturday. Her hair looked flayed and her eyes were muddy with old makeup. "Jake," she said. "Can we talk?" Jake was puzzled that Gillian had come over as they had never been close, and he neither liked nor trusted her. He was touched, though, by the unsteadiness of her voice.

"Sure," he said. "But actually, could we do it a bit later? I'm just on my way out. I've got to do a baptism up at the Head of Westport." Jake stuttered as he spoke. He was afraid that the ceremony would not go well; Maggie's recent coupling with Grenville was all he could think about, and it had capsized his soul. When he was full of troubled longing it was hard for him to concentrate enough to perform a ritual; when the correct focus was missing he could not say the words so that they would get their strange grip on him and pull him up with them, out of his own matter. Instead, lacking that focus, no matter how loudly he spoke, he remained where he started.

At first Jake had found baptisms wrongheaded, like funerals, because the subject has no choice in the matter, unless it was an overage baptism—and that felt even stranger, as though the person were spiritually retarded. Jake preferred weddings: the result, he presumed, of rational participation and decision. That was how he thought when he was much younger. But now he saw baptisms as forming a marriage between generations, and weddings between peers had come to seem somewhat dangerous and irrational. He was never good at funerals; he felt like such a charlatan performing rituals of loss for other people when his own heart was scraped and scarred by wanting.

For him to preside at funerals seemed to be a grotesque attempt to outwit or deny his own burden.

That particular Saturday when Gillian came to his door, Jake was so sure that Maggie was going to run off with Grenville that he felt cleft, amputated, and when Gillian spoke to him he was less harsh than usual with her.

"It can wait, but can it be today? I think you're the only one who could possibly listen," she said.

"Ah, Gillian . . ." Jake could see that she needed gentleness and he just wanted to flee from her. Gillian was small and bookish but she could play physical proximity like a harp. Her skin was electric. She could widen the pupils of her eyes so that he would be drawn right in. Standing beside her Jake felt clobbered by her sexuality.

"No, wait," Gillian said, now. "There's two things—and I can't speak to anyone at the farm. There's Maggie for one: she's gone all strange this summer. Have you noticed? You must have seen it. And then there's—well, look, did you ever think you knew everything and then you go and meet someone who turns it all upside down?"

Two things or one? So now Gillian was part of this thicket.

"No," Jake said. "You wait. Or else I'll be late for the Leacocks' baptism. You can stay here if you like until I get back. I should only be an hour or two. Or you can come with me. I can use your help— I have to christen twins. I'd welcome your company."

"I'll come, if that's OK," Gillian said. She didn't want to be alone.

"You have just time to wash up a bit," said Jake. She looked awful, he thought. She would scare the baptismals.

Gillian took so long in the bathroom that Jake wondered if she had fallen asleep or slit her wrists. He didn't know whether to try to hurry her. He went into the kitchen and washed up the breakfast dishes. Finally he knocked on the bathroom door.

"Are you OK?" he called.

"In a minute."

When Gillian came out she looked just the same: she hadn't washed or brushed anything that Jake could see. He took her by the elbow and steered her back into the bathroom. There he combed her hair and tied it back with a clip that Sally had left behind. He then proceeded to wash her face, wanting to get the smudged eye makeup off, but trying not to rub too hard. He wasn't sure how to do it, but did the best he could. She still looked owlish and haunted but she didn't look so slept-in.

As Jake opened the door of his brown truck for Gillian, he wondered if bringing her with him to the ceremony would lead to disaster. But he couldn't leave her alone.

"I should warn you, it will be kind of absurd," Jake said as they drove up Drift Road. "The Leacocks insisted on 11 A.M., so that they can go back to their house and have a big lunch party afterward. I told them that the tide would be dead low at the head of the river. They wouldn't listen."

⌣•

Helen and Guy Leacock and about twenty other Leacocks in summer frocks and white flannels were waiting at the landing. They looked like a sect from another era. Helen, the new mother, was a photographer. Jake had always found it odd that she included nude portraits of her husband in her gallery shows in Providence and New York. Somehow, it was not the same as if a male photographer included nude portraits of his wife. Women, photographed naked, tend to look grand and elemental, while men appear simply unprotected. Each year Helen documented her whole tribe down at the beach wearing Victorian clothes—parasols, eyelet lace and gauzy cottons, which looked as though they had been washed in tea to antiquate them even more. The year before, Jake had watched Helen photograph them all one late afternoon: first walking in the foam at the water's edge, then standing on the dunes looking windswept. The babies and the grandparents looked miserable; the pubescent girls looked worldly wise and sheepish; a towheaded boy in knickers sulked in a shaded hollow refusing to come when called. Jake couldn't understand why more of them didn't rebel, but then he also didn't understand letting your wife put you naked on the walls of fancy galleries.

⌣•

The tide was out. The muck reek of August sun on river bottom hovered in the air. Salt, clay, and sulfur: fire and brimstone. Jake knew he should have insisted on a different hour.

He pulled up behind Guy Leacock's truck and walked around to open Gillian's door. "Are you OK?" he asked her. "Can you make it?"

"Don't worry," she said. "I'm glad to be here with you. I'll be fine. As long as we can talk afterwards."

"That's part of the deal," Jake said, helping her out. "Hand me those books, there, will you?" Guy Leacock wanted God the Father and Helen Leacock wanted Jesus. Jake had asked them if they didn't really want a more mainstream cleric, as he charged more for services containing that particular Father and Son, and more again if he had to use the Book of Common Prayer. But the Leacocks said they wanted him and they would pay whatever he wanted, a phrase that set off in him tintinnabulations of greed. Since Jake had no fixed income except the quarterly payments to stay out of his natal Newport, his finances depended on ministering, on renting canoes and kayaks, and on general scrounging. Hoping they would refuse, Jake told the Leacocks it would be 500 dollars to baptize their twins, at the head of the river, at low water, with the Book of Common Prayer. The check had come that morning. Later, he offered to return it to them, but they refused.

Helen Leacock walked slowly toward Jake and Gillian, twirling a beaded parasol. She was only slightly deflated from pregnancy and she carried herself like Queen Victoria. Her cream-colored dress flowed with a certain grace, though sweat stains had appeared under her arms. The day was already heavy, the sun lurid and on the attack. She held out both hands and, indicating the guests with a motion of her chin, said, "Oh, Jake. Isn't it all so lovely?"

Jake introduced Gillian as his assistant. There were, of course, going to be photographs. Helen had set up her view camera by the stones at the edge of the landing. Jake asked her if she was going to take pictures or hold one of the babies during the service.

Helen turned to look at him. "Oh, God," she said, as though she had forgotten she couldn't do both.

Gillian came to the rescue. She said she could handle a view camera, and that it was more fitting for Helen to be in the photographs.

Helen wanted the ceremony to start with the entire party arriving at the landing in punts and canoes, and she wanted pictures of this procession. Guy Leacock protested that there was not enough water in the river. The boats were tied up a bit downstream, at the second landing, and Helen claimed they looked perfectly afloat to her. The party chattered gaily during the embarkation. Helen and the twin babies in one punt, oared by her oldest son; Guy Leacock went with Helen's parents and the dog, Haskell, in the other; a bestiary of large and small children in the canoes; straw hats, bonnets, parasols, and boaters; gauze scarves, lace, cream-colored froth. Helen, in the bow of the first punt, waved to Gillian to take the first photo. Gillian consulted Helen's light meter, set the lens, and disappeared under the black cloth. The shutter clicked.

Helen called over to Guy, "Have you more water over there, dear?"

Twenty humans in turn-of-the-century dress sat stilled in the middle of the narrow river. Two punts and four canoes encountered, at the same moment, the August mud. The dog, a border collie, barked; paddles churned but did not propel.

"Jake." They called on him as though they thought he had the cure, being proximal to God or other power. However the only cure for low water in that lovely old river is to sit and wait for the sun to crawl. All the Leacocks knew this as well as Jake did. But their border collie didn't know it. Haskell flung himself out of the second punt and ran around the boats trying to get them to move. He slithered in the mud, then tried to swim to shore. He waffled.

"Oh, Mom, Haskell's drowning," said one of the long-legged, high-waisted girls, as she tucked her skirts into her sash and leapt out of her canoe to save her dog. But you don't leap out of a canoe without incident, and this canoe went over on its side, spilling Cecily's two brothers and her four-year-old sister into the slimy clay.

"Cecily, get back into your boat this instant."

Cecily, disregarding the maternal advice, continued on her mission, muck-thumping after the collie. In the lead punt, a baby yowled. The other baby joined in.

"Guy?" Helen called. "Do you think—perhaps—that the grown-ups should get out and pull the children to the landing?"

Pant legs and dress hems—folded, lifted, tucked—were fringed with black mud, straw hats askew. Helen sat in the prow of the leading punt; she carried both twins in her arms, looking like the figure-head of some legendary ship. Gillian, still under the black cape of the camera, was documenting the dragging of the boats, the smirching of the clothes. Helen noticed and called out to her, "No, no. Please don't waste plates on this. We'll need them for the ceremony."

But Gillian remained under the cape of the camera.

Seeing this, Helen raised her voice: "Stop photographing us, dear. Jake, would you kindly get that young woman to stop what she's doing?"

Jake went over to Gillian, and she pulled her head out of the black cloth and dropped the plate she had just pulled out of the camera onto the ground. Her shoulders twitched as she hissed, "Would you tell that bloated cunt that she can take her own fucking pictures from now on. If she doesn't stop yelling at me I'm going to throw her damned camera in the river."

Jake looked over at the party on the river to see if any of them had heard this outburst, but they were all advising one another on how to pull the boats toward the landing.

"Hold on, sweetheart. Just hold on," Jake said. He put one hand on Gillian's shoulder firmly to still her as he whispered. With the other hand, he pointed toward the near bank of the river, and to the slow procession of boats full of children being dragged up the river by overdressed adults. He wanted it to look as though he was explaining something visual about the ceremony that was to come. Instead, he was saying, "I told you it would be absurd. I feel worse than you do and I need you to stay calm and help me." He rubbed her shoulder. "I promise we'll talk as soon as this is over, but you've got to help me get through it first. When things get like this, I feel like a buffoon. I'm not sure I can make it without you. This ritual is meant to be a wel-come, a sort of promissory note—from the family to the babies—and instead I suspect that you and I should be providing those babies with amulets to protect them from their own family and its pageants." He stopped for a moment to breathe. "But who am I to judge? I am taking their money for doing this."

Gillian drew back a bit and looked at him, wide-eyed and thinking. "OK, kiddo," she said, inhaling and drawing herself straighter. She took Jake's hand from her shoulder and shook it as though they had made a contract. Then she grinned. It was a smile of collusion and forgiveness and it was enough to keep him going.

The Leacock tribe gathered around Jake, shaking out pant legs and dress hems. Their clothes looked like markers of the last highest tide, like that lobster shop down at Westport Point with a penciled mark on the wall showing how high the waters rose during Hurricane Bob.

They all stood on the grass beside the landing with the muddy boats pulled up beside them. Helen Leacock held one tiny baby in her arms, and Guy held the other, and Jake read from the black book and the words rose up and pulled him up with them, sucked him out of his body and out of his rational mind and made him hover somewhere high above the landing at the head of the river; he was looking down at the people in their oyster-colored and mud-striped clothes, and hearing his own voice that now seemed to come from somewhere else, from some other body not his own.

Jake was only brought down when Helen Leacock turned to him, touched his arm, and said, "Jake, dear, I think it would be proper now if we actually dipped the children in the river."

Jake didn't say, "Helen, look: there just isn't any river to dip them in." He said, "Ah. Whatever you like. Whatever you think best." He said, "I will go down into the river, and you and Guy can follow me, with the twins." He knew the mud was precarious at low tide, slippery and unpredictable, but he was thinking about Maggie, his love, who was in a state of sexual turmoil over someone who wasn't Jake and who wasn't her husband. She had slept with Grenville, and now she might run off with him. Maggie's daughter, whom he didn't trust, was by his side, and in her own terrible need. So Jake ignored the possible treachery of the river floor, and forgot to wonder what had happened to Haskell, the border collie, and prepared to wade out from the riverbank.

It was Jake's job to be aware of things—essentially his only job, and he knew that if he took money from people to perform a ritual for them, he should do it properly, not with his spirit off somewhere else, wondering who his cousin was bedding down with and whether she found him worthy. Of course, the man wasn't worthy. And, of course, Jake shouldn't be hovering over her determining this.

Jake rolled his pants up, took off his shoes, and stepped into his beloved river. It is always an act of embarrassment to walk into a river without its water. It feels like witnessing a friend pleading with his lover over the phone. A red-tailed hawk soared overhead, silent.

Jake beckoned to Helen and Guy, and they, carrying the babies, followed him. Baking black mud exhaled its sulfur into the air, eons of organic decay rising to the surface as they moved. A hermit crab with his foolishly eccentric shell lumbered over Jake's foot and he wondered what the crab was doing this far upriver.

Guy grunted as he stepped, muttering, "Easy there, that's right, soon be over."

They didn't need to go far, just to where the water still trickled. Jake turned to face Helen and took one of the babies from her. "Which one is this?" he asked her. It was important to keep them straight. Twins have a hard enough time as it is.

"Hillary Penstemon," Helen said.

Jake wondered how Helen knew which of her daughters was which. Or was this baptism defining them? With the tiny Hillary in his arms, he bent down to touch the dark water. He marked her forehead and spoke his words and had just gotten to the only part he really liked, *and of the Holy Ghost,* when Haskell the dog, barking and growling, leapt onto his shoulder. Haskell was protecting the baby from him. As Jake stepped back to regain his balance the mud gave way, and with flailing and splashing and baby shrieks he was on his back. He clutched the baby on his chest and she seemed safe there until Haskell clamped his teeth into Jake's upper arm. Without thinking, and without being able to restrain himself, Jake flung arm and dog and baby away from him. Guy, still holding the other baby, leapt to pick up Hillary. But you can't do anything quick in this kind of wet clay, there's odd physics present here: rapid movement sheers the surface. Guy slipped, glided, finally stretched out beside Jake. Both babies squalled, lying on the riverbed. Helen approached, flat-footed, careful. "Oh, my darlings," she murmured. "How awful." She picked up the twins. "Here, Jake," she said. "I'll ward off Haskell. You finish up the ceremony." She hesitated a moment, looking at the babies. "This one is Rosemary Jessamine."

Jake stood up, wiped his hands on the front of his pants, which were not yet dirty, refused to look at his dog-bitten arm, and took the baby from Helen. He bent down, gingerly, mindful of the mischief his river was capable of. He wet his fingers and welcomed Rosemary Jessamine into her community of family and neighbors, into Christ and His family, and noticed, as he spoke in his loud clear celebrant's voice, that among the other smudges there, her forehead was already marked with a cross. He had already baptized her as someone else.

As soon as Jake's words were done, Guy came over and took the baby from him, and as Jake tried to whisper to Helen what had happened, she mistook it for apologizing about the mud and whispered to him, "No, no, it was all my fault. I should have listened to you about the time and the tide. I am so sorry. I don't want to hear another word about it."

Jake lost heart. His neck itched. His arm hurt. Helen asked him if he would bring Gillian back to the reception at Leacock House, but he told her they had another engagement and wouldn't be able to make it.

"I fully understand, dear," Helen said. "I hope you won't be angry at us for long."

"Not at all," Jake said. "It's really not that at all."

It was noon. The sparrow in Jake's throat raced. He had baptized one of the Leacock daughters twice and the other not at all. He had given one of them two identities and stolen the name from the other. What would happen to these twins? Would he ever be able to admit it to either of them? He would watch over them as they grew and make sure to tell them only if they needed it. Perhaps he was over-wrought and making much out of nothing: no one else believed in the magical power of words the way he did.

Jake couldn't talk all the way home in the truck. Perhaps Gillian didn't notice. Perhaps she didn't know what to say. When they got home he offered her a shower, but Gillian said she didn't need one as much as he did. Standing in the shower sluicing the mud off, he saw that although his arm was sore and bruised, the dog had not broken the skin.

Finally, dry and dressed, he took a couple of beers from the fridge and opened them. He put crackers into a bowl and brought it outside.

"Jake," Gillian said. "Please, Jake. I need you to tell me some things."

He sat her down on the bench while he kneeled on the ground and weeded the grass. He still hadn't learned how to listen to people without doing something else. He realized that this was the most important component of conversation: to stay oneself from moving, from accomplishing; to simply look and listen, but he was not able do it yet, and with Gillian that day he scooped at crabgrass with the blade of his knife and ate crackers until she burst into tears.

"Now then," he said, getting up and joining her on the bench. He put his arm around her. Her hair had a sharp musky smell. Her shoulders were thin and small compared to Maggie's, or Sally's. One's arms can get so habituated to hugging one body that any other seems hefty or absurdly frail.

"What is going on?" she said.

Oh, Lord, he wished he knew. "What do you mean?" he said.

"I asked you before we set out, remember? I met this person in the woods and now I don't seem to understand anything and besides," she paused for breath.

"Besides?" He cupped her shoulder with his hand and rested it there.

"What is going on with my mother?"

Jake didn't want to suggest that Gillian's mother might have met the same man in the woods. "Maggie is moody these days," he said. "But I don't think she's gone crazy." This was a lie.

"She watches me," Gillian said. "At meals."

"Is this what has got you so bothered?"

"No. OK. Forgive me; this is so puzzling to me. I don't understand anything anymore. I used to know how the world worked. Or felt that I did." Gillian stopped and inhaled and sighed. Jake was afraid she was going to cry so he moved his hand to the back of her neck, rubbing it gently.

"So," she resumed. "There's this guy. He's been living in shacks along the river, or in boats. He grows grass for money. He's hard to get to know, but easy to go to bed with. Upstairs in the boat shed. After we have sex we eat Oreo cookies. We watch the moon and drink tea and eat Oreos in his bed. He has a one-gallon tin full of them. Like Mom keeps in the pantry."

"How many do you eat?" This was not what Jake wanted to ask at all. How could he ask what he wanted to know without sounding leering and fanatical?

"Do you mean, how is the sex?"

"Any way you like."

"The sex is . . . I'm not sure."

Jake asked how often she visited this man.

"Almost every night. I leave the house when everyone is asleep. Paul and I are on the ground floor of the barn; it's easy to get out. I've always taken walks at night when I can't sleep. People are used to me leaving."

"Well, it can't be all bad if you go to him every night." Jake tried to keep the sneer out of his voice but Gillian caught it and began weeping again. Oh God, he thought, these women with their tears on toggle switches. Men have such different machinery for weeping: heavy gears and cranks. He was cynical and sneering and yet Gillian was beginning to affect him, with her unhappiness and her olive skin, her thin pale arms coming out of her black T-shirt.

"Jake, don't be this way. You've got to help me. I can't ask anybody else. Who is this guy, really? Will you find him? Will you talk to him for me?"

"No, Gillian. I won't do that." Jake was dying to find Grenville. To talk to him. To throttle him until he explained to him why he had caused all these disturbances in their quiet little lives. But he wouldn't talk to him for Maggie, though she had been asking him to do so all summer, nor would he act as go-between for her daughter Gillian.

"What should I do, then? Sometimes when I go to find him, he isn't there."

Of course he wasn't there, the tall black-bearded bastard. He was off sailing Maggie to Cuttyhunk. He was off sailing Maggie. John Hiram Stuart Grenville not only had too many names, he had too many women. With his sexual athleticism and his smooth-tanned skin, he was a menace to the neighborhood. Jake went into the kitchen and got them each another Sam Adams and a pile of paper napkins. He came back and said, "Your new friend—Paul, is it? What does he think of this?"

"Don't play games," Gillian said. "Just tell me what to do."

"Dry your eyes and drink this."

Maggie's daughter was in Jake's summer garden. Maggie's daughter smelled of tears and musk and ginger.

"What are you working on these days?" Jake asked.

"Work," she said. "Hah."

"Poems?" he asked.

Gillian took the paper napkins and wiped her face. "I've been try-ing to do one about the old story of the hunter who saves a crane—from a trap in the marsh. You know that one, don't you? It's not getting anywhere, though. It's terrible. Oh, Jake, what should I do?"

"About the poem?"

"You are such a shit," she said, bursting into tears again. "You promised that you would talk to me but you keep sidestepping."

Jake knew that he was stalling. He had no language for talking about Grenville to Maggie's daughter and felt incapable of giving her any advice about love. At this moment he felt that love had to do with watching and observing, and he didn't feel that it would be helpful to tell Gillian to watch someone she couldn't even locate, and then, if she did observe Grenville, there was a distinct possibility that she might find her own mother in his arms. Jake wanted to lead Gil-lian away from the whole idea of Grenville. "OK, OK," he said. "Come here, I want to show you something."

Gillian looked at him.

"Wait a minute," he said. He went over to her and dried her face with his hands. It seemed to him that he had spent the day taking care of her face, washing it before the disastrous christening, and now trying to dry it and keep the tears away. He wanted suddenly, horribly, to kiss it. Instead, he took her hand and led her into the garden. He picked a bunch of pale yellow coreopsis and stuffed it into the pocket of her black T-shirt. "This variety is called 'moonbeam,'" he said. "But that's not what I wanted to show you. Come this way." He put his hand again on the back of her neck and she allowed him to keep it there as he led her to the edge of the blue garden. "Sit down," he said. She obeyed him and sat cross-legged while he kneeled beside her, without saying anything more.

"Are you going to tell me anything?" she asked.

"This is Russian Blue Sage," he said, "These are delphiniums, this is a geranium called 'Johnson's Blue.'" He pulled a broken delphinium stalk toward him and twisted it off. Then he plucked the small, sky blue florets off and began tossing them at her.

Gillian winced. "Why are you doing this?"

"What?"

"Playing the buffoon instead of telling me what you know and what you think."

"These are what I *know*. They are what I *think* important. I throw them at you to get you to look at them, but you ignore them. These flowers are more important than your guy in the woods, though it's hard to remember that fact, and it is always gone when you need it most . . . besides, I would like to see what you would look like covered with flowers. Here, smell this." He handed her some catnip and showed her how to crush it in her hands. He broke off the purplish blooms and tossed them onto her.

Gillian gave a puzzled giggle.

Then he stretched out on the grass beside her. "What happens next?" he asked.

"You tell me," she said.

"I meant, in your story about the hunter and the crane."

"Don't you know it?"

Jake shook his head.

"It's very well known. In Japan. Anyway, the hunter sets the bird free," she said. "And it flies off. The next day a beautiful maiden appears at his door. He takes her in and she weaves beautiful clothes for him, in exquisite unknown patterns. Perhaps they become lovers.

But she tells him he must never watch her weave; she always does it in a closed room. One night, of course, he spies on her, and sees that she is really a crane, and is plucking her white breast feathers and weaving them into the cloth she is making for him . . ."

At this point in the story, Jake reached up for Gillian and pulled her down beside him.

"What is it?" she said.

"This," he replied, kissing her. "And this." He smoothed her black hair away from her face and let his fingers tangle in the coils. The more he kissed her, the more he wanted to, each kiss satisfying and renewing his appetite.

Finally, she kissed him back so fiercely that he rolled with her into the edge of the blue garden and began to unbutton his jeans.

Then something made Jake look up, some creak of sound, some imbalance, some new shadow.

It was Sally, standing there with her picnic basket. Since the previous Saturday's trip to Capernaum Island, Sally and Jake had been very happy and close. They had not argued, they had talked on the phone each day. Jake had known that Sally would be coming over on Saturday; he knew that was today. He knew it and yet he had forgotten.

Sally looked as though she might have been there for some time, observing the damp urgent couple among the stalks of the blue flowers. She gazed at them for a few moments longer, as though they were strangers, as though they were birds, then left without a word.

Chapter Thirteen

MAGGIE COULDN'T WAIT ANY LONGER to meet Denise Grenville; her clipboard bulged with what appeared to be responses to her survey underneath a typed list of names and addresses. In her clean slacks and white linen blouse she looked as though she could have come from town hall or the state university or some private concern looking to market an ecological chocolate bar.

"Hello, my love. Where are you off to?" Hugh came out of his study waving an open newspaper at her as though apologizing for having gotten too deeply into it. "Is it that committee thing you talked of the other day, then? Shall I make myself lunch?"

"Mmmn. Yes." She kissed him, grateful that vagueness born of old habit meant that she didn't have to actively lie about where she was going. She wondered what "committee thing" she might have mentioned, and whether she was forgetting something important.

Where was she off to? As she hurried the red Volvo down the rutted half mile of driveway, she realized that she would have no way to explain to Hugh this expedition to meet Grenville's wife, since she never had told him that Grenville had showed up one day, naked in the laundry sink.

The car thudded down the uneven drive, its undercarriage complaining of bumps and possible damage as Maggie tried to outrace her second thoughts. She didn't know what she intended to learn from visiting Denise Grenville; for days she had been unable to think of anything else.

The wind, after veering to the northwest the afternoon before and howling in the chimneys all night, now whipped the August morning, harassing the trees, making each leaf shimmy in the sharp-cornered sun, spinning breath and air into a crazed dance that seemed to heighten perception even as it pried loose control. Grass clippings and puddles of sand were whisked into low-traveling clouds that showed the shape of each gust. On days like this, arms and fingers tingle with ideas and desire; mind and body feel clear and vast and waiting.

⌣·

Denise, at the door, seemed dubious: she didn't ask Maggie to come in. Maggie felt unbalanced by this and by her own recklessness, as though the space around her had lurched to a sudden stop, making her drop her clipboard. The papers scattered. As she crouched to gather them, she looked up at Denise with a shy smile. "I really haven't done this very much before," she said.

This virginal self-exposure seemed to rid Denise of her misgivings, and she said, finally, "Look, why don't you come in? We can be much more comfortable inside."

Grenville's wife did not look the way Maggie expected. She was small and wiry, her black hair cut short at the neck and tousled on top. She wore a yellow-and-white-striped jersey and looked foreign and knowing. Maggie wasn't sure what kind of a doctor she was. She had imagined someone more forbidding. She restrained herself from inspecting everything and looked down at the kitchen table, at her clipboard, as though she had blinkers on. There would be time to examine things. The table was made of thick pink granite. Denise was confident, unusual; she was not a woman one would think of leaving, she seemed too smart and funny and complicated for that.

They sat at the kitchen table and proceeded through the questions. Denise asked Maggie if she wanted some coffee. She filled the Italian espresso pot and put it on the stove. She already had a bat-house—she answered, smiling—nailed up on the garden shed. She preferred the lines of wooden boats, she said, but didn't like sailing in them because of the smell.

"Do you mind if we talk about marital status?" Maggie said. "Oh,

Lord, I don't know who thinks these things up." She blushed, relieved that her embarrassment would be taken for prudishness rather than connivance. "We can skip them if you'd rather."

"Heavens, no," said Denise. "Don't pre-censor. I'll tell you when I don't want to answer."

Finally the question about separation.

"My husband is gone," Denise said, getting up from the table and walking about the room. She opened a drawer, took out two tea-spoons, and closed it sharply. "He disappeared about three months ago, without, as they say, a word. He had gone for a weekend on somebody's boat. Then he never came back. The boat is in the harbor, at its usual mooring. He is not there, nor are his things. If he had drowned, his things would still be onboard. The police say that it's more likely that he's run off with some younger person—that that's what men of his age do—and less likely that he's dead or turned into a wandering amnesiac."

"Is that what you think?" asked Maggie. "Do you think he's run off?"

"I don't know. Yes, I would like him back, if that's what you mean. He was, or is, a good man. A moody bastard sometimes, but gentle and good. But I can't talk about him anymore. It's pretty hard. Let's talk about you. You know, I didn't catch your last name. I don't quite understand who you're working for."

Maggie hadn't come with the idea of telling Denise that she had sighted Stuart Grenville; she wanted to get information rather than give it, to be alone with his wife, talk with her, watch her. But now that she had done that, she found Denise as puzzling and appealing as Grenville. It suddenly seemed devious and horrid to keep what she knew to herself. She faltered. Maggie knew that she was jeopardizing her relationship with Grenville: if he went back home, she would probably never see him again. She did not want to imagine what it would be like not to look forward to his visits.

"What if I told you I'd seen him?" Maggie said.

"Seen who?" Denise got up from the table and walked to the sink. "What do you mean?" She turned around sharply, then walked to the other side of the room, came back to the table, sat down.

"He's not dead, not amnesiac," Maggie continued. "Not even living with another woman." She paused. "As far as I know." She blushed again.

Maggie and Denise looked at each other. The espresso pot on the stove made a muttering noise as the water bubbled up into the top section. Neither woman moved.

"Leave now. Out of here." Denise said.

"Excuse me?"

"I said, get out."

"Don't you want to know how I know this?"

"Out."

"I didn't say it to hurt you."

Denise pointed to the door. "I need to be at the clinic in twenty minutes. I didn't invite you over here. You come in here. Into my kitchen. You sit at my table and ask me an absurd battery of questions. And you proceed to tell me you've got my husband. I don't want to hear about it. I don't want to talk calmly about it. You are a creep and a shit and I want you out of here."

"But I don't have your husband. I didn't say that." Maggie's voice trailed off. Her heart was flailing about. "I have a husband of my own." But that statement seemed too proud and self-important, so she added, "As far as I know." The dark smell of just-made Italian coffee filled the space between the two women.

Denise pushed her chair back and walked to the farthest corner of the kitchen. "Are you getting a kick out of this? Who are you anyway?"

"What do you mean?" Maggie fiddled with her spoon on the granite tabletop. The coffeepot began to burn dry on the gas ring.

"Power of information, asshole. You come here and you lord it over me with this secret information you've been harboring, that you know where my husband is, when I don't. Why don't you spit it out? If you're so anxious to tell me, then tell me, bitch. Tell me your fucking story and get the hell out of my house."

A reek of overheating steel and burnt coffee came from the stove. The silvery pot was now blackened up the sides. Maggie got up and edged toward the door. "Look," she said. "Perhaps this isn't the best moment." She picked up her clipboard and slipped out the door into Denise's yard. When she heard the door open again behind her, she ran toward the street.

"Come back here, scrawny bitch." Denise called, running after her. "You get right back in here." Denise caught up to Maggie at the gate and lunged for her, embracing her in an ungainly tackle. Both women lurched into the fence, trampling on a stand of yellow foxgloves. Maggie wondered why she couldn't hear the expelled breath of the flattened yellow trumpets. Then Denise pulled Maggie toward the house.

"Let go of me," Maggie said. "Get your hands off me. You have no right."

"Get inside and tell me what you have to tell me."

"Look, I really don't think it's the right time."

"There is no right time." Denise paused. "There's no right time to tell someone whose husband has disappeared that you know where he is. Or that you and he are lovers. Or whatever it is that you are. What are you anyway, asshole?" She paused, breathing. "Oh, never mind. I'm sorry. Please come in."

As they entered the kitchen the air was thick with the stench of burning: the bakelite handle of the coffeepot. Maggie rushed to the stove and turned off the gas. Denise yelled, "Don't touch it," but Maggie had already picked up the coffeepot by the handle. She flung it away from her. "Oh, shit. That was so stupid. Oh, shit. It doesn't hurt."

The coffeepot skittered across the floor sending up an arc of boiling coffee that splattered on Denise's legs. Maggie knew she hadn't thrown it that way on purpose, and hoped Denise would know that.

Denise said, "Cold water; quick, run your hand under cold water. I'll get some ice." She went to the refrigerator and pulled out an ice tray, and found a plastic bag to put the cubes in. "Here, put your hand on this; it stops the burning." Denise stood up and made a face. "That coffee is still burning me through my pants." She unzipped and peeled them off. Then she made another ice bag for herself.

A puddle of evil-looking coffee lay on the floor beside the Italian metal pot. Denise took paper towels and mopped up the coffee. Then, holding it with damp towels as though it was capable of more hurt, she took the coffeepot outside and set it in the yard. The women sat at the kitchen table, with plastic bags of ice on their burns. Maggie debated what to tell her. Although she had rehearsed this visit in her head for the past week, it had not occurred to her that she might end up liking Grenville's wife, that she might find her own loyalties multiplying or dividing.

~·

What is it that two women who love the same man do when they meet? How do they spar? What do they measure as they size each other up? What makes their hearts sink?

At first, they measure everything. Maggie laid her left hand on the table so that she could compare it to Denise's. Her own hands were full of veins, freckles. Denise's right hand was on the table; she had bitten all her nails down to the nubs. Maggie wondered if she had always done this or if she had begun in response to Grenville's disappearance. Denise's yellow jersey made her breasts seem full, even though her arms were thin and muscular.

Women in this configuration check each other over as though they are competing for a position on a glossy magazine cover. Hair, eyes, skin, flesh. But soon something else follows, because they know the man too well: they suspect that to him all women are attractive. Just as they know they can be attracted by anyone, for any reason. Then, too, it is never reason that is being appealed to, in the case of attraction, but something deeper, older, lower down. And so the calculations, the measurements, do not make very much sense, and for a while they stop. Then Maggie notices an irresistible curve in Denise's arm and wonders if her own arm would look that way if she held it so. But that, she recognizes again, is only dog-beauty, and so she begins to look for odder things: dimples, freckles, and a nose that is pointy and slightly small. These calculations of what might make another person lovable to the man one loves—in the end they lead to laughter or despair.

"Now what?" said Denise. "Where are we? Where do we go from here?"

~·

Maggie spent the rest of her time with Denise trying not to betray Grenville, and trying not be too dishonest with his wife. She said she had seen Grenville, once or twice. In a bar, though Maggie, in fact, had rarely been to a bar. They had fallen into talking. He hadn't told anyone else, he said, about what had happened to him. He wasn't flirting with her, she said, but he seemed to need someone to talk to; he seemed puzzled.

"Do you want me to carry any message, if I see him again?" Maggie asked as she got up to leave. What a skunk he was, she thought, to let his confusion cause so much trouble; what an ass.

"I don't think so," said Denise. "Not yet. It's too soon. I have to have time to think about all of this. Could I take your phone number, though? Would that be OK?"

Maggie wrote down her number and address. Her heart heaved as she started writing down the name of her road, but it would have been perfectly clear, if she stopped now, that Grenville was living with her. Yet, in writing it down, she had banished privacy; she might as well have built her house of glass. Denise could drive up at any time. What had she done? It was too late to take it back.

A flock of small birds scattered from Denise's garden as Maggie walked down the path to the street. She walked slowly. She wondered if she had betrayed Grenville. She wondered if she had lost him.

Chapter Fourteen

ASIDE FROM HIS DISAGREEMENT with Sally about possible uses for it, Jake's secret room in the forest led to further troubles, but on the mid-August morning of Maggie's birthday it still seemed like a fine idea, a felicitous construction. Hugh led Maggie to the newly planted cedars early in the day and she sat cross-legged on the springy bed of pine needles that Jake and the children had transported there by wheelbarrow. Hugh poured coffee from the old green metal thermos, and set out bread and cheese and strawberries on white-enameled tin plates. They talked and ate, and after breakfast Maggie lay with her head in Hugh's lap, looking up at the sky, listening to him.

～·

That afternoon Maggie took another walk in the woods. The blueberries had ripened and she carried green cardboard berry boxes in her wicker basket, along with a galvanized pail. The basket was already half full of wildflowers and she looked like a midsummer goddess as she strode toward the walls of dark pines. Jake happened to be there, too, walking in the forest, not following her exactly, but happily present and trying to keep her in sight. The forest crackled with insect chatter. As Maggie moved past the row of densely planted evergreens she caught glimpses of something light-colored from within the enclosure. Overhead, a pair of gulls mewed. But who was there in the room? A crow flapped noisily. Maggie stepped more carefully. Who?

A couple, a pair, pairing and coupling, cleaving and cleaving. "Oh, yes," the man said.

And, "Oh, yes," said the woman.

Maggie was stunned. Curiosity pulled her. Along with dread. She laid down her pail and her basket of flowers and peered between the trees. There the two sprawled, naked and laughing. Clothes flung haphazard. Heaving with laughter, with arousal—oh, the humor of it all, that disheveled cosmic game that we call the sexual act. Her daughter Gillian, that sly one. Gillian. And that bastard, Grenville.

Maggie took a breath in and it seemed too much for her lungs. She was drowning in her own inhaling, but if she let it out, it would howl. How dare Grenville make love to her daughter. How dare Gillian make love with her Grenville. She wanted to part them, screaming, to jump in through the wall of bushy trees and throw things at them, baskets, pails, stones. The air crashed down on her; a blackness of *being* descended, a thick shawl falling onto her heart, weighting it down and crushing it like an iron grating.

Maggie leaned over carefully to pick up basket and pail and began to step backward from the tree-lined evergreen room. Stalk away. Slink away. The box was in the basket beside the flowers but not crushing them, and the basket was over her arm and she held the bucket in her other hand; she'd forgotten why she'd even brought the bucket with her, something to do with the stream, something had needed water. It was hard to carry all these things now, she felt as though any quick or sharp move would tear her apart. She stopped. She had not seen enough. She had not filled her eyes. She turned back to look between the branches once more. They were still at it. Gillian was very active. She coiled around Grenville like a snake; then she raised herself and coiled another way. She sat on him. Her back was shaggy with pine needles, her breasts smudged with loam; she looked almost furry. The pine needles had come from an old stand of pines in the forest. Now they were being used for this. If you make the perfect den for making love, lovers will find their way to it. Count on it. The two copulating bodies looked as though they belonged to the forest. She could go to the stream and fill her pail with water and then she could throw it on them. Was that why she had brought it with her? Fucking hell.

Maggie had never watched other people make love before. She

wondered if *she* looked like that; if she had looked like that when she was younger. She wished her daughter were not so lovely. She wanted to kill them. At first she found it more humorous than arousing. We are animals and sometimes that fact is inescapable. It was funny and black and she wanted to kill them. Then, too, part of her wanted to join them. Laughable and grim, and the grimness took over until she wondered if they were having any fun at all, or if there was only desperation involved. If she didn't hate him so much, she ought to warn Grenville about Gillian: Gillian was a tormented soul, and she usually brought the horrors with her to anyone she touched. Come along, children, she wanted to say, finish up now. She wished they would finish so that she could pick up her bucket and pick up her basket and resume her walk. But she had to keep watching. Why did Grenville have to choose Gillian, of all people? In Maggie's green forest room. So sly. Couldn't they do it somewhere else? She wondered where else they had done it. It stabbed her that Gillian probably knew where Grenville slept—without even searching. They had probably made love all over the farm; Maggie suspected that Gillian was never careful, that she had a tendency to do it anyplace. This was betrayal. Jake had made this room for Maggie. It was Jake's room and hers and Hugh's. The moment she saw it, early this birthday morning, she had also wanted Grenville to see it, but she had wanted to be there when he did. Had she wanted more?

The answer was a simple pain in her throat. A bleak murderous ache. Reason told her she didn't own him. Rationally, she couldn't even begrudge him her daughter. Gillian had always been sly. Gillian had always been treasonous. Gillian was young and lithe and full of poetic torment. How could Maggie compete? She couldn't. She could only scowl. She could only lurch through the forest with her basket over her arm, dragging her bucket on the ground, letting it scrape dark grooves in the leaf mold. She hoped for rain. Sudden immediate torrents of rain, pelting and hideous, turning their bed of pine needles to mud. And wasps. The rain should hold off just long enough for the wasps to come and find them in their frolic. She knew she was getting ridiculous. She was deep in the blackness of love and she hated Grenville with all her heart and she hated her love for him.

She should have strewn nettles on the floor of that room. Innocent-looking euphorbias and other rash makers. She should have saved her poison-ivy plants just for this.

"Oh, there you are. I've been looking for you."

The quiet voice behind her made her jump.

"Hugh, dear. But I thought . . ."

"The wind is up." he said. "Small-craft warnings. How are you, my love? You look a bit grim. Are you feeling tired?"

"Actually, I just realized how late it is, and I have to pick some berries. Won't you come with me?" Had Hugh seen what was going on inside the cedars? Had he seen her watching? She had certainly stood there long enough. What would Hugh think if he knew? If he knew what—that his daughter Gillian was sexually cavorting with a stranger in his room? That the stranger was no stranger to Maggie, but rather someone she herself had made love with a few weeks earlier on a borrowed sailboat on a night drenched with stars? That Maggie's life had been spiraling around this stranger for the past few months? That she now hated this stranger with all her heart? "You know you like to pick blueberries once you get into it," she said. "The mosquitoes aren't out yet." She tried to keep her voice from quivering. She felt shaky, as though the forest was suddenly too tall and its floor tilting and spongy; the light was confusing her by dappling all the leaves. She handed him her basket and started walking away from the evergreens.

"Well, yes, of course, dear," said Hugh, following her. "But I was wondering what you were looking at back there, at the trees."

"At the trees?"

"Yes. You know. The cedars Jake planted for you. What were you watching?"

"Watching?"

"Yes. Well, I thought you were. You had put your baskets down and were standing there. It seemed like you were peering, actually, through the branches."

Maggie's impulse was to say she had been stalking a bird, a raccoon, anything. How terrible to be seen watching.

But what if Hugh had seen what was going on inside.

"Well, it was Gillian actually. She was making love with someone. I couldn't see who it was."

"Well, how nice. How awfully nice. Don't you think so, my love?"

"Yes. Of course. I suppose so." She tried to jolly-up her voice.

"But we shouldn't say anything about it, should we?"

"No, dear. You're right. Better not."

The blackness of heart was coming over her and crushing her, and she took Hugh's arm and held it. She needed his warmth and his strength and his goodness to carry her through.

Jake joined the Giffords at the farm for dinner that night. The wind had backed to the east and it was chilly, so they ate in the dining room, all except for the youngest ones who were already in bed. Maggie was oddly tender toward Gillian. Yet she blushed so whenever Gillian spoke to her that Hugh finally asked her if she felt feverish. Finally Turko and Storm came up behind Maggie's chair and both tried to throw their arms around her at once.

Later, when they had coffee and dessert, Maggie said she was feeling like some air and she would walk Jake back to his place. As soon as they got into the darkness of her long driveway she broke into tears of fury.

Jake did not tell her that he had been in the forest that afternoon, hidden there behind an oak tree, watching Hugh observe his wife observing Gillian and Grenville, their watching embedded like nested Russian dolls. Jake didn't tell her because it might seem too odd that he was there, as well. He had just been walking through his woods, which bordered on her woods, hoping that he would find Maggie there.

Chapter Fifteen

WHAT HAPPENS TO FORMER BONDS OF LOVE? Are they there in negative if not in positive, like a ghost knot, some tangling of black ropes in the darkness of the soul, until finally that lack itself becomes a thing, a hollow outline that distorts or reshapes the space around it? Each time we reach out, trying to grasp it, we pass right through contacting nothing. Yet still we grope.

⌣·

Maggie came over to Jake's house the day after she had spied on Grenville and Gillian in the forest. Maggie was pale, in the territory beyond tears.

That was it, she said. No, she didn't want tea. She wanted Scotch whisky.

Jake gave it to her. He put a bowl of crackers on the table but she didn't touch them.

She'd had it, she said. Suddenly she saw what it all meant. She smiled. This betrayal of Grenville's was radiant and glowing. It had illuminated, for her, what he was, and showed her what he would always be, and what they both would be like if she stayed in contact with him: she would grovel and he would be mean-spirited. And so, she said, this beastliness of his seemed warm and golden and full of goodness: for it freed her from having to love him anymore, from having to try to make him love her, from trying to engender sweetness in him. The searing pain of watching him make love to her daughter had sliced out that piece of her heart which she could now see had been diseased, that piece she had turned over to him. The rest,

smaller, thinner, hurting, and numb, would recover. She would recover. She would think about him less and less until finally her days
would be free and her nights would be free and the obsessive coils of
her brain would be smoothed out and could be used for something
other than longing.

Jake told her that when the soul has been torn, even the healing
hurts.

Maggie said she didn't mind the hurt, in the face of the freedom it
gave her. She was soaring. She said Grenville had been beastly. He
had always been beastly. Why hadn't Jake told her, she asked, that
Grenville was that way?

Jake kept silent. He filled her glass with Scotch.

She had constructed her vision of Grenville to dignify herself, to
make her desire for him seem not so rotten, so ill-conceived. It was
not Grenville's fault: he had not led her on; he had not made prom-
ises or even demands; he had simply provoked her desire. Now she
was free. She would use all her time for the perverse sewing projects
of which she was so fond. She would finish her mermaid. The people
over in Providence at the School of Design wanted to put it on exhi-
bition. She had been squandering time, and that, after all, was sin
against mortality. Against the universe. She knew she had always
done this, she said. When she had been very young, all her relation-
ships with men had been like this: they had always said: Thank you
so much, but how do you find the time? She had stolen the time from
herself to give to men, and they had lapped it greedily like cats from
the cream pitcher.

"Oh, Jake," she said. "How I hate all that giving. I hate the caring.
All senses. If I could only scrape love from my being like cow shit
from my boots." She could do without, oh Lord yes. Now she was
through. She would sew; she would garden. She would show her
natural fondness for her husband. Other than Hugh, the only things
she felt like talking to were trees and lettuces and garlics. She saw
Jake's expression at that point, and turned to him and said, "And you,
Jake. Don't misunderstand. I don't include you in all of this venom."

She felt so different that she wondered if she were dying. Court-
ing Grenville, looking for his approval was an irritation she had lived

with so intensely that its absence was suspect, its hollow a shape. She played it like touching a hole in her tooth with her tongue. All that energy suddenly loose. She hated herself, she said, for having been so devoted not just to Grenville, but to the idea of loving him. She was grateful that he had let his beastliness show this way, rather than interspersing it with hints of possible sweetness, playing out the line to keep her beguiled and in a state of hope. She was burning with energy, freedom, and time; she would enter the white heat of sculpture. Where before she had used her time to work on dialogue with him, replaying past conversations, making up future arguments, cooking imaginary meals for him, now all that time was free, now it would go toward incandescence. This was the way the men she knew worked anyway: they put their work first. Their work was the stuff of self. Their women were their play, and the two activities were connected only when they let the notion of their women inspire their work. For them, the women made the work go better. With her, men, except for Hugh, had always demolished the work.

Oh, men were sly. They let you think what you wanted. Their pricks waved like fish in the ocean. Desire of desire. Women were sly. Their cunts waved like bait. Evolution was sly, getting them all to stop thinking and jump on top of each other. She was out of that now, she said, for good.

She would be out of it, Jake knew but didn't say, as soon as she could stop thinking about it.

～·

After Maggie left, Jake went outside. He was dazzled with hope. Too old to be innocent or surprised or to believe that it would never come again, he staggered, that summer, with love's crippling gait, sick with the heaviness of wanting and the paradox—still and always—that absence has weight enough to crush the heart.

It seemed to him, at that point, that perhaps Maggie would be freed from Grenville. It was evil of him to rejoice in his beloved's distress, but oh, he was very glad. Of course, there was still Hugh, the steady and much-loved husband. Jake ignored the question of Hugh.

He danced a bandy-legged jig in his garden and then set out to walk to the river.

◡·

How does love color the fields, the sky, resolving the visibility so that all the edges burn with sharpness around the fizz of molecules in the light? Jake knew how this was, and he didn't want to admit it—that love distorted everything and then distorted the prism of vision, giving the illusion of clarity. He wanted to pull off his old skin somehow, change completely. He knew this light was dangerous, the cyclone that followed too black. He needed some shadow, but the fronds of corn were so luminous in the sun, radiant as brass, that he couldn't look away. The sky trumpeted overhead. He could see the south wind as it danced through each row of corn, lifting and whirling the tassels, then letting them go.

What does love do to the fields and pastures? Everything pulses against the elemental dance. Resolution, definition: is it the senses newly bathed, or perhaps just a new creation of the world? Clangor and shimmering on fields and rivers. Nothing is quiet even in the breathlessness of the wind subsiding into stillness, quivering again, then still. Only the sound of love pulsing, the definition of planes and edges against the green blackness of the distant forest. Oh, this is when the texture of things is almost too much to bear.

Chapter Sixteen

JAKE WOKE IN THE NIGHT, startled by something—an owl, a cow in heat, some other moaning cry in the far meadows. He lay in bed, listening. But it wasn't an animal, or even a noise that had jolted him. Anger is sometimes hard to recognize, and when it clings to everything it can be hard to see where it is spreading from and where it is heading toward. Jake was furious at Grenville for turning the quiet neighborly quadrille into a frenzied bacchantic rite. Grenville had stolen Maggie from him—although she had never really been Jake's, he knew that—and from her husband, his sweet friend, Hugh. Grenville had tasted Maggie's daughter, Gillian, luring her into the boat shed with the moon and Oreo cookies. Jake was mad at himself, of course, as well: for wanting Maggie as much as he did, and for trying to seduce Gillian, and for doing that exactly when Sally was to visit. He knew that Sally was much too good for him, and wondered if Grenville would get involved with her as well. Jake tried to link his last disaster with Sally to Grenville's presence, but he couldn't. His own raging mindless appetites were to blame. Realizing this only increased the night's whirling malevolence toward Grenville and toward himself.

Loud with midnight heartbeats, Jake got dressed. He made himself some tea and wandered outside. It had rained, but now the wind had shifted to the west leaving the air thick and damp. Patches of clear sky chased after the clouds. He sat on the porch and listened to the tree frogs.

Tony and Jake had talked about Grenville that very afternoon. They had been working on Jake's toolshed and after a couple of hours they stopped to sit on the back porch and drink some beers. It was hot and quiet, with just a single green hummingbird whirring the scarlet flowers of the bee balm. They drank and listened to the ornithopter-like vibrations. Finally Tony said, "What's your opinion of this Grenville character, anyway? Why is he living on our farm?"

"How do you know about Grenville?"

Tony explained that when the whole family arrived at his parents' place for the summer visit, things got "too jovial" sometimes, by which he meant too populated with his siblings and relations. He said that he tended to spend a lot of time in the woods when this happened. There were always things that needed doing in the forest, hacking brush, chopping wood, cleaning out the stream beds. One day he had come upon a scruffy-looking guy and because the man didn't seem to be just passing through, Tony followed, and watched him carry things through the forest, dump them at the base of an oak tree, and then leave. Tony went to inspect and saw that he had been transporting sash weights, which had probably come from Hugh's shed. Soon the stranger returned with another load, and then he began tying them with clothesline to a limb of the old oak, where he suspended them in an uneven row. When he was done, there were about twenty iron weights hanging from the branch, looking like so many sausages. At last, Tony walked up to the man and asked him what he was doing.

"He said he was making a wind chime for hurricanes. And then I had to laugh, because that's exactly what it looked like." Both Tony and the stranger had picked up rocks and thrown them at the weights to make them sound their odd clangor. "But when I got around to asking him what he was doing there, where he was living, he got pretty quiet and said he had to go, that he'd come up by boat from the river, and he knew he was trespassing and all."

That was the first time Tony had seen him, but there were other times, and soon it became clear to him that although Grenville never admitted it to him, he must be living in one or another of the out-buildings of the farm.

"You know," Tony finally said to Jake, "Grenville has a truck. He spoke of it one day when he told me about leaving home. He drove it to the boatyard when he did his disappearing act on his friend's sailboat. But then, of course, he had to leave it there, if he wanted it to seem as though he had drowned or disappeared. Besides, it's so distinctive that somebody would have noticed him sooner or later—it's that turquoise Chevy pickup with Rhode Island plates, at the end of the yard by the trees near the back drive. Must be early seventies. Have you seen it, blue-green like an old copper roof?"

Jake said he had seen it. He had wondered whose it was as he passed it on the back path to the beach. Tony asked him again what he thought of Grenville and his inhabiting the farm.

"I don't know," Jake said. He couldn't answer without stripping bare too many hearts. He echoed the question back at Tony, asking his own opinion.

"Well, I think it's strange as hell," Tony said. "Grenville told me that Maggie knew he was living there, and that she wasn't against it. He doesn't seem like a crook, he's not demented, really, or mean. But who in hell does he think he is? A hermit in a grotto? A gypsy? What do you think we should do?"

"You know," Jake said. "I think we should wait it out a bit."

◡˙

That was how Jake had felt in the afternoon. Now, in the middle of the breath-stricken night, he knew that the waiting was over. His keys were in his pocket. The night throbbed.

From the newly shingled work shed he took canisters of acetylene and oxygen and put them into his faithful chocolate pickup. Turning from Cranford into Westport, he took Horseneck Road to East Beach, past the trailer homes, where the river backs up against one side of the road and the sea stretches out from the other. His veins tingled.

At the marina Jake parked beyond the last boat shed so that no one would see him. Crushed shells and sand underfoot. The moon slipped out from behind a cloud. He draped an old steel chain around his neck; it had once hung across Maggie's driveway. He lugged the canisters, walking slowly so the chain wouldn't clink against them. He wasn't quite sure how Grenville got around now that he didn't use his truck anymore—maybe he just paddled up and down the river, maybe he walked. Or simply sprang from bed to bed. That was more likely.

Jake tried to breathe normally but the air had filled with cotton mist and his lungs already rasped with fright; he kept turning around to see if anyone was there. The shipyard was full of its own breathing noises: halyards clinked against metal masts; hulls flopped against water. Above loomed the dark bulks of fishing boats perched high on cradles, waiting for repairs.

Grenville's pickup was at the farthest edge of the yard, next to the bushes. Jake looked up at the sky for a moment. The wind had backed to the east, which meant that no one on the docks at the other end of the marina would hear him. He listened for footsteps, trying to think of some reasonable story to explain what he was doing. High clouds scudded moonward. Between them, stars roared. Waves clasped the sand of the dinghy beach.

Sometimes a truck is what you have to take it out on. Your anger. At the turbulence. Even a 1973 Chevrolet the sea-green color of old copper. He couldn't see the color in the dark.

The first thing you do when you want to slash a truck is to take that rusty chain which used to run across your cousin Maggie's drive-way and flail it across the windshield. Then, there's no turning back: your anger sears until you smell something burning, and you have to keep at that old truck until one of you goes under.

When the chain greeted its surface, the windshield crazed, buckled—then that cold skating noise, the conversation, almost wordlike, of glass chip on glass chip chattering onto the dashboard. Jake reached through the hole and pulled out Grenville's coffee mug—ceramic, heavy. In the moonlight he could see that it was filled with the glitter of shards. His hand wanted to bring that cup to his lips even though he knew it had been roasting there all summer long. It would not have any liquid, but only dry circles of mold and glass. Still he wanted so much to drink from it that he threw it away from him, into the bushes. Clearly there was something wrong with his appetites.

The side and back windows come next: they don't really look right next to a smashed windshield. There's a disturbing imbalance of intactness.

Jake was tired of the chain. He took a rock from the edge of the parking lot and heaved it through the back window. That worked, but it was remote action. For the passenger-side window he took a rock and tapped it—like cracking an egg—to see at what point the glass would give. The answer is: five taps, if you increase the force slightly with each one. The window wasn't like an eggshell, though, it was tougher, thicker, designed to stay whole, like a skull.

Jake had never done anything like this before. Except for ripping up letters or bills that had a threatening or otherwise unpleasant tone, or throwing stones at the woodchuck before he erected a fence around his kitchen garden, he had never set out to destroy anything— at least not anything important or symbolic or belonging to someone else. He had never felt murderous. It was as though he had been born without the sense of anger, the way some people are born without the sense of smell. Now, anger had bloomed, roguing him like an elephant, making him forget, except for brief shudders of clear-sightedness, his fear.

The tires gasped when he stabbed them with his pocketknife, the truck sighing as it settled a handspan lower onto the crushed shells of the yard. He lit his canisters and turned up the acetylene until he could hear its hissing voice. This sound comforted him, and he tried to listen to it rather than to his own blood pounding. When the flame had blued inside the yellow, he held it to the Chevy's haunch until he could smell heat-peeled paint and the roasting metal underneath. Then, turning up the oxygen, he began burning right through. He cut off the left front fender and carried it over to his own truck: he needed it for a trophy.

Jake was working smoothly now, humming to himself under the hiss of the gasses, while the truck metal first creaked and pinged at the heat, then screamed and clanged across the sleeping blackness of the shipyard and he was afraid it would wake the people who lived on their yachts or the night watchman who slept in a cottage by the docks. He told himself that the wind was carrying his noises away from them, but his skittery body wouldn't listen, veins and arteries felt as though they were carving out new pathways in his arms and legs. He stopped to wipe his hands on his pants, but they, too, were damp with sweat. He sliced through the other front fender, and then through the humps over the rear wheels, afterwards placing all the pieces tenderly in the bed of Grenville's truck. Then he changed his mind and carried them over to his own truck, spooked, of a sudden, not entirely rationally, by the thought of fingerprints. Of course, he was leaving prints everywhere. He was not efficient at this; he was losing time; it was all he could do to keep at it. And where he left any of that Chevy intact, he seared the paint until even in the changeable moonlight he could see it blister and darken.

It was time for Jake to engage with the inside. Damn thing was locked. This shocked him: in his rage he had assumed that Grenville would have left it sitting there, doors unlocked, welcoming Jake to come and savage it. What kind of nut, Jake wondered, would want to lock his truck from him? He reached through the broken glass on the passenger's side and pulled the lock up, but the handle still wouldn't turn. Twisting from inside didn't work either. He pulled at the handle until it came loose, catching his fingers against the door and slicing across all four knuckles. Skin for skin, blood for blood. He wrenched that handle back and forth like a tooth until it popped—so heavy it seemed meaningful—into his hand. He slipped it in his pocket, then went back to his own truck to get crowbar, sledgehammer, bolt cutters. Enough work with bare hands.

After jimmying the driver's door open, Jake noticed that its window was still in one piece. Standing outside the truck with the door ajar, he slid the point of the crowbar up and down, scoring the glass, up and down every half inch or so, feeling the scratches with his thumb to make sure they were deep enough, then using the handle he had ripped off the other door, he tapped until the window collapsed in slivers and tinkled onto the ground.

Then he was inside. The breeze coming from the docks blew straight into his face. Time to pluck out the dashboard gauges: gas, oil, speed—place a screwdriver at the center of each one, tap with the sledge, then pluck it out, drop it onto the glassy floor. No more powers of rational measurement for this vehicle.

At the sound of footsteps Jake froze. He ducked down, placing his face gingerly on the glass-covered seat. The interior of the truck pulsed with the drumming in his ears. The dash clock said exactly one o'clock. That made him nervous, even though he doubted it was correct. Sitting up and looking shyly around at the night outside, he saw no one. He had heard his own fear. He considered the clock again. Finally he scraped a triangle in the glass with his screwdriver and punched it in as though he were trepanning to relieve some pressure in the temporal lobe. With a delicate forefinger he moved the minute hand away from north. When he could breathe again he thought a little bronchodilation would be a good thing, and after a couple of whiffs he forced himself to sit there for a while, inflating and deflating, until the wheezing stopped.

Jake got out of Grenville's truck, brushing the glass off his pants, shaking and patting his beard. His bolt cutters had been waiting quietly in the moonshadow.

He now committed dark surgery under the hood—snipping the trachea-like wire-stiffened radiator hoses, then battery wires, fuel lines, and the thinner brake lines—until all those dark tubes pulsed in the night, swaying with released tensions as their useless fluids oozed and bled.

Jake was about to get his sledgehammer so he could work on the engine but another idea intruded, threatening and insistent, stronger than anger, displacing even his fear. What had begun, when he had set out to meet with Grenville's vehicle, as fury and glee, fizzy and wild, with darkness only around the edges, had now transformed itself into something more physical and groin-focused. In this lonely nocturnal demolition Jake found he had gotten so hard that he could no longer stand straight. Such arousal did not seem related to the wild love-need he felt with Maggie, the flagrant joy he knew with her tormented daughter Gillian, or the sweet slow deliberation he experienced with his now rightfully distant Sally. This sudden sexual hysteria stabbed with urgency more than excitement. We are animals, he thought, and we should be walking on all fours.

Jake got back into Grenville's Chevy, clearing the glass onto the floor with his crowbar and wiping the seat off with a filthy rag he found above the sun visor. Wide-eyed with necessity he slid over to the passenger side. He rubbed his hands on his beard to get rid of any glass particles, then he unzipped. Howling softly he opened the glove compartment—that one female pocket in the roaring maleness of the pickup truck—and then he groaned his seed into it.

"Oh, Grenville," Jake whispered. "You planted my beautiful women; I planted your ravaged truck. How could I?"

~·

Finally Jake took his things back to his own truck and covered its bed with a tarp. Maggie's chain lay coiled on the sand like a snake; he shook the glass bits from it and put it in the cab. The easterly breeze brought calming noises: water slapped against pilings. Boats rubbed on bumpers.

His skin felt singed and smutty. His fingers didn't smell like him, or like sex; they stank of torch and oil and burnt metal. He needed a swim.

On the path to the beach the boatyard noises faded; just the massaging wash of the incoming river tide, and farther off, across the dunes, the enticing roar of the ocean. Bullfrogs thrummed old rubber in the puddles beside the track. Salt hay smell tangled with bayberry as the dune sand squeaked under his boots. Noticing these things reassured him that he had not gone out of his mind.

To the left stretched the whole bight of Horseneck Beach, its fringes of surf white in the moonlight. To the right, the mouth of the Westport River. The surface of the river should have been smooth and black, wind and tide caressing it together. Instead it coiled and jittered with silver.

Jake came down from the dune and took off his boots and pants, carrying them under his arm as he walked along the beach to the river mouth. As soon as his feet lit up with phosphorescence it was impossible not to jump and splash like a madman.

In the black water of the river luminous flares heaved and roiled, streaks of phosphor on the dark bodies of harbor seals. Jake stripped off the rest of his clothes and walked in. Seal bodies glided into him, around him, smooth-pelted flanks, palmlike flippers, barking to one another, talking to him. They were playing, thumping their tails and flippers to ignite more planktonic sparkles. They churned their wakes at him; he flutter-kicked back at them. They barked. He lay back and floated, looking at the moon and laughing.

They played, the seals and Jake, until he was exhausted, and then, as though they could sense his fatigue, they saluted him, raising their heads out of the water and barking. Then they dove into streaky blackness and were gone.

～.

Back in his own truck, undiscovered, out of the boatyard and onto the highway, Jake was hungry and he wanted a drive. The sky clouded over as he left the sea. All along Route 6 into New Bedford the neon signs glowed drunkenly, nonsensically, fuzzed by mist. At the docks, the Vineyard ferry was tied up for the night; one of the big fishing boats was all lit up, its crew getting ready to go out. The fog had settled in, smelling of salt and engine oil under the warped funky fish smell of dried nets. Creosote. Finally he parked and walked the rain-slimed cobbles of the Historic Section, past the Seamen's Bethel, the Zeiterion Theater.

The street was dark, its lamps inexplicably gone out. The wind blew in from the sea smearing his lips with salt. A man in a dark jacket approached with a black dog trotting beside him. Jake asked him if there was any place where he could still get a drink.

"Sure is," he said. "I'm just going there myself. If you don't mind me stopping home to get some cash."

Jake said he would follow him, if it wasn't too far.

"Far?" the man said. "It's just around the corner here." At the door of a triple-decker he pulled out his keys. "Come on in, why don't you? I won't be but a minute." He led Jake through a hallway and up a flight of stairs that should have smelled of cabbage and fried fish; instead there was a hint of chocolate. He opened a door and motioned Jake to go in. "Make yourself at home in here," he said. "Back in a jiffy." It was the best room, the one that no one ever uses except for funerals and occasionally engagements—but instead of being full of high-backed chairs draped with antimacassars it appeared to be dark and empty except for a line of standing clocks around the edge of the room and a birdcage with a large parrot, asleep or stuffed, in the middle.

Jake paced. He stood still. He put his hands in his pockets and then took them out again.

He had left his watch in his truck, in preparation for his assignation with Grenville's Chevy, and he had forgotten to put it on afterwards. Here, in the gloom, he could just make out the clockfaces. Each showed a different hour; none of them ticked. The parrot lifted his head and spoke distinctly in a language Jake didn't know. He wanted to turn on the light but felt somehow that would be wrong or inappropriate. Minutes stretched out, feathering the distance around him. He wondered aloud if he should go or stay. The parrot made clucking noises, cocked his head at Jake, and said, "Sufficient unto the day is the evil thereof." At least Jake thought he said that. But the bird might have been talking in some foreign language, and Jake could have been imposing English on top of his words. In any case, Jake thought that the parrot sounded much more convincing as a minister than he did. Now the bird turned his head and uttered: "Well, look at you: you're all dirty. What on earth have you been up to?"

Footsteps in the hallway, then down the stairs. The front door opened and clicked shut. Jake wondered if that was his guide. He wondered if he'd been forgotten.

The bird bent his head down, scratched his neck feathers, then said in a radio announcer's voice: "It's midnight in the city. Do you know where your child is? Do you know where your mother is?" He paused, stepped side to side, from one clawed foot to another, as though testing which was stronger. Clearing his avian ministerial throat, he said again: "Sufficient unto the day. Fish for dinner, is it? Do you want some more cabbage darling? Son of a bitch. Son of a bitch. You *and* your mother can't cook worth a tinker's damn." He put his head back under his wing.

Then more steps in the hallway. "Sorry to keep you waiting," the man said. "The good woman wanted to know what I was up to. Shall we go then?" He gave a low whistle for the dog. "Come along Maelstrom." Claw taps on the wooden floor.

The fog had thickened while they were inside; it spilled up the street shrouding the streetlights, which were working here, and form-ing a wall of mist at the end of the block as though this were the last street in the city. A few houses away a party was letting out, with billowy light flooding from an open door; departing guests ambled unsteadily in twos and threes. A thickset man lurched toward them out of the gloom. Maelstrom stopped and sniffed his groin. The man looked at Jake and his guide for a moment, then said, "Too late, too late. It's all over, you know?" Then he was gone. A woman followed him; her skirt was short and flounced, her heels spiky. Her hair was pulled up on top of her head where it was bound with a ribbon before it tumbled down her back. As she ran past, Jake could see her dark lip-stick and he found himself unable to guess her age. A neon sign hung in a window, *Food and Drink, all ours.* In front of the same establish-ment, lit by a single bulb, a painted wooden sign rocked back and forth in the wind; *All Hours,* it said, but the room inside was dark.

The man turned to Jake: "Are you a stranger here?"

"No," he said, too loudly. The mist had been tossing their voices, magnifying, then losing them. Jake said he was from Cranford. "I came to New Bedford all the time, when I was younger." He named some of the bars near the fish piers.

"That's a long time ago," the man said, giving him an intense look. "They've all shut down."

"Even The Grotto?"

"Had a fire last month. If they can scrape some money together, they'll open again. Always having fires, though. Bad wiring."

Jake asked the man what he did.

"Odd jobs. Repairs. Guide. I take people fishing, Blues, Marlin."

The air had gotten too thick or too thin. The fog closed around them, creating a barrier between mouth and lungs. Here the street-lights were haloes in the gray. They were barely trying to illuminate.

At sidewalk level, a light from a low window with bars over it, some sort of kitchen behind; three faces peered out, two men and a woman, they were from a different place. Asian eyes.

They walked until Jake's feet seemed imperfect and his head filled with mist. Was it even Grenville's truck he had attacked? How many old Chevys were sitting near the bushes in the marina that night?

Which bushes? What color would that truck be by daylight? It must have been exactly 2:00 A.M. for him to launch into worry like that. The exactness of the hour passed. He knew which truck. This was an idle transitory anguish. That pickup had smelled of Grenville, though Jake had never met him.

"Are you sure we shouldn't get my truck?" Jake asked.

The man didn't answer. Jake looked at his face to see if he had heard, but they were between streetlights and he couldn't really see. Jake asked him again.

"No, no. You're a young fellow, this can't be too much walking for you."

"My name's Jake," he said.

"You told me that already. Jake Beecher, you said."

Jake didn't remember introducing himself. But then he wasn't tracking very cleanly; the sadism of what he had done to an innocent elderly work vehicle was making him feel queasy. To console himself he tried arguing that at least he had not been attacking the man he wanted to murder, he had only killed his truck.

"Did you tell me your name?" Jake asked.

"Nope. Don't think I did."

This was a relief. "Ah. What is it then?"

"Donahue Pereira. You can call me Donahue."

"Where are you taking me, Mr. Donahue? Will there be any food there?"

"Oh, Lord, yes." He said something about the fishing in New Bedford having gone to the dogfish, but the fishermen still knowing how to eat.

Maelstrom, the dog, had been off on a mission, but now he jingled back to them, sniffing the air. Jake never liked it when black dogs exhibited their white teeth and nuzzled his crotch. It was impossible to walk with the dog's nose between his legs. Jake pulled at the animal's collar. Donahue Pereira gave a sharp whistle and the dog slunk off. Jake was a cat man, himself; dogs ruin things with all their plunder and wild digging. Dogs yearn far too much.

The city had changed. Jake's old hangouts were gone: closed and boarded-up, burned-down and charred. He hadn't showered after swimming, and now the salt had dried on his skin, twisting his hairs and tickling him, gossiping to his flesh and making it mutter. His beard was crusted with glass particles; his hands smelled of burning. The earlier giddiness he had felt at setting out to destroy Grenville's truck was gone; gone, too, was the anger. Jake had not recognized himself as a destroyer before and he felt as though he had been handed a new sort of mirror, which he did not know how to read. A cubist face looked back at him. Perhaps he was wasting his life. He wondered if he should be doing something else. Building something. Loving differently, loving someone besides Maggie. He was glad the mist was so thick that Donahue Pereira would not be able to see him. Jake Beecher, destroyer of trucks. Embracing and hacking apart: were they the only gestures left?

"Your face is all covered with soot, you know. Were you at a burning earlier?" Donahue Pereira's voice startled him.

"Oh, is it?" Jake felt his chin. "Yes, I was. Had to cut apart a truck."

"Truck chopping? Friend or foe?" He seemed to take it as an ordinary occurrence.

"Foe," Jake said.

"Was it the first time for you, then?"

"It was."

"Well, there's always a first one. Trouble is, when you destroy your enemy's transport, you better make sure he's far away from where you live."

It alarmed Jake that Donahue Pereira seemed to think that truck chopping would now be a regular part of his life. Jake asked him what he meant.

A woman's voice sounded in the distance. Donahue stopped to listen and then said, "Well, if he's close by, and you cut off his wheels, well then, you're stuck with him, aren't you? He won't be able to leave you."

"That's a bad thought," Jake said. As though it was Donahue's fault Jake had destroyed the truck without first making sure Grenville was gone from the neighborhood. Jake was hungry and he was annoyed at Donahue for taking so long to get where they were going. In the blackness Jake aimed a foot at the dog.

"Don't go kicking Maelstrom," Donahue said. "That dog didn't do anything to you."

The voice got closer. A woman singing.

Donahue gripped Jake's arm and pulled him into a darkened doorway. "Psst," he said. "Keep quiet, now."

It was the same woman Jake had seen earlier—was she fifteen? Forty? Foreign-looking, with that cascading Portuguese hair.

Donahue waited until she was far down the street, then said, "The wind always shifts to the east when she is out at night."

Jake snickered. He couldn't help it. But he also couldn't stop himself from looking up at the sky. The cloud scud showed that Donahue Pereira's direction was correct. "Why?" Jake said. "What has she got to do with it?"

"Haven't you noticed," Donahue said, "that the only thing that explains the weather is the behavior of certain women?"

Jake guffawed so loud it echoed and Maelstrom came back, crooked tail high, to see what was going on. Jake covered his crotch.

Donahue continued. "I can make it veer south again, and west, if I get down to the fishing docks in time, but Smeralda Gutierres can back the wind to the east simply by walking the streets of New Bedford after midnight."

"How long has she had this power?" Jake asked.

"Since she was old enough to look men in the eye and know what she meant by it."

There was a whole chain of command and cause whose links were missing here. Jake wondered what he was getting himself into. And he had been in this man's house. In the dark. With his parrot who muttered from the Gospel of Matthew. "Do you ever try to keep her inside, your Smeralda Gutierres?" Jake felt insane for asking.

"We have all tried, from time to time. Our fishing depends on the weather, and the weather depends on the winds. So we have sweet-talked her, married her, paid and implored her. My mother's brothers, Donahues all, wanted to take out one of those contracts on her— shows you how much the Irish know about the sea. What if they'd killed her when she'd gotten us into a Nor'easter? Then it would blow forever instead of just the three blasted days of dirty rain. Now that the cod and pogy are gone from these parts—and the blues and the haddock, also—there's hardly anything but dogfish left—and the dogfish are eating what remains of the others—well, we need Smeralda Gutierres more than ever."

Jake asked Donahue why, if he needed her so much, he'd been hiding from Smeralda, in the doorway, just then.

At first it seemed as though Donahue wasn't going to answer. Then he said, "Sometimes, women . . ." he searched for the right phrase as they walked. "Sometimes, men . . ." They kept on through the mist. "Sometimes, we just aren't strong enough to face them."

They turned the corner and Donahue touched Jake's elbow to lead him into a bar. A neon sign in the window had most of its letters missing. Three men sat at the counter, hunched over their drinks. Jake ordered a cheeseburger and a beer. Donahue ordered whisky.

"This is ridiculous," Jake said, stopping to face him. "Women don't control the weather. How can you think that?"

"Now don't distort what I told you: she doesn't control it in every way. But when she is out in the street after midnight the wind will swing around to the east. Then it's up to us to set it right."

"Does she know what she is capable of? Does she walk the streets on purpose?" Jake felt ridiculous: he needed much more alcohol to have this conversation.

"Depends on what you mean by 'on purpose.' But no, she doesn't know. No woman knows the effect she has. We tell her, but she doesn't believe it."

"Aren't you, well, overdoing it a bit?"

"And you, my fine truck murderer: what caused you to char your face and blacken your heart earlier this evening? Was it because of a woman that you were feeling the need to bring a truck to its knees? Or were you just wanting to sample a little demolition for the hell of it?"

"Not exactly." Jake wasn't sure how Donahue had gotten such a clear idea of what he had done. The latter part of their talk had been so queer that it was blocking out anything he might have told him earlier.

"So, then?"

"OK, it was a woman." Hunger and tiredness filled Jake's voice with resentment. "But she can't influence the weather."

The barman came out of the kitchen with Jake's food.

"Don't try to think, OK?" Donahue said. "Just swallow this good stuff down."

The cheeseburger must have come from some other world. It was the best Jake had ever tasted. He made the mistake of saying so to the bartender, who gave him a strange look and grunted. Jake ordered another one, then asked the bartender if he knew whether The Grotto was going to rebuild.

"The what?" the bartender said. He'd never heard of it. He went back to the kitchen and brought Jake's second cheeseburger. Who was back there cooking at this hour? This one tasted so good Jake got scared. Cheeseburgers are not supposed to have a taste; they are supposed to present enough heat and grease and bulk and bready softness and tough-meat smell to make you think you are holding a meal between your hands. But this beef was charcoaled and crunchy on the outside, the roll was crisped in butter, and the cheese was sharp and thick. This was what man the hunter had been looking for since he first swung down out of the trees and chipped flint for a bison spear. The hair stood up on the back of Jake's neck and he felt as quivery as noon. As Donahue slipped off his stool to go to the head Jake noticed that the clock above the bar was frozen with both hands hanging straight down at six. He was still clearheaded enough to know that this was an impossible time: the hands couple in the southern quarter only at 5:27 and at 6:33. No one here would know the time, from the look of them, so, paying careful attention to the placement of his tongue and the sound of words, Jake said, "What is the name of this place, anyway?" He wanted to be able to find it later, when he was sober and more sane. His one beer felt like half a dozen.

The barkeep laughed and shrugged and pointed to the neon window sign. From the back it looked like Arabic.

"What street?"

He said something that sounded like Rodman Street, but Jake knew Rodman from one end to the other. Finally he stopped asking and cradled his empty beer bottle in his hands. Donahue had not come back. Jake went to the men's room expecting to find him passed out on the floor but there was no one there. He pissed and then went to the kitchen, which was empty and dark. In the bar, the other men had left. The bartender was turning out lights.

"Are you closing up?"

"That's right, fella," he said. "It's about time."

"How much do I owe you?"

"Don't worry about it. Your friend paid."

"Mr. Pereira?"

"If that's what he told you."

"Did he already go then?"

"About an hour ago."

Jake's sense of time had tilted, but he was sure it hadn't been that long since Donahue had left the room. It was too difficult to pursue, however, so Jake asked the bartender how to get back to the fishing docks from there.

"Easiest way is up the stairs at the end of the alleyway. Can't miss it."

⌣·

Outside a mackerel dawn was breaking, piercing and dappled with a hint of glory to it. Jake turned back to look at the bar's sign in one last try at catching its name, but the neon was off, now, and all he could see was a tangle of thin glass tubes in the darkened window.

He climbed the wooden stairs, two flights of them, and found himself in the middle of the fishing docks. The fleet had left. Overhead, speckled clouds caught the sun in yellow and orange. He walked along the quays with their smell of rot and wet and fish until he found a pay phone to call Tony and invite him to breakfast at the Shawmut Diner.

⌣·

There are times when one needs Formica tables rimmed with metal, counter stools that spin, and the spit of frying of pig fat. Fried eggs with chorizo. Rivers of unreconstructed lard.

Tony looked happy and well-slept. "Hey, man, what's up?"

"I wanted a breakfast so heavy it wouldn't be safe to go it alone," Jake said.

"Like oatmeal?"

"Worse," Jake said. In spite of the cheeseburgers he was ravenous, so hungry he felt wobbly. The diner clock said six sharp.

Doris brought their platters of scrambled eggs and chorizo, hashed browns, toast, fried tomatoes. Mugs of coffee. "Sit with us, sweetheart," Jake said, grabbing at her tough hips with both hands but catching only the edge of her apron. Jake had just realized that he would have to tell Tony about his murderous involvement with Grenville's truck, as well as the Matthew-spouting parrot, and the conversation with Donahue Pereira and his belief in Smeralda Gutierres. Jake felt newly bewildered and incapable. He wanted Doris to join them so that he would be prevented from having to talk.

"I can't, Jake," Doris said, detaching Jake's hands. "Isabella's late and I'm alone on the floor." She headed back toward the kitchen. She blew him a kiss as she went, leaving him alone with Tony.

Now, in the sharp and radiant language of daylight, Jake would have to find a way to talk of his tangled engagements in the dark.

Chapter Seventeen

LATE THE NEXT AFTERNOON, Sally came over to Jake's house. Jake was in the shower and Sally yelled to him that she had come for the rest of her belongings.

When Jake emerged, he found that she had made a pot of coffee. It was about a week after she had caught him in the garden with Gillian, and they had not spoken since. Jake sat down at the kitchen table.

"I had always thought," Sally paused for a moment, then put her head down and wept. She seemed brave and destroyed and Jake was not sure what to do. He knew he was to blame for her destruction and understood at that moment that he had loved Sally for years. He had never loved her the most, though, and because of that he had always felt mantled with guilt when he was with her. Over the last few years she would leave him, because he wouldn't marry and didn't want children. And then she would come back to him. This was a mystery. It implied either that she was not as bright as she needed to be, or that Jake had some virtue he himself was unaware of. There must have been men out there who were much more suitable. But she would come back and they would take up again exactly where they had left off, except for a small measure of new bitterness. It was a sweet bitterness, though, and contained humor and acceptance, even if Jake was never clear about what was holding him back. Perhaps he would have liked to have children with Sally.

This time it seemed different. Sally had made them one last coffee, and they sat there mostly silent, fingering the old grooves in the wooden table. Jake was feeling like a dog who has been discovered raiding the pantry and pulling down the cereal boxes and overturning the flour bin in an effort to reach some doggy treats. He sat there wanting to yap at her and make her laugh but his heart was slinking into another room.

"I've been really dumb," Jake said.

"Worse than dumb."

"I'm really sorry, Sal."

"Well, I hope you'll be happy with your young cutesie."

"She's not mine. She's not cute. She's got nothing to do with anything."

"So why were you humping her. In *our* garden?"

Sally was right: she and Jake had dug and planted that plot together. It was the blue garden: scilla in early spring, then sky blue and cobalt delphiniums, balloon flowers and carpathian bellflowers, gray-blue sea holly, silver-leaved Russian blue sage, and finally the deep purple-blue monkshood that blooms late, after everything else has given up. It was a strange and haunting place. The answers to unutterable questions were on the tip of his tongue whenever he walked through that blue garden of theirs.

Jake didn't know how to respond to her. Finally he said, "I was lost. I lost my way."

"Can't you get lost and still keep your prick in your pants?" She toyed with the sugar bowl, tilting it this way and that. "You think it's some kind of beacon? A flashlight to help you find out where you are?"

Jake found Sally's image funny, and he laughed. This was not the right thing to do. Sally raised the sugar bowl she had been playing with and flung its contents at his face. Jake winced, shutting his eyes. This filled his eyelids with crystals. His nostrils were clogged. He wiped at his nose but did not dare breathe. His beard was still wet from the shower and now the sugar stuck to it and coated it. Flailing about, he got up in a cockeyed squint, both eyes smarting and scratchy, and pawed his way to the bathroom.

When he wiped the steamy mirror he saw himself, transformed, or exposed: an ancient white-bearded guy, both eyebrows white now, bleary-eyed. With a wet washcloth he cleaned his eyes and nose, but he left the glowing white mass on his beard and came back out to the kitchen. It snowed on the table as he sat down.

"Well, am I good enough to eat?"

It was the wrong joke, and he knew it as soon as it was half spoken.

"Your poet friend Gillian may think so," Sally said. "But she can't tell sugar from dogshit."

"Oh, Sal, which of us can?"

But his lament was lost on her. Sally bundled up her books and a few old sweaters and let the screen door slam behind her as she left.

Chapter Eighteen

WHAT DO YOU DO WHEN THE MAN you hate most in the world shows up one morning in your kitchen?

You say: "Coffee? Tea?" It's either that or kill him.

Then he will say, "You don't have to feed me, I didn't come here for that."

"Still and all. What would you like?"

"What are you having?"

If only he hadn't been so polite, then Jake could have thrown something. "Coffee, then. Toast? English muffins?" Jake gestured toward the different parts of the kitchen; he tried to keep from buffooning.

"If it's not too much trouble."

"No, no." People were always feeding this guy, Jake thought. What was it with him? His very presence must be a feeding trigger like the open beaks of nestling birds.

᠆᠁

An hour earlier, Jake had been at the marsh just after dawn: not a breath of wind. The moon-tide had brimmed to fill the lowest marshes, widening that intimate part of the river to an oceanic expanse reflecting the heavens. The great blue heron veered toward his usual stakeout in the salt grass. He landed, saw that it was too deep for him, and took off again with cartilaginous flappings, hearty and furious. The sun whispered on Jake's back. He waited a bit to see if the heron would return. The great blue felt like an emissary and Jake was always mindful in his presence.

When Jake returned to the house, a man was standing in his

kitchen, looking out the window. Jake twitched, startled. He knew the man must be Grenville, but he looked so different from Jake's mental picture of him that he wondered if Grenville had disguised himself for this visit: he looked thin and inconsequential—willowy—if you can say that about a man. Blackish hair gone to white at the temples, shaggy, bearded or simply unshaven, it was hard to tell. Jake put on his ministerial voice and said, "Hello, there. How's it going?"

"I thought I'd visit you."

"Oh?"

"I wanted to talk to you."

"Oh."

"Maggie trusts you. Gillian trusts you."

"Ah," Jake tried not to snort. "Trust."

Grenville turned out not to be so very large. All summer long Jake had imagined a tall archaic god, striding across the fields and into the beds of women, and instead the real Grenville looked like a being who moved sideways and disappeared behind trees—his gestures were quick and darting, arms expressive; hands electric, brilliant. Not beautiful, really, or not at every moment. Where, then, did his power, his attraction, come from? Was it that he was always in motion, even after he sat down at the table?

Grenville wore old jeans and a faded green cotton shirt, which seemed very familiar. In fact, Jake had lent such a shirt to Maggie one day when they had gone kayaking and her clothes had gotten wet. So, it probably was his shirt that Grenville was wearing. Had Maggie given it to him? Had she thrown it out? Had Grenville stolen it from her clothesline? Had she invited him into her closets after making love? The love-fevered brain can always uncover infinite pathways of treason.

Keep breathing, Jake said to himself. Listen for the wind. And do not believe that women control the way it blows. Except possibly Miss Gutierres, in New Bedford.

There was no wind. Still.

Jake thought of sword dances, throat singing. He wanted to rave in obscure languages. Instead he said: "Sit." He grinned. Partly because that was how he would say it to a dog. And partly because, after all—next to Maggie telling Jake that she loved him—Grenville's story was what he most wanted to hear. He needed it to make sense of his world. The kettle whistled. He ground the coffee.

Jake had never seen Grenville before this moment, and had been actively avoiding him all summer. Dodging around Grenville's presence, Jake had felt he could not bear to meet him. Maggie had tried to make Jake stay when she knew Grenville was about to appear. She would ask Jake to go down to the river or to the boathouse with her to try and find Grenville. He had bowed out of this so often that it became a joke between them. There were moments when Jake disbelieved in Grenville's very existence and presumed him a collective figment: Maggie's, Gillian's, his own. Perhaps he preferred to keep the stranger thus. For a while Jake thought the man would be less of a threat if he never actually saw him. This was wrongheaded: the way the imagination of jealousy works, Grenville became, of course, much more dangerous in the abstract. The menace of the absent unknown rival is infinite, incalculable, endless. In the end, Grenville had caused such upheavals that he had to be real.

Jake wanted desperately to misbehave: he could tip over the kitchen table and jump on its underside; he could gargle his coffee and then spit it at his visitor. Instead, he said, "Do you take milk?"

"A bit, yes, please."

How often do you get your enemy sitting at your kitchen table, ready to tell you all the things that mystify you? Listen first. Hear him out. And then tie him to the tall humped rock they call the Knubble, at the entrance to Westport Harbor, and let the ospreys eat his important parts.

Jake did know how to listen. In this tripartite calling of his: minister of the dim light, ne'er-do-well, and remittance man, he had learned to nod his head at intervals and to hold his tongue. By listening he had found that the women around Cranford had words for things, though their menfolk were blocked and dumb. The men talked when they were drunk: they became maudled, inflated, and debased themselves, and got nowhere. Jake knew he was no better: when he gathered wood in the forest with Maggie's husband Hugh— whom he counted as his friend despite, or perhaps because of, his intense desire to steal his wife—the two men exchanged grunts and ideas but not souls. When their son, Tony, came to help Jake build the toolshed, by the end of a few hours Jake knew what was on Tony's mind, but he could never begin to tell him what was on his own. You do not tell a grown man you want to run away with his mother, no matter how well you get along.

Now, here was Grenville. Perhaps he had the words. Perhaps he could tell why he had carried away Jake's flock of beauties, stolen the women Jake wanted. Jake now counted Maggie's daughter Gillian among his flock, even though he didn't always like her, and even though by attempting to make love to her in his gardens he had betrayed Maggie and lost his true friend Sally. Sally was the only one around who hadn't been seduced by Grenville's hairy charms. Or had she? What was he waiting for? Jake wondered. He hoped Sally had better sense.

Perhaps, Jake thought, Grenville would explain things to him. But that would mean sitting still and Jake was too nervy and couldn't sit down just yet. He plucked the first two English muffins from the toaster, put in another pair, moused around the fridge for butter, opened the cupboard and found some blackberry jam.

"I'm all out of sugar," Jake said. "You can use this jam if you like."

⌣

What would Maggie say if she knew Grenville were here in his kitchen? Would she be pleased? Had she, in fact, sent him, since Jake had always refused to go and meet him? Had Maggie heard about the destruction of Grenville's truck? Had *Grenville* even heard about his truck? Had he guessed that it was Jake? Was that why he was here? If Jake killed Grenville, would Maggie mourn him forever? How could she have slept with him? How could she have enjoyed the awesome and ridiculous act with him?

"What do you want?" Jake asked Grenville, with a smile. Always that damn smile. What did Jake want? Jam *and* butter. And Maggie in his bed. But he had lived long enough to know that you don't really wish for things unconditionally anymore, once you've reached the middle regions of a man's age. The genie in the lamp is too full of willful spite and if you have forgotten to state the correct conditions of your desires, you will be condemned to regret, in perpetuity, their fulfillment. If Jake wished for Maggie to want him as much as he wanted her, then that would double the pain unless he also wished for a way for them to resolve that desire. He wanted her to be constructing her cloth mermaids in his own house, then talking to him all night long, greeting the dawning river with him. He wanted her to be playing in his gardens with all her grandchildren. And Hugh? Jake wanted him to be turned into some kind of happy black puppy, jumpy and avid for scent trails in the forests. Or perhaps Hugh could sail off somewhere and disappear, as Grenville had done. Maybe Grenville would take Hugh away. But then Maggie would not be the person Jake loved: a piece of her would be missing and what remained would be full of grief. So his wishes concerning Maggie were not to be uttered, even to the imp in the lamp. Except certain nights, when he could no longer bear the shackling of his wants, and he told the evil one to just lead Maggie to his bed and he would take it all from there. Just bring her, Jake commanded. Here. Now.

As one who didn't live by the rules, Grenville had immense power over those who did. And yet he was outside of life, on the edge of things. Outside, looking in. Except for the few times he got to sample it. Sampling Maggie, for example. Or Gillian. A few occasions were too many.

Jake wanted to ask Grenville if it was important to him that he was living by the edge of the river. Jake knew that he sailed—he had taken Maggie to Cuttyhunk, among other voyages—but he didn't know if Grenville was conscious of the edge. When you mess about with very small boats then you are playing with flux and with time. In large boats you go away, you head for the horizon, out there, in the offing, you have a destination, and except when you are in harbors the tides do not matter so much, the margins lose meaning. With the small boats, though, it is the edges that define. With kayaks and canoes, those indentations and channels cut in the marsh grass, those hidden bays, are what pull at you.

There was a sandbar near the mouth of the river, a sometimes-island made of gulls and gray sand. The local boys swam to it against the riptide, proving, over and over, their manhood. Jake would beach his kayak on it and pace about there on the sand and eat his lunch as though the ground were forever and not bordered so by time and the will of the river. This was the line that interested him, that temporal boundary, that phase shift of the elements.

Jake wanted to ask Grenville if that was why he chose the shacks along the river, or if they were simply a convenience and the plywood and linoleum cabins of any empty motel far inland would have felt the same to him. Jake wanted to find all that out, and why Grenville was fucking Jake's cousin.

The second two English muffins popped up. Jake put them on another plate and brought them to the table. He gave them each a knife and a napkin, then sat down.

"Look," Grenville said. "I'm desperate to talk to you." He smiled. "I don't really know what to do." He shrugged. "I'm totally confused. You must think I'm a crazed person. I'll go." He put his cup on the table and stood up.

"No. Come back," Jake said. "Stay." If only he had remembered those words when Sally was leaving him.

Grenville turned around and sat. He gripped his coffee cup. "Without rudder, keel, or compass," he said.

Jake didn't know which of them he was referring to.

"Does Hugh have acetylene torches?" Grenville asked.

Jake told him that even if Hugh had acetylene it was doubtful he would know how to use it. "Why do you want to know?" he asked.

"They wrecked my truck." Grenville spoke in a whisper as though it were an embarrassment. As though it were some failing, some impotence, of his own. "Demolished," he said. "Burned."

Jake brought his fingers to his nose. Usually he did this out of sexual nostalgia. We are dogs after all, he thought. Sometimes he could smell a woman days later if he was careful not to wash too thoroughly. But now he wanted to see if the burnt metal scent was still present. They just smelled like fingers. He could have offered them to Grenville for a quick sniff, but didn't.

"Why?" Jake asked. "Why would anyone cut up your truck?" The words "cut up" were a mistake. Grenville hadn't used them. "Did you say 'burn' or 'cut up'?" Acetylene implied cut up, and Grenville *had* asked about acetylene, but the kitchen was suddenly booming with heart-thumps. Jake got up to walk around and he wondered if Grenville was going to savage his house now, but Grenville only jumped up and darted over to the counter and poured himself more coffee and asked Jake if he wanted some. Then Grenville sat down and began to tell his story.

⌣·

Grenville lay on the mattress in the loft of the boat shack, his hands crossed behind his head. The night was still warm and the soft west wind carried the salt-mud smells of the river at low tide. The marsh and the meadow were full of noises: katydids scratched and the tree frogs bleeped and bullfrogs strummed their improbable membranes. Out his diamond-shaped window he could see a sailboat with a single mast tilted, resting on the riverbed, grounded by the receding tide. The moon hung, caught rocking, just past full.

The Gifford farm was full of people these days. He liked their shouts and calls and laughter; there was a smoothness to them at this distance that he was sure would turn into texture if he got closer. Then he would see snags in the smoothness, complexities. At first he only knew Maggie. With her, he could begin to see the tangles and the prickles and they delighted him even while they frightened him. How angry she got at him. She saw the horror of what he had done leaving his wife, and she presented it to him, almost daily. She said he was morally wanton. Grenville hadn't known men could be wanton. Was her constant badgering part of what kept him there? She asked him how he could be jealous of her marriage, when he had abandoned one just like it. But no marriage is just like another one, and his had dwindled; he and Denise had forgotten to plant and plow, harrow, weed, fertilize. Lack of husbandry. He was jealous of Maggie's marriage and of her garden, which he now raided each morning before dawn, at first for lettuce and herbs and later for beans, peas, carrots, and tomatoes. He had begun to raid the marriage, too. Hoping for something to rub off on him, happiness, perhaps, or knowledge. He greeted Maggie's flowing anger as though he were parched for it. It was the opposite of absolution.

When he had seen Maggie's daughters in their kayaks that Sunday, Grenville had known immediately who they were. The blond one with Maggie's sharpness was Connie; the troubled one, the poet and wild neurotic, was Gillian, who would, when she met him, keep flirting with him and backing off. He had known Gillian would hunt him down. When she found him on the marsh one day she kept asking, "But where do you live?" as though she already suspected they were practically roommates. Farmmates. Maggie hadn't warned him about her daughter's beauty.

As Gillian told Grenville about the poem she was working on, about a man who is told by a water snake not to look into a pool of water, as she sat there beside him on the marsh, he felt as though his skin had developed eyes, as though his skin was watching her skin. She was using the nearness to make him feel her breath, her gaze. He was sure she knew what she was doing, and it made him wonder if Maggie, too, was conscious of this art of sexual beckoning.

Grenville made sure that Gillian didn't visit him on the farm. He moved for a while to the Cooksey place, farther down the river, and told her he lived there. He still had the keys from when he was a real estate agent. He showed her the path along the water, through the reeds.

One night he awoke before dawn to find her sitting on his bed. "You'll get cold," he had said. "Come under the covers."

She had been slinky, cold and hot, undecided and decisive. He had been oddly out of it; perhaps it was the hour, perhaps he didn't really want her. Flattery and intrigue could go a long way, but not far enough to make him lose himself. Perhaps he was waiting for Maggie. He did not apologize. He did not go all abject. He pretended to fall asleep and softly snored.

Sunrise came and she said she had to get back to her boyfriend, Paul. "If I come by again, will you be here? Will you be alone?" she asked.

He looked into the blackness of her eyes. "Try me," he said.

That was the last time Grenville kept his head with Gillian. After that he needed her and wanted her and did everything but stalk her.

It was as though her need for sexual intimacy had contaminated him, and suddenly he wanted her all the time, her limbs coiled around his body, her damp tangled hair, her musk. He still didn't know how much of his attraction to her was because she was Maggie's daughter. Perhaps he was using her, his involvement with her, to help him figure out what it was that he wanted from Maggie, what kept him living on her property, at the edges of her life.

Meanwhile, Grenville asked Gillian to leave Paul and come away with him. Perhaps she guessed that his offer wasn't real. He did not tell her that he was married, or that he had parted from his wife without saying anything, or that he had lived now essentially without money for half the summer. He also did not tell Gillian he had recently asked Maggie to go off with him.

That had happened just after he and Maggie had come back from their weekend sail to Cuttyhunk. It was before he had involved himself with Gillian. Hugh was off sailing, the whole Gifford brood was at the beach, and Maggie had been on her way to join them when Grenville appeared on her driveway and hitched a ride with her.

"I want you to come away with me," he said.

"I've been away with you," she said, smiling. "Cuttyhunk."

"I don't mean that. I mean really away. Longer. Life."

She was silent for a long moment. "You know—you act as though the act of flight was in itself a life. It's not. Not for me, at least. Being in motion doesn't resolve life when it stands still."

"What am I now, running or standing?" he asked.

"Neither," she said. "Somehow you've slipped between. You're watching my life."

"I'm sipping parts of it."

"What will you make from them?"

"A hive. A life."

"But you leave things dangling, you know. Like leaving the phone off the hook."

"But that noise eventually stops; it just goes dead, doesn't it?"

"Not a good way to end things: alarm, agony, going dead. Not good. Invent some other way. Stay here with me. Live on the farm."

Days later, in the boat shed, when he asked Maggie's daughter,

Gillian, to run away with him, Grenville wondered if he had lost his mind.

Gillian had refused. She said life was confusing enough. Like her mother she asked him to live on the farm. She suggested the boat shed. It wasn't clear if she knew he had been staying there. It had a bedroom upstairs, she said. And there was probably a burner for cooking, even electricity, though he would have to be careful. He didn't tell her that he had already lived there above the boats, but said he would think about her suggestion.

Grenville knew that people don't live like this. It was as though, slipping through the mesh of allowable behavior, the very structure of civilized being had come apart. He wondered how long it would be before he took to robbery, mayhem, eating babies. He looked on himself with horror. Each day was full of choices.

～·

When he had finished telling his story, Grenville looked at Jake. "I've got to go now," he said. "I've been here long enough. I know you can't tell me what to do. I just wanted to utter my confusion. I think I'm only making trouble."

"I wish I knew what to say," Jake said.

"I'll visit you again, if you'll let me."

"Anytime," Jake said. Grenville seemed to have no ballast, no anchor, and Jake found that frightening and even disgusting. He wanted to be rid of Grenville so that he could do a reckoning of his own. As he saw his visitor to the door he felt cold and clammy. The wind had risen out of the east. A chill.

Chapter Nineteen

SEVERAL DAYS AFTER GRENVILLE'S VISIT Jake noticed that his blue garden was shrinking. The flowers seemed to have lost their voices, and the stalks looked shorter, as though they were being eaten from below. There had been no rain for several days and he invented an explanation having to do with drought, that the plants had retracted along the spine, like old people, in a sort of longitudinal wilt. He was late for dinner with Maggie and Hugh so he didn't take the time to look closely but just set the soaker hose going and didn't think of it again until the next morning.

For Jake, gardens were mood temples; each one was planted with a different intention and gave off its own spirit. This animus ought to be evident, he thought, even when he couldn't define it. The blue garden always made him feel fine-bladed and hard; he took a sharp intake of breath whenever he looked at the delphinium spires, or the sea-holly thistles with the dusting of amethyst on their spikes. When he worked in that bed, existence was on the tip of his tongue.

If Jake didn't visit one of these gardens for a day or two he would get anxious that he was missing some fresh geometry uncoiling—some new petal, buoyant, thinner than air, fierce with color. He was supposed to take notice and give witness but instead he had been avoiding the blue garden since making love with Gillian there.

The next day it rained and he stayed inside reading and writing letters. He paid the utility bills. He received an odd telephone call from his mother. They usually talked once a year on Christmas afternoon—after the family in Newport had all finished their mammoth bloody roast of beef and their Yorkshire puddings crackling with fat, after the svelte long-armed women had honked and tinkled at one another, and the men, bursting their waistcoats, had brayed and snorted into their goblets. Jake didn't often speak of his family. It broke his heart to think of them.

Each year, on Christmas afternoon, his mother would telephone when his father has taken his sons and sons-in-law into the library to smoke cigars and drink brandy and talk about futures and markets. Jake's mother, who was named Glone, would have let Cook and Maidie—yes, that was really what the family called them, though the last ones Jake had known were born Theresa and Colleen—go home to their own families, and his two sisters and their two sisters-in-law, feeling liberal and Christian, would do all the washing up. Meanwhile, their red-faced men waggled their smokes and guffawed, speaking in brandied grunts from swollen leather armchairs. That was when his mother called him and he tried to be decent to her because she probably loved him even though neither she nor his father would allow him in their house. Jake liked to think that his mother had enough other children so that his defection from the pinstripes was not devastating to her; still, beneath all their talk her puzzled dismay hummed like static on a bad line.

The reason Jake's mother was calling—out of season—on that rainy August Friday, was to invite him to have lunch with her in Newport. It would have been bad manners to ask her if his coming into the city would invalidate the legal terms of his agreement to keep away. He knew that she had better things to do than to try to lure him into insolvency, but he was afraid that she might do it inadvertently. Jake was leery of going into Newport and he invited his mother to lunch at his place instead. As he uttered the invitation, he pictured days of housecleaning and rearranging, even though such work would be hypocritical and useless: a clean house cannot bleach a black sheep.

His mother did not want to come to Cranford; she refused the offer, asking him to come to Newport on Monday.

Jake smiled. "But I would like to show you my gardens," he said, trying not to sound young and eager. He was fifty, after all, his hair was mostly gray, one of his eyebrows was white. Glone was seventy-five; when he left home for the last time she was still blond.

"Another time would be better for your gardens, dear." She made them sound like Tinkertoys.

Jake asked if the old man would be at lunch, too.

"No, dear. It is just you and I. Just a little chat. We have got rather a lot to catch up on, don't you think?"

This last she said as a question, and it made Jake realize that he didn't know what she was up to. Was she sick? Or the old man? Perhaps one of his siblings or their troublesome spouses. Jake had never been allowed to meet any of their children, his nieces and nephews, though he had heard that they were both numerous and gifted.

Jake told his mother Monday would be fine. He picked at the whitest hairs of his beard, pulling them out, then he went back to his rainy-day occupations: reading and scheming to make money without having it look like work. Perhaps, as minister, he could convince some long-married couples to renew their vows. He would avoid baptizing any babies for a while, but he could easily christen boats, or large mammals. He could expand his very small marijuana garden on the tiny rock of an island that his grandfather had deeded him. He would change over to the shade-tolerant strains that had been developed in Holland and extend his planting farther under the canopy of scrub oak. The federal helicopters never dawdled over the river, although they inspected the cornfields by Jake's house, row by row. He pondered raising chickens, for a moment, or growing more exotic garlics.

The next day was rain-washed, brilliant, the wind a galloping westerly. After watching the river Jake drank his coffee and went out to the blue garden. The mood of that bed had never been connected to the blues; it had never spoken to him of mortality or loss or even troubled love. He and Sally had planted it when they were effervescently hopeful. But now it looked forlorn. He had left the drip hose on all through the rain and the color had dissipated: indigo had faded to navy; cobalt slid over into marine; sky had gone milky; the violet muted to gray. The leaves were dull, the angles wrong.

Jake turned off the hose. He thought of rigging up a serpentine contraption using the sump pump from the basement to suck the extra moisture from the earth with giant straws. Instead, he sat down beside the plants letting the wetness from the grass soak through his jeans. Then he prayed for the wind to blow hot and desiccating, and went to inspect the other beds.

The vegetables still looked robust: tomatoes and beans in need of picking, zucchini on the rampage. The garden out by the wall next to Maggie's property was studded with blue lupines and pink and purple loosestrife. It was easy to be lulled by the sweet warmth of summer: the hummingbirds still whirred in the garden by the porch, sipping from the scarlet grooves of some late bee balm; the deep blue flowers of the catmint were bouncing with small white butterflies.

On Sunday, before kayaking, Jake tried to convince himself that colors were elusive and variable, and his memory inexact, but the garden was truly fading and awkward. He took his breakfast outside and ate it on the grass, like eating at the bedside of a sick friend. For once there was no mold on the phlox. He pulled up a purplish Geranium Ann Folkard and looked at the roots. With a hand lens he checked stems and leaves for parasites, but could not see the problem. The blue garden had begun to smell like death.

~·

When Jake drove into Newport on Monday to meet his mother for lunch, he felt like a ghost, as though the dying garden had penetrated him, weaving itself among his own molecules.

For this occasion he had washed and brushed his hair. He trimmed his beard, clipped his nose hairs, clipped the hair of his white eyebrow, which was bushier than the brown one. His suit had gotten musty and he had let it hang on the back porch for a few days to air out. He borrowed a pair of black shoes from Hugh. They were long and skinny and felt awful but Jake doubted they could cause serious damage.

Jake was to meet his mother at her club, The Spinnaker, in the dining room. He wondered if he would recognize her, not having seen her since his uncle's funeral, fifteen years earlier, but he found her on the far side of the dining room, sitting at a table by the window. He crossed the dark blue carpet, tiptoeing in a mincing dance—

that one where demons insert marbles between your toes—hoping that no one would notice his gait.

Glone Beecher tilted her face back for a kiss. Jake gave it, patted her shoulder. She looked good, the old girl, white-haired and fine and nervous as a doe.

"Are those bunions, dear, or did you borrow the shoes?"

"How are you, Mother? How is Dad? How are my affluent siblings and their well-dressed spawn?"

She looked at him and said nothing.

"I'm sorry," Jake said. "I shouldn't start by insulting them." She was looking around the room, so he turned to see what she was scanning for, but it wasn't obvious. He had never been in her club. White tablecloths, cobalt tumblers. On the walls: early American portraits, those faces peering through the varnish with the sly ambiguous smiles of poisoners. Only three other tables in the large dining room were occupied: at each of them an ancient woman sat opposite a middle-aged daughter. It was a women's club, after all. When they were children Jake and his siblings had called it the Spinster Club. The room smelled of paintings and face powder. His mother was wearing a perfume he didn't remember, and it seemed exotic on her. He had an urge to take her hand, although that was not in the catalogue of his family's gestures—which included holding a woman's elbow during dangerous curbside maneuvers—but the grand advantage of being known to have no manners is that you can reach across the table and grab your mother whenever you want. It was only as he held her thin vein-mapped hand in his own fleshy, calloused palms that he realized she was not wearing any rings.

"Mrs. Beecher, ma'am—would you care for a drink before lunch?" The waitress had short red hair and a carved face. An imp, an angel. Jake felt a sudden leap, like a raising of spirit flags; he wanted to follow her into the kitchen and do something inappropriate and glorious.

He turned toward his mother, whose hand he still imprisoned in his own. "A drink?"

She asked for a dry martini.

"Make that two," Jake said.

Actually, he hated martinis. For one thing, the glass they come in was designed only for breaking or spillage. Then, they taste like bad salad dressing, with that iron taste of juniper in the gin; juniper belongs to the architects, those men who push little models of trees around cardboard constructions. True gardeners rarely drink gin because they dislike juniper—its very touch is so noxious that when a branch brushes over naked skin it can raise a rash that burns for days. Come back redhaired missy, Jake thought. Come, my fine-featured girl, and let me stroke your neck and let me change my misbegotten order.

She didn't come back.

Jake let go of his mother's hand, excused himself for a moment, and followed the imp-girl into the kitchen. The waitress saw him right away so he didn't have to dodge among the chefs and skillets; she came over to the swinging door.

"I'm sorry," Jake said, breaking out into a sweat. "But could you cancel my martini?" He really wanted beer but that seemed lummoxy among these thin-necked people. He asked for a glass of the house red.

He made his way back to his mother's table like a kangaroo in ballet slippers. Humbling himself he said, "I remembered that I'm allergic. I had to change it. Sorry. Where were we?"

Jake had been holding his mother's hand, that was where they had been. Why had he been doing that? Something about her face, looking about the room, skittish and wild, and her perfume, unseemly and sensual. No rings.

"Perhaps we should order," she said.

Jake studied the menu. "What's good?"

"Flounder," she said. "And the bouillon to start."

He nodded.

The redhaired one brought the bread basket: melba toast and Ry-Krisp. An iced silver dish of butter curls. Jake promised himself to go for a decent lunch as soon as he left here; this was just tongue teasing. Then the girl came back with bowls of soup, her wings bound and flattened to her body under her white blouse.

Glone had called this meeting, let her talk, Jake thought, looking at her and seeing with a start that she didn't have blue eyes—they were green. He had always thought they were blue and she had always carried herself as though they were. A flicker of doubt as to whether he was at the right table. Who was this woman and what was he doing lapping bouillon out of a tonsillectomy spoon, when he could be having fish and chips on the other side of town? He was half a century too young to be eating in this dining room. It was 1:00 P.M. Jake began to shiver lightly. He drank some wine. They finished their thin broth in silence.

"I wanted to ask you about something," Jake said. "I think one of my gardens is dying. Every plant has suddenly gone dim, as though the life is being sucked out."

"We shall talk about your gardens later," said Glone. "First, I have things to tell you." She whiskered some butter across a piece of melba toast and bit the corner. "And to ask you." She sipped her martini, looked at him, then drained it.

Jake wondered if he was that scary to talk to. Or could she—his mother—be a bit of a lush? He remembered his father getting red-faced and fumey, but not her.

"No," she said, looking at him sharply, although he had not said anything. "I am not an alcoholic, and yes, it takes a certain amount of courage to say what I am about to." She scanned the room again.

Their fiery-haired angel in her black skirt and white tuxedo blouse chose this moment to bring their main course: a pair of defenseless flatfish, lightly crumbed, with only the tiniest sprig of parsley beside the cloth-wrapped lemon half. A small mound of green peas. A single red potato. Oh, angel, thought Jake, your timing is perfectly bad. Do you know it? Do you read our body language, and only bring on the disturbance when I am holding this old woman's hand, or when she is leaning toward me with the hint of tears in those eyes that are now, and perhaps have always been, green?

"Thank you, Angela. That will do very nicely. White wine, if you please, for both of us, the Sancerre."

They took their lemons and spurted the lemon juice through the yellow lemon cloths into each other's eyes. They daubed. They pried with fish fork and fish knife. His mother leaned toward him and had started to speak as Angela returned with the white wine, but then she sat back, silent, toying with her water glass until the young waitress took herself away toward the kitchen, her white stockings whispering mysteries.

Glone looked at Jake and grinned. "I think we're safe for a while. Anyway, I don't know how to say it, so here it is: I am leaving Newport," she took a breath, then took some wine. "I'm going to get away from this place." She made a sweeping gesture to the swags of blue velvet above the windows, the white-painted half columns, the thin-lipped portraits. Another breath, then, "I am leaving your father." She looked around the room. Her face and neck got very red. She blotted her forehead with her handkerchief but the blush remained.

Jake put down his knife and fork. He drank some water and tried to swallow.

"I wanted to ask you a favor, actually," she began. "You see, it's uncomfortable living in the house at the moment. I need a place to stay, and I would prefer it to be a place where your father cannot reach me. Do you think I could stay with you in Cranford for a few days? Do you have room for me?"

"You can't do that," Jake said.

"I can't stay with you?"

"No, I mean, you can't jump out like that."

"What on earth do you know?"

Jake spluttered, "You're seventy-five years old."

"That has not escaped me. It is part of what drives me."

"To do what, exactly?"

"I am divorcing your father."

"Haven't you waited a bit long?"

"I am going to live in Egypt."

Jake drank more water, swallowed it the wrong way, and his coughing gave him time to think of saying, "Good God, why Egypt?"

She looked around the room. Two more tables now had elderly women and their younger female companions. None of them were watching her.

"You mean," Jake said, in full voice, "you're running off with an Egyptian? I assume it's that, rather than taking up archaeology? Pyramids? But I don't know you well enough to even guess, do I?"

"Speak softly, dear. It isn't the pyramids. It is a man."

"Oh, I see. And what does he do, this Egyptian man?"

"I'd rather not say."

"Oh no. You can't back out now. If you won't say, then either he's working class, or an artist of sorts, or perhaps in secret work for some government. Is he an actor? Vaudeville? Do the Egyptians have vaudeville? Is he, by chance, a circus performer?"

"Perhaps I shall tell you some other time."

She looked around to see if the portraits were listening, or the other white-haired ladies. They ate for a while in silence. Jake finished his fish and chewed on his beard. The wine was all gone. Angela came and asked about dessert. Glone ordered fruit salad with sherbet for both of them.

"You did it," she said, when Angela had left.

"What did I do."

"You left this debilitating family, for one thing?"

"Leave?" Jake said. "I didn't leave, I was tossed out like garbage. Remember?"

Glone said nothing.

"Perhaps you don't remember why I was sent away," Jake said, getting up from his seat. "But I do. And I didn't do it in order get myself thrown out of the family. I was young and selfish and didn't foresee the consequences. But I'm not sure anyone could have."

Jake pushed his chair in, and left her without saying good-bye. He hobbled with as much dignity as he could over the blue carpet and went out through the white-enameled columns and then down the rose-lined brick path. Once outside the main gate, he took off Hugh's narrow black shoes and walked barefoot on the sun-warmed pavement to his sweet brown Nissan truck, which he had parked several blocks away.

Chapter Twenty

IN THE BLUE GARDEN there was a deathly quiet. Not an insect. Nothing hovered. Blooms flopped, stalks huddled, all green gone, sap fled, as though they had been drained. The very sunlight seemed poisoned: it no longer danced over the foliage. No butterflies. No praying mantises or ladybugs. Not a beetle. The stark silence of no more bees. The air, hungover and sodden, pressed down on Jake's no-man's-land. The day before, he had had twelve gardens, if you count the shooting stars and dogtooth violets he had been putting in under the pine trees; now there were eleven and who knew what would happen to them. Sixty-five acres and nothing purposeful growing except the kitchen garden — if it was still growing. He went to inspect it. He fingered the tomatoes, stroked the Hungarian pepper plants and the giant red mustard. They were fine, bursting. He sucked a lettuce leaf. It tasted correct. Whoever was killing his flowers did not want to starve him. He kneeled among the tomato plants and wept with gratitude and with loss and with fear.

A sudden rush of loneliness: who would visit him if all his gardens died and even the insects avoided him? His mother had asked to come and stay with him. How atrocious he had been to her at lunch, shocked, unable to listen or respond to her news except with a viciousness that now made him shudder when he thought of it. He had used an unimaginative and poisonous conventionality as a means of revenge. Perhaps he could still reach Glone before she left.

Chapter Twenty-One

THE FOLLOWING DAY Jake went to that house he had once called home, now forbidden, in Newport. He went under cover of broad daylight. The road from Cranford was loud with messy sunshine and the pocket radio, which he had wired to the antenna of his truck, caught only snatches of the university radio station on which students talked earnestly about something he couldn't quite hear.

In the center of town, crows cackled around the top of the Viking Tower, harassing a pair of gulls back to the harbor.

The house was exactly as Jake remembered it: white clapboard, black shutters, sturdy scrollwork framing the elegant captain's lookout high above the main entrance with its black enamel door. The verandah, which wrapped around the sides of the house, still had its ceiling painted clear sky blue. Moss-covered terra-cotta pots held mauve petunias beside the front steps.

Jake didn't go in the front gate, but followed the high stone wall around to the back. He went slowly up the back driveway, hoping that his ratty brown Nissan would be mistaken for a workman's truck, and that if anyone saw him they would think he was making deliveries or doing repairs. He parked by the greenhouse with its proud weather vane, an old rooster with splayed tail feathers, blue-green with age.

Another flock of crows took off from the copper beech on the back lawn as Jake got out of the truck. The greenhouse door was ajar, letting out the sound of the overhead fans working against the heat of the sun. A cracked pane from an old soccer-ball kick of his was still not repaired. He fought back an impulse to go and inspect his mother's orchid collection, and wondered what would become of them all after she left.

Above the kitchen steps, mourning doves still roosted in the eaves, muttering and purring. As Jake stood at the back door he could hear the sound of a food processor that he hoped would cover the actual sound of his entering the house. It could still be the same cook from his childhood who was at work there, though he had no scars from youthful exploits with gods or wild beasts by which she could recognize him, and the domestic beasts—his father's beagles—had always hated him and would not distinguish him from any other housebreaker. With luck, those ugly and ridiculous dogs would be locked away in his father's study or in the fenced kennel outside by the compost enclosure.

Jake opened the kitchen door. The old cook, Theresa, stood by the sink. He couldn't resist tiptoeing up behind her. He blew on the back of her neck, whispering the old spell she had taught him when he was very young: *"Whoosh whoosh: Is it My Lover or is it just the West Wind?"*

Theresa dropped the pot she was washing into the sink, spraying soapy water over the side. "Jesus, Mary, and Jacob Ezekiel Beecher," she said. "Is it you?" She turned off the water and wiped her hands on a dish towel. "Well, there's a breath from the distant past." Then, looking him up and down she said, "Good Lord, look at you, you're an old man, now. You've gone all gray and you're still not tucked in. What are you doing here? They'll be so mad if they catch you."

"Give me a hug then, Cookie, and stop talking."

As Theresa embraced him Jake could smell the old mix of lily of the valley and tobacco and roasted meat. Those were the earliest smells he could remember.

"Is my mother home?" he asked.

"She is. She's in her bedroom."

"And nobody else?"

"The rest of the help has gone out; no one here but myself and Purley. And he's in the garden spraying the roses."

"Is she packing?"

"She's just about finished, I think. You've heard that she's going traveling?"

Jake told her that he knew about Glone's trip and wanted to talk to her before she left.

"Well, go on up quickly then so that you can be gone before . . ." Theresa didn't finish the sentence.

Jake went up the backstairs and made his way along the hallway. Here the rooms were smallest just over the kitchen and got larger nearer the front of the house until finally the suite of rooms overlooking the main garden contained the vastness of his mother's bedroom, her dressing room, his father's bedroom, and his study.

The whole upstairs was hushed. No sounds came up from the kitchen. All but one of the rooms were open. On the south side, light flooded through the windows, reflecting off the white walls and white-ruffled curtains, spilling out into the hallway. A beige and pink Persian carpet muffled his footsteps so that he couldn't hear himself walk. Jake had forgotten how light-colored the rugs were. Without thinking, he stopped and wiped the soles of his boots against his pant legs.

The rooms that had belonged to Jake's two sisters were now full of neatly arranged children's toys, for the nieces and nephews Jake had never met. Each of his brothers' rooms now had double beds, and, in one of them, an old exercise bicycle stood in a corner, seduced and discarded.

Jake opened the door to step into his old room, but stopped short on the threshold. There was no floor. The room was gone—though its window remained, now out of reach. A dark-walled stairway leading down had taken the place of his bedroom. He stepped back, closed the door and reconnoitered, counting all the rooms that had once been inhabited by his siblings. Dizzy and nauseous, he opened his door again just to make sure. How could a whole bedroom be gone? Where had they taken it to? Where had they put his bed? His insect collection? He sat down on the top step. His room had been obliterated, transformed into a flight of wooden stairs painted black with white banisters. The walls were a dark eggplant purple. This was absurd: the house didn't even need a stairway here, there were already two others, the back one for children and servants, and the front one for his parents and their guests. Still sitting, he leaned against the railing, wheezing for breath.

Somewhere, in the silence of the rest of the house, a clock struck noon. It must have been the grandfather clock in the downstairs front hall, the one that showed the moon always on the wane. This was so baffling: being annulled. When had they done it? How long had it taken them to decide? The old panic lunged into his heart, clashing about his head and ears. He sat up straight on the top step bracing his hands on his thighs to keep his chest upright as he tried to breathe.

The thing that usually kept Jake from drowning himself at noon was that he knew that within five minutes his scalp would quiet down, his irises contract, and his lungs would trust again that the air was sufficient unto the day; he would stop heaving. If he was safe at home, grooming the tomato plants and cutting the hornworms in two with his clippers, then it was just a matter of looking down at the soil and waiting for his lungs to ignore him. He would think of the names of things—Red Toch garlic from the Republic of Georgia, deer tongue lettuce, *Zucchetta rampicante*, that climbing Italian trombone squash—and the music of the names anchored him and chased away the shakes. Here on an impossible staircase in his childhood home, he was unable to ground himself in the things of the earth, and when he got up to go and find his mother he was still weak-kneed and breathy. He rubbed his hand over his head, and found that his hair was still sticking up straight. Noon was always the worst hour. He tried to massage his scalp to make it relax, but that only worked sometimes. Perhaps, he thought, if he walked slowly, his pelt would settle and not frighten the woman he was come to deliver.

⌣·

Jake's mother's door was ajar. He could see her standing beside her suitcase on the bed. She had on a hat with feathers and she was struggling with the suitcase, trying to make it stay closed. She was also weeping.

Jake rapped softly on the door. "Hello? May I come in?"

Glone stepped back in alarm, hands down beside her, as though she didn't want to be seen touching the valise, which, jostled, now looked like a live thing as it opened itself, slid off the bed, and spewed its contents on the floor.

"I'm so sorry," Jake said. "I didn't mean to frighten you." He tried to smooth his hair.

"Oh, Jake," she said. "Oh. I was so startled. I was afraid . . ." she didn't finish, but went on. "I'm so glad it's you."

"I wanted to come and apologize," Jake said. "I'm really sorry for the way I behaved at lunch. I'm here to invite you to my place, if you want. I'm here to take you."

"I'm so glad you've come," Glone said, dabbing at her eyes with a handkerchief. "I don't know. I don't know when I last used this suit-case. I can't get the damned thing to stay locked." She went over to her dressing table and took off her hat. "Have you seen my handbag, dear? It's the small white one."

Jake looked around the room. "Do you have any line?" he asked.

Glone looked over at him without really focusing on his question.

"Rope," he tried again. "Or do you have any string? Something we can use to tie up your valise, until I can fix the locks?"

"This place is really such a mess. I've left the bathroom in utter chaos. I really ought to clean up a bit . . . under the circumstances, don't you think?"

"I never clean under the circumstances."

Glone looked at him.

"Sorry. No. Don't clean up. But what about some heavy twine, do you have some?"

"Dear?"

"I'll be right back," Jake said. "Don't move."

When he returned with the rope from his truck, Glone hadn't moved. She was sitting at her dressing table, opening lipsticks and looking at the colors. "I'll only take one, that's what I'll do," she said. She pursed her lips and looked at herself in the glass. "If I come to your house, I can never come back here," she said, sweeping her hand to indicate the ruffled bed with its Indian silk bedspread, the dressing table with its three-paneled mirror, the view of the gardens out the windows.

"Is that what you want, to come back here?"

"Not at all. But . . ."

"Let's pack before anybody comes," Jake said.

Then they kneeled on the floor by the fallen suitcase and Jake folded and packed things he had never seen before, or never felt before, of lace and silk. He had always known that his parents were of another era, but it seemed more like a different century as she let him put his rough hands on those pieces of cloth. He did not know why she let him touch them, unless it was her general state of confusion. "That was my mother's shawl," she said of the last piece. "Made in Kashmir." The gossamer wool was robin's egg blue, with paisleys and fountains stitched in white silk.

Jake closed her suitcase, finally, and tied it with his own ropes until it was secure. "So, you'll come to my place, then? I have plenty of room."

Glone found her handbag in her dressing room. "Yes, take me there, dear. I can cancel the hotel from your house. You do have a telephone?"

Jake assured her that he did.

"And I'm sure they have lipstick in Alexandria," she said. "I'll buy new ones there."

Jake tied the second suitcase with more rope, although Glone said its locks were fine.

"What about your hat?" he said, gesturing to the one she had been wearing when he came in.

"Should I take it?"

"Definitely," Jake said. It was a fine mustard-colored, layered thing with pheasant feathers and a broad yellow ribbon. Someone must have felt brilliant and happy concocting it. "In that hat you ought to feel ready for anything."

"Yes," she said. "I suppose I do."

As she stood by her two valises, with her handbag over her arm, Jake asked her whether she had anything like jeans or pants to wear for the few days she would be in Cranford, as the beige linen traveling suit she had on did not look very promising for life at his house.

"Oh, yes," she said. "Don't worry. I have rough clothes packed as well as smooth ones."

Jake put his mother's bags in the back of the Nissan, covering them up with the old blue tarp. Then he helped her into the passenger side. She closed her eyes for a long moment, then opened them and looked around at the house and lawns. Theresa stood waving from the back steps. Jake blew her a kiss.

As they started to move, Glone said, "Wait, dear. Could I get out? Just for a moment."

Jake stopped the engine and went around to let her out. She ran over to Theresa and the two women embraced. Then she walked back to the truck where Jake was waiting by her door. "I said all my good-byes this morning," she explained. "But it was time to do it again."

Chapter Twenty-Two

THE PULSE OF JAKE'S UNIVERSE went wild, life began darting like a shoal of startled minnows. Driving his mother from Newport to Cranford he was curious about her. Physically she seemed in good shape, even if her eyes continued to look green instead of the blue he had always thought they were. When Jake got Glone to his house he looked for abnormally dilated pupils; he smelled her breath; he kept watching for tremor in her limbs, involuntary shudders, quivery eyelids, discolorations. He didn't know what was new for her, had no idea what was normal. He put the roped suitcases in his back room and took her out to see his gardens.

For a while they simply wandered, and she engaged in that oldest of garden pleasures: naming. In her gravely purr Glone appreciated the hummingbirds in the bee balm, the pink rose growing out of the myrtle. At the compost heap, Jake showed her how he had stenciled the names of the seven deadly sins on the boards that formed the enclosures. She approved. Jake smiled. He walked her to the snotty moon garden. Snotty not only because of its pretensions of class, but because some of the white flowers were tinged with green. Snot was a much maligned fluid, Jake thought, and probably it was underutilized. He showed her the vegetable garden, the raspberry canes, the blueberry bushes in the boggy place near the brook, the bank of poppies now gone to seed behind the late daylilies. He saved the blue garden for last; there, each plant had shriveled into angular brown awkwardness. A single late delphinium stood tall and sapphire blue. His throat closed in.

"Who did this?" Glone asked.

"What do you mean?"

"Who killed everything in this bed?"

"Why do you think it was done by someone?"

"A garden doesn't just die like that. Not all at once." She looked at Jake as though he were five years old, he thought, except that she would be nicer to a child. Glone told him that if a whole garden died because of insects or fungus or microbes, one species would die out first, then either related ones or neighboring ones, then those farther away, genetically or spatially. The blight would start somewhere, and one could usually trace the spread. Some species would survive, and occasionally one individual. "Here," she said, "everything, except that one delphinium, is racing toward death at the same damn speed. Can't you see?" She sounded angry at him, or at the garden.

"But no one would kill my garden," Jake said. "Who would do a thing like that?"

Who wouldn't? Sally had caught him making love with Gillian beside this, her blue garden. Grenville might know, by now, that it was Jake who had demolished his truck. Gillian herself could be angry that Jake had destroyed the truck of one of her many lovers. Maggie could be angry about Grenville's truck, or might have found out that Jake had almost done the slithery deed with her daughter Gillian. Hugh could have figured out by now that Jake was turmoiled over his wife. Gillian's boyfriend, Paul, could have found out about his cavorting with Gillian. Had he left anyone out? Grenville's wife, Denise? Surely she could find some reason to have murderous thoughts toward him. Nonsexual offenses must also exist, though relatively rare: what about the Leacocks—perhaps they had found out how he had bungled the baptism at the head of the river and christened one of their twins twice and the other not at all. The only real surprise was that no one had acted sooner.

Jake was struck with the vertigo of his own wrongdoing. The drooping plants in front of him feathered apart into atoms; the sky separated into particles, scintillating into a textured haze until finally the ground tugged him down.

"Dear. Are you all right?"

He opened his eyes.

"It must be such a shock."

Jake sat there on the grass feeling completely punished. Over the years, he had established a form of conversation between himself and those blue plants and now that whole language was extinct. He knew several answers to: *Why me?* He just couldn't narrow it down to any single why. He had betrayed Sally in this garden. Would she, therefore, kill it? She might. But was plant murder a proper revenge for sexual errancy? He wasn't sure. He considered, for a moment, burning down Sally's house.

Jake's gardens were all he had to show for himself. He couldn't show his misdirected love for Maggie. He couldn't show the process of gardening: the working with matter and then the witnessing of change—they cannot be exhibited. Only the product, and now all that was left of the blue garden was husks, and the outline of dark earth in the green of the grass.

Jake wondered about his other gardens: why had they been saved from this blight, this maniac? Should he sit up nights with a shotgun? If the blue garden was the only casualty, then wasn't it clearly Sally who had done it?

"What do you think about the other beds?" he asked Glone. "Will they die, too? How long does it take the poison to work?"

"Get up off the grass, why don't you; we'll go and take a more careful look."

Jake followed his mother across the lawn, docile and full of dread.

"You can kill a garden by salting it out," Glone said. "Water it with sea water or pour table salt on it, or rock salt. But your plants will probably die at different rates. Is there any residue of salt? Have you tasted your soil?"

He looked at her. How did she know all this? Was this what she had been doing in the three decades since he had been chased from home? "Taste the soil?" he said. "No, I haven't." He bent down, pinched some dirt, rubbed it between his fingers, licked them.

"A little more than that," Glone said. She scooped up a handful and nibbled at it. "Pphuh," she exclaimed. "It's hard to tell if it's salty or not." She took a blackened leaf from a dead Johnson's Blue Geranium and crumbled it. "Smell," she said. He couldn't smell anything but soil and dead leaves.

"Of course, another way to kill a garden is Agent Orange—true Vietnam-style."

Jake felt as if he were drowning. He forgot how to breathe as Glone talked about trucking out the dirt to keep dioxins from contaminating the groundwater. She explained how to get the soil tested by the county agents.

He knew all this. He didn't want to hear it. He said nothing.

Glone saw his face and smiled. "I am nattering on. But if I had wanted to get at you, I would just spray Roundup. Such a benign sort of weed killer. It kills the present—everything except pine trees, I think—but not the future. Or not much of the future; that is, you still might want to truck out the surface of your soil. Things can grow back a little crumpled if there's too much glyphosate present, no matter what the label says. It's fast, it's easy, and if you don't spray a plant's leaves, Roundup doesn't kill it. That blue delphinium in the middle—untouched—that could be the signature of your killer and his weapon."

The blue spire stood there, second growth of the season, singled-out from death, erect and green-leafed in the midst of everything brown. Jake had never thought much about the symbolic use of flowers, but this lone blue candle seemed to be declaiming a message for him. "Prick," it said. "You are such a prick."

If Roundup was the murder weapon, then all he had to do was pull out all the dead plants, get rid of the top six inches of soil, add new manure and compost, and start again. He had no cash to buy perennials, but he would beg plants from friends. He would start things from seed. He had spent most of his July disbursement from his parents on the rest of the bill for the trees for Maggie's birthday room; what was left had to last him until September. He wondered if his father would cut off his payments when he found out that Jake had been to Glone's club in Newport, or that she had stayed with him before fleeing to her Egyptian. Jake was getting on in years to still be receiving payments for staying away from his home. It was time to think of growing a cash crop. Perhaps he would row to his island in the river and plant it all over with forbidden salad.

⌣·

It was odd to live with his mother in the middle of all that was going on that summer. It would have been strange at any time, to try to catch up after a lifetime of separation, but that summer Jake was a stranger to himself as well. She was not a relaxing person, Glone—to even glimpse her in the distance made him stand differently; he would pat himself to make sure he was buttoned and wonder if his gut had an overhang.

Glone was away most of the next day conferring with her lawyer. The following day she and Jake had breakfast together. They sat at the little table on the porch and Jake fed her coffee and blueberries and yogurt. He toasted some English muffins for her and brought them out. The sun was in her eyes and she put on a straw hat. She blurted out, finally, that her Egyptian was not a circus performer, as Jake had cruelly suggested, but a poet. He was world-renowned, in certain circles, and very well-to-do. Jake sat, tongue-tied. Here she was, and she wasn't intending to stay long and it felt as though—out of limitations of time or propriety—he would only be allowed to ask her two or three questions. He didn't know what they should be. Three wishes. How do you find out what someone's whole life has been like, when you should have been there with them all along? He didn't want to ask her what triggered the change in her life, in her outlook, because triggers themselves were often completely irrelevant. The sand grain has nothing to do with the pearl. He sat there trying to think, feeling silly, fiddling with his spoon.

"Well?" she asked. She had all the secrets, or some of them, and she was about to swim through his net and escape and he would never again be able to find out anything about her. Letters would probably come, in the future, from Egypt, on crinkly blue tissue paper, but he did not know if they would answer the questions that lay coiled and hissing.

"Well," Jake said, at a loss. "What should I ask you?"

"Should?"

"What would you like me to know about you? If you go off, there, to Egypt, to your poet, I don't know when we will meet again and I don't really know you. Never mind. I'm sorry. I'm being melodramatic. Forget it." Thrust and parry. But parry what? There was no counterthrust. Jake was doing it all. They had not achieved a language to talk in.

"Do you suppose we could walk while we talk?" Glone asked.

So. She couldn't simply sit still and talk. Like him, she had to be *doing*. Jake smiled at this particle of knowledge, this hint of relationship. He was glad for her to set up any sort of conditions. He grabbed his clippers, a basket.

They strolled over the grass. "When you were nineteen," she began, "and Harvard asked you to leave and not return—on account of the business with the camel in the dean's living room—well, I thought it wasn't very nice to the camel, but oh, God, I laughed until I wept. I was alone when I got the news. Then your father came home, and he simply wept. Without laughing. As though you'd been lost at sea."

Jake had always been able to make his mother laugh. Back when she towered over him, he could crack her up even though the next words she said were always, "Oh, Jake! How could you?" Then she would tell him how serious it was, his offense, and he would be sent to his room, to boarding school, to Harvard—or away.

He had to stop this line of conversation. It would work around to his final expulsion from the family, and he didn't know how to talk about that with her. His term as a remittance man had begun on the evening of the day that should have been his brother Jeremy's wedding day. He had since taken that passage out of all the weddings he performed, that phrase that no one ever answers, that question that causes a lurch in the belly of everyone who hears it, and perhaps also a knowing snideness, but no one says anything except in the old movies, the melodramas, where the messenger on horseback arrives. Well, it was Jeremy's bride Felicia who spoke up, in that voice of hers like a clear young bell, ringing and intelligent. And, as she talked, it became clear what she had learned from Jake that she should not have, and over how long a period of clandestine time, and how it all compared with what she thought Jeremy would teach her in the future. All eyes were on Jake while Felicia was talking, and then on her as she turned from the altar and walked the length of the aisle, alone and blond and tall. If only she had sounded overexcited everyone would have put it down to nerves and discounted the implications of what she had said. But she was sober and calm and there was nothing for Jake to do but follow her out of the church. When he got outside, he walked the streets looking for her, bewildered that he had affected her so profoundly.

That was enough for the family. As far as Jake knew, they had never found out about Annabelle—the fiancée of his other brother, Morris—who had approached Jake earlier the same year. Jake didn't know why he had gotten into such complexities, except perhaps from a misguided hope that he could show those young women a different view of life than what his brothers could offer.

After a quiet, almost wordless, scene with his father in his study that night, Jake packed and left. His father had told him the lawyer's checks would follow him—as long as Jake stayed out of his parents' house and out of Newport—and his father had proved true to his word. While Jake regretted leaving the women of his family, he did not miss the menfolk, nor his parents' part of Newport, nor their friends. The structure, the life, that Jake had built over the years in Cranford had always seemed both more lovable and more solid. Until the blue garden died.

⌣·

To keep his mother now from talking about any of those harrowing times, Jake began to chatter about the dinner party he was giving the following night: he had invited Maggie and Hugh to see Glone, as she was, after all, Maggie's aunt. Now Jake took Glone's arm and they went into the vegetable garden.

"By the way, Mother," Jake asked. "Do you eat meat?"

"Glone," she said. "You are middle-aged and partially gray, dear, and it is time you called me Glone. Yes, I do eat meat, except for very small birds, with their heads still on. I don't like it when their little eyes look at me."

Chapter Twenty-Three

FOR THE DINNER PARTY IN HONOR of his mother Jake made clam cakes, ambrosial fritters the size of baseballs. Earlier in the afternoon he had taken Glone to the beach with him so he could gather quahogs. These plump purple-shelled clams, heavy as bricks, were not exactly legal—that is, you are supposed to have a license from town hall if you want to look for quahogs, and if you should happen to scoop them up by mistake—while shuffling your toes in the black silt by the harbor mouth—it's punishable. Jake didn't have a license, so he didn't use a galvanized clam basket, or one of the handy contraptions made of floating inner tubes with a net hanging beneath. Instead, he put his harvest in his mother's tote bag. Who would suspect a proper-looking skinny old lady of poaching the town clam bed?

⌣·

Glone strolled up and down the beach in her navy blue-skirted bathing suit while Jake, in cutoff dungarees, shuffled along the tide line feeling for that thick-shelled roundness, heavy and full of sea-meat. It felt strange that they were both at the beach but walking separately and not talking to each other and he wondered if they were squandering their short time together, but he wasn't sure either of them could have stood it—being together every moment now after thirty years apart.

When they got home, Jake scrubbed the quahogs and put them in a bucket of saltwater; to spiritually cleanse them he threw in a handful of cornmeal and stirred it with his fingers. Mollusks are reputed to love this grain, and as they swallow it down, they expel the mud and grit they ate for their previous meals. And who wouldn't rather eat a clam full of cornmeal than one full of motorboat fuel and river leavings? So, Jake encouraged them to eat in the bucket all afternoon. He changed the water every hour or so, to get rid of toxic remnants, and by nightfall their innards were all yellow with corn.

In the afternoon, Jake made the salad while his mother swept the kitchen and the front hall. He had never seen her sweep at home in Newport; broom in hand was not an image he had of her. He tried to ask about her Egyptian lover. But it was hard. Again he felt as though Glone were the teenager and he the aggressive parent. What did he want to know, after all? Glone said her lover was a few years younger than she, but not much, so his youth was not a factor. He was well-to-do but not absurdly, stinking rich. Some things, she predicted, would be more luxurious in Alexandria than at home in Newport; others would be more primitive. But what it really was—what made her fingertips lust for him, she admitted, what made her toes curl with delight—it was hard for Jake to hear her say this and not blush with her—was the man's voice, his talk, his curiosity. He had read everything, Glone said, and was still reading. She didn't know if their affair would last forever. She was afraid, she said, that he would tire of her, that she would not be able to keep up with him. Then why was she chancing it? Why was she leaping out like this? The abyss was wide and dark and full of ocean monsters.

"I have paid my dues," she said.

"That is a cliché," said Jake. "Which ones?" He was steaming the quahogs in a shallow pan of water, to open them.

"Sorry. I know it is. I meant the ones you refused to pay."

"There was a price," Jake said. "Even so."

"Yes," said Glone. "I know. There still is. But it is different."

"Yes," he said.

"A matter of choice, now," she said.

"Yes."

"I finally realized," Glone said. "It's all a matter of rules: once you have paid by behaving well, really paid, I mean, then you can hop right out like a rabbit and take your leave and do whatever you damn please. If you've got enough time left. If they haven't sucked the marrow out of your bones. Do you realize how boring they are, the rest of your family and mine? How small-minded and frightened? I am not a terribly smart woman, but it felt, finally, as though they were pouring cement into my brain. Through the ears."

"They?"

She watched Jake chop the clams. "Your father. Your brothers. Their low-slung automobiles that smell of ozone and leather polish. Their wives. Your sisters."

"Are my sisters as bad?"

"They depend, so, on the bigoted philanderers they married. I failed to teach them not to."

"But you got out."

"Money helps," she said. "Besides, they would have had me locked up if I had stayed."

Jake looked up from chopping.

"Oh, you know." she waved her hand, imitating them, or herself, dismissively. "A delightful place, with some bucolic-sounding name: *Windemere. Haslingfield.* Discreet, gastronomic cuisine, everyone in tweeds, dress for dinner."

Jake mixed the fritter batter and left it to rest. They set the table.

The afternoon light was shifting. Jake asked Glone to come walking with him down across the meadow. He took her arm and they went to the river.

Jake didn't tell his mother that watching the river at dawn and at dusk informed his spirit. He supposed that he was testing her, to see if she would understand without his explaining anything.

Glone did well. She remained silent and stood there beside him, watching the tide come in—tiny ripples swallowing the edge of the marsh, nothing violent, just an incremental seep of black water between the green stems of the grasses. The sun glancing off the reach had softened, ripened, to the warmth of a fruit skin—apricot, mango. It was still early for Jake to go down to the water, there was no real sunset, yet, but he knew that with dinner guests coming he wouldn't get to speak to the river until night had fallen.

Glone shuddered suddenly. Jake didn't know whether the river had finally forced itself upon her, or whether she felt a dart of fear about her plans; perhaps just a passing current of cooler air. He took her arm and led her back across the meadow. They didn't speak until they got home.

◡·

Candlelight bounced off the old wood of Jake's kitchen. Perhaps Glone had dusted the cobwebs, the corners seemed sharper to him. Maggie and Hugh were telling Glone about their river trips; they asked her if she wanted to accompany them on Sunday.

"I'd love to," Glone said. "My plans are set, finally, and I leave on Monday. I shall have to occupy myself on Sunday, otherwise I'll think about it all too much. Have you a boat for me, Jake?"

Jake asked her if she wanted a kayak or canoe. Glone said either was fine; she had kayaked as a girl, though not the modern plastic kind; she was pretty sure the muscles would remember even if the mind had forgotten.

Hugh asked Glone where she would like to go, and she said that there was one thing that had always intrigued her, though she realized it wasn't at all the sort of pastoral trip they had been describing.

"Where?" Maggie asked.

"Well," Glone began. She stopped and drank some wine. Then she reached for the pepper grinder and began to play with it. Jake realized he had never seen her fidget before. She looked girlish and intent as she asked them if it would be possible to explore the harbor in Fall River to see where the water came out from under the city, the water that flowed from the reservoirs outside of town, and that had once powered all the old textile mills. "Well, it's probably completely silly and boring," Glone said, "but do you suppose we could paddle around the harbor there, and see if we can find the outlet?"

Jake was breathing in and out. He drank his wine. He pulled apart a potato chip into as many pieces as he could. They keep such secrets, parents.

They agreed to kayak in Fall River. Hugh said they could use the public boat landing near Battleship Cove. Then he turned to Glone and her future. Hugh had been to Egypt when he was in college, an uncle of his had been an archaeologist on a dig there. He and Maggie were able to ask Glone more direct questions than Jake had managed. It turned out that Glone had never been to Egypt; she had, however, engaged a tutor and was now learning Egyptian Colloquial Arabic.

"In Newport?" Jake was stunned.

"No, dear. In Providence."

Jake did not know why all this shocked him. He kept trying to tell himself that just because someone turns seventy-five doesn't mean they have to stay put. Consider Sally's parents running away at age seventy. But a new language? All those swirls? Didn't the brain stop taking things in after a while? What about loss of memory? What about sex? When?

Hugh got excited, now. He was spouting guttural phrases and doing funny things in his throat. "Can we visit you, do you think, Maggie and I? Once you're settled in, of course. Do you think Ahmad has room for us?"

So that was his name: Ahmad. Possibly this man would become his stepfather and Jake had not been able to ask his mother what the man's name was.

"Of course you can come, I'd love it." Glone said.

Jake felt wan and displaced. Arabic goes backwards. What did Arabic have to do with coastal Massachusetts and Rhode Island? What would Maggie do there? The kitchen clock struck nine.

"What about you, Jake?" said Maggie. She grinned at him.

"The oil is ready," Jake said, pushing back from the table. "I should cook."

"Yes," Maggie persisted. "But what about coming to Egypt with us?"

It felt as though she had asked him if he wouldn't like to go jumping into volcanoes on bungee cords, or some other new sport, rich in cost and danger, poor in meaning. What did any of this have to do with him? Who were these people, anyway? His mother; his cousin—the love of his life; her husband—his friend and neighbor. Why did they want to change things?

Jake's kitchen, paneled in sweet old wood, now filled with the smell of frying ocean. That hissing burble of deep fry. He did love fry. Sally used to say—back when she was still talking to him—that Jake was the last unreconstructed cook. "Watch out," she would taunt him, "soon you'll be round enough that your palms will face backwards when you walk." Visiting Egypt would mean leaving his gardens. Perhaps in winter?

As each clam cake browned, Jake scooped it out and drained it on paper towels. He turned down the gas. "Go to Egypt?" he said. Alarm flooded through him as breath fled. He panicked with homesickness. He wondered how Maggie felt about it. He had not had a passport for twenty years. He was no longer supple or good at change. He tried not to sound petulant. "Is there a river?"

Hugh grinned. "Would the Nile do?"

Jake's heart lightened. "Oh, well," he said. "In that case." Jake had relaxed even before Hugh had spoken. He had realized that Maggie would be away from Grenville as long as she was in Egypt. Maggie's even wanting to go was a good sign. And then, too, she had invited Jake to come along. Hugh seemed to want him to come, as well. One had a duty to rivers, after all. It wouldn't be for a long time. Probably in winter when his gardens wouldn't need him. Jake's own fear at the idea of travel was now more frightening than the notion itself. How had he gotten so hidebound? How could someone as tall and bearded as he was be so brittle?

Jake served the clam cakes on his white platter in a bed of parsley, with malt vinegar and Sally's old bottle of organic catsup on the side.

～·

The next morning Jake slept late. When he got to the river the air already shimmered, dazzling with dragonflies. Water skeeters printed their circles on the calm water surface. On the way back, bees droned in the brambles and in the multiflora rose by the stone walls. But wherever he had cultivated, in all his gardens, there was unholy quiet. The same dimness had overtaken them, pointless attempts at color, the feebleness of the dying. Everywhere but the kitchen garden.

～·

Glone had made breakfast when Jake got back to the house. It still felt odd to have her in the middle of his life. Things were complicated enough, with Maggie and Grenville. Having chopped apart Grenville's truck, Jake had felt he was on a new plateau of peacefulness, that he could get on with life. But now garden grief had settled in him.

Glone had put toast and jam and butter on the kitchen table. Jake was glad she had not set the porch table because it was too awful to look out onto the browned hummingbird garden, the bee balm and the cardinal flowers lolling and flaccid. As though to make up for the heaving silence out there in the gardens, Glone chattered as she finished pouring boiling water onto the coffee grounds. Jake didn't really listen until his mother said, "How long have you been in love with Margaret?"

Jake put his coffee cup down and looked toward the sink. "In love?" he stalled. "With Maggie? Does it show?"

"I didn't say that."

"How did you know, then?"

"You listen to her, even when she's not talking. Men usually don't listen to women at all, unless they lust after them. But you have your antennae trained on her all the time, even when you're not watching her. That is more than simple attraction."

"Oh." he said. He looked around the room, careful not to look outside. "Guilty."

"How long have you felt this way?"

"A hundred years."

"Then it's kind of dull and comfortable?"

"It is as sharp as *now*." He pushed his chair back from the table. "I am breathless, flayed."

"What are you going to do about it?"

Jake got up and took his coffee cup over to the stove where he filled it. He motioned to Glone's cup but she shook her head. How could he answer this old woman who had barely talked with him for thirty years—except for those Christmas calls, fluting and shallow, with the voices of his sisters who were washing the Christmas-dinner dishes in the background—and who now wanted to know how he was going to deal with his soul's agony. And his gardens, dead. His mother was a new tornado of clutter in his already confusing existence. His absurd and vengeful father would hear that his fleeing wife had been with Jake, or that he had been to her club in Newport. Jake was going to have to earn money like a normal person. Perhaps start a cult for the rich summer people. Or take up raising chickens or exotic vegetables.

"It's pretty complex, actually," he began. How was he to respond to his mother's question? He had never talked about Maggie with anyone. The whole world, though, felt so strange, so quaggy, that he no longer saw the point of secrecy. Especially with this stranger, his mother, so soon to leave for Egypt. And so Jake recounted to Glone everything he had understood so far about this summer.

When he was finished, Glone asked him what Maggie thought. Jake told her he thought he would know if Maggie felt the same way about him, but that instead she yearned only for Grenville.

"And Hugh?"

Jake explained that Hugh didn't yearn, as far as he knew. He dabbled with young women at his boatyard, the "mermaids," Hugh called them, but as far as Jake could tell, Hugh did not ever tear himself apart over anyone.

"Do you talk about this with Maggie?"

"It would destroy the ease between us. This way, as long as it's unspoken, it can hover, coloring the air, an optical illusion—there and not there. Speaking would shatter the possible."

Chapter Twenty-Four

HUGH AND TONY RIPPED UP Jake's gardens with him. They loaded the blackened, wilted stalks into Tony's truck and into Jake's, and then they drove both trucks into the woods, where, in a clearing, they burnt their dead. They sat on fallen logs drinking beer that Hugh had brought as they watched the plant carcasses smolder and give off an oily smoke.

"Well," said Hugh, taking off his hat and scratching his head. "Who do you suppose did it, after all?"

Jake stood up to rake outlying branches into the smoking pile. "My friend Sally," he said, looking at Tony and hoping he would not disagree. "She seems to have gotten jealous. She thought I was seeing someone else."

Tony smiled, and Jake was sure that he knew about Sally catching him with Gillian beside the Russian Blue sage, though he did not know who could have told him.

"What a shame," Hugh said. "I've always liked Sally." He paused, examined his can of beer. "How are you going to get her back?"

⌣·

The gardens looked like claw marks left by a giant bird. Tony borrowed a dwarf tractor from the vineyard where he worked, and they used it to dig out the top few inches of soil, which they dumped in the woods on top of the charred remains of their fire. Then they tractored some fine old cow manure into the dirt and followed that with dried seaweed that Jake had collected from the beach, and dug that in as well, finally covering each of the beds with hay to keep the weeds down. The sudden ripping away of color made the grounds seem as though the ache of winter had been grafted onto summer, spinning the seasons and skewing time.

Jake's mother offered to pay for replanting one of the beds. Jake told her he was grateful, but somehow he couldn't bear to start growing things just yet. Later he would start almost everything from seed; the perennials would take, most of them, two years to flower. He would seed annuals among them, and Maggie would give him cuttings and he would beg from friends.

Jake had found the few old photographs he had of the whole place and tacked them up in the kitchen so he could think more clearly of the way the grounds had looked. He had constructed the gardens over thirty years, but now he was thinking of replanting all at once, and was suddenly unsure of what he wanted. Or if he wanted to do any of it. He thought of moving to Providence, and looking for a job—to revenge himself, as though blaming the plants for getting themselves killed, or for his own love for them. These thoughts didn't last long; even he could see through them.

Jake went over to Maggie's. He just wanted to sit with her in her kitchen, or, if he could bear it, in her geometric herb garden. He found her alone, working on her mermaid, which lay across the kitchen table with its head in her lap. The tail was completed now, scales embroidered onto the green velvet. The breasts running up the chest were all in place, and the long graceful arms ended in lifelike hands, slightly cupped as though offering food or solace. Maggie was embroidering the ears, stitching a heavy wheat-colored thread over question marks of twine she had glued in place.

"Well," she said. "What have you got to say for yourself?" She was harsh and Jake's innards crumpled.

"Can I have some of what you're drinking?"

"It's iced coffee. There's more in the pitcher. You'll find milk in the fridge." She made no move to help him.

"Mags, you're not angry, are you? Don't be; I couldn't take it right now."

She was. She looked up and didn't say anything.

"We just burned all the dead plants," Jake said.

"Damn fool."

"I had to."

"I mean, to let them get killed in the first place."

Jake said nothing.

Her voice was too quiet, too still and flat. Jake waited for her to jab her needle into the cloth, but she sewed calmly. He expected her mermaid to jump each time she pierced the skin around the earlobe. "I loved those gardens," she said, dropping her voice. "They were my favorite place to be."

"I'll grow them again."

"So that one of your lovers can poison them again?" There was such bitterness in her voice that Jake's heart leapt. Of course, there are many reasons for bitterness and in her case sexual jealousy about him was not the most likely one. Still he hung onto the possibility that she might be jealous.

"One of *my* lovers? Or one of yours?" Jake got up from the table and stood at the open kitchen door, looking out at the lawn. Maggie's own gardens were sun struck, lilting with bees. The wind, now no more than an air, gentled out of the southwest. "Maggie," he said, leaning his forehead against the screen. "Oh, Maggie."

Jake hated how deeply the stranger had entwined himself in their lives. He wanted to say something cutting and bitter. "Oh, Maggie," he said. "Oh, God."

She finished one ear of her mermaid, and turned the whole figure over so she could work on the other side, pulling the head back down to her lap.

Jake sat there with her, wondering how to speak.

⌣·

The next day was Sunday. They went by caravan to Fall River: Jake's chocolate Nissan, Hugh's blue Ford, Tony's old Dodge. Gillian drove the older children in the red Volvo; the younger ones stayed home with Connie, David, and Gillian's boyfriend, Paul.

At the boat landing on North Davol, Jake helped Maggie unload her kayak, looking forward to being beside her on the water all day. How could he gaze with longing at so many women? He could see

Gillian bending over to stow her steel coffee thermos and her sandwich in the bow of the yellow canoe. She was going to ride with Hugh. Jake didn't love Gillian. Or even her bare legs, which deserved constant watching. The fact that Gillian could vortex him with her eyes, the fact that he got hard whenever he saw her, no matter what the situation, the fact that he would gladly have led her into any closet or out to any shed was simply the beast in him answering the animal in her. They called directly to each other in some unmindful language that bypassed reason. This was not love. Gillian was much too bookish, coiling into poems and avoiding the outside world. But yes, she was one of the women Jake yearned for. To hear her name mentioned, to see her in her boat up ahead on the river, was to feel a current of desire sparking through him, short-circuiting thought.

Maggie was different. Jake's desire for her was a slow ache that was always with him, full of love and of thought. That ache had come to define who he was. The way he did the things in his life, the way he executed them, was in order to please some ideal form of Maggie, whether or not she ever learned of them. Even when he was completely alone, when he cooked for himself at night, he would set the table for one, with a place mat and a flower in a bowl of water, as though some shadow self of Maggie's were watching, or as though she might enter his kitchen at any moment and look upon what he had done. Perhaps it was partly in hopes of making her love him when she saw how well he performed the dailiness of life. The state of Jake's love for Maggie gave to all those small acts a grandeur—the euphoria of little events.

Then there was Sally. Hugh had said, "How are you going to get her back?" He was right, Jake would try. It had been more than two weeks since she had thrown the sugar bowl in his face.

᠆·

Over the Taunton River the sky hung textured and beige. The water slopped and bent like metal, tarnished and unprecious. Gillian had folded herself into the yellow canoe while Hugh held its stern, then he got in with her and pushed off. Maggie carried her own green boat down the cement incline, but waited while Turko and Storm loaded themselves into the green canoe. Tony took off in his fiberglass kayak of his own design. Jake helped his mother into the wooden kayak, the mandolin.

Just as Jake was carrying his own boat to the water, a Dodge Ram Magnum drove onto the landing, throbbingly new, black and chrome. Sally jumped out of the passenger side and ran down to where Jake stood. The driver was a man he had never seen before.

"Hugh called me," she said, breathless. "He invited me to come with you all. He said I shouldn't miss this expedition—that it would be worth a truce."

Jake knew he didn't deserve her company. He was glad to see her, though he did not want to tell her that. His arms wanted to hug her, but he still linked her with poisoning his gardens, so he kept still. The other reason he didn't hug her was that the man Sally had come with had gotten out of his shining vehicle. He had his ears back, and was watching Sally closely, so Jake didn't tell her he was happy that she came, but he did grin a bit. He kept his hands in his pockets to keep them from touching her arms or lunging to hug her.

"Who's your friend?" Jake said.

"Oh," she said. "That's Randy. Hugh said it would be OK to bring somebody. It is, isn't it?"

"What?"

"OK that I brought him? He borrowed a boat." She gave a fetching smile and Jake wanted to hold her and lift her and carry her to his truck and drive off with her. He wanted to take her to a Portuguese dive to eat oily crab and get their faces messed with red oil and hot peppers. He also wanted to burn her house down in exchange for killing his gardens.

"Hell, yes. It's a free river. You can bring hundreds of Randies if you like."

"Jake?"

"Sorry. Listen, when we get out onto the water I'd like to introduce you to my mother." Jake could see from Sally's expression that she thought he meant he intended to capsize her, so he pointed to the multicolored boats bobbing and backing near the landing. "In the mandolin, there: Glone Beecher, lately of Newport, Rhode Island;

soon to be of Alexandria, Egypt. I'll explain later." If Sally would let him. If she would give him time. She was probably about to run off and marry this Randy fellow and produce little Dodge Ram lambkins for him, and tend his hearth fires. Jake wanted to go off with her and talk somewhere, or jump on her and lick her face, but so much had been going on that he felt shy and hobble-tongued. "Introduce me to your friend," he said. "I'll behave. I promise."

Sally led Jake over to Randy, who was locking up his very broad truck. Jake remembered how annoyed he had been with Donahue Pereira for assuming that Jake would make a habit of torching trucks. Randy was very clean. All his clothes were new, straight from some white-water catalogue with leaping salmon on the cover. No white water here, bud. We're after something else. No mountain high. No pristine streams. Look yonder: we're into soup-colored water here and our sky is the shade of old tea with milk.

Jake made a sheepish gesture when Sally spoke their names so that Randy wouldn't assume that he was going to shake hands. Randy. Couldn't she have a friend named Ernest or Rich? At least they each had separate kayaks. Jake helped them launch, and explained where they were all heading.

Maggie had been waiting all this time, paddling in circles around the landing until Jake put in. They set out downstream with the wind snuffling against them. The hills of the opposite shore, rounded and green, bounded their gray water. They did not usually explore big city rivers—instead their haunts tended to be hidden and bucolic. Here everything seemed spread out and visible, with half-submerged wrecks along the jetties, then coves of fishing boats and pleasure craft, and finally a full-rigged sailing ship painted in bright primary colors; in the distance, toward the Bragga Bridge, ghostly hulks of warships and naval vessels. But near the landing, just starting out, they found themselves skirting chunky bulwarks of masonry as fiberglass speedboats whined past, engulfing them with huge choppy wakes.

Jake liked to watch the shifting groups of their little boats on a river: two come together, then three, then someone splits off, or stays behind to smoke a cigarette, then another group forms, until a channel is found that only one boatsman finds it necessary to explore. Up ahead, Gillian and Hugh had turned into a cove formed by two jetties. Tony went after them, followed by the children. When Maggie and Jake caught up to the others, they were circling a sunken boat. It was a tug, made of steel. Only the pilot house was above water, the glass broken, the metal plates rusted. They edged it like sharks, so close to the pilot house that the sunken hull lay beneath them.

"Bet we could buy it for almost nothing," Hugh said.

"Ours for the raising," said Tony. "I've talked to the harbormaster. I've asked around."

Eyes glinted. Hugh angled the yellow canoe over to Tony. Dreams of polishing engines. Draining and scouring. Steel wool and oil. Visions of the exploring the Mississippi by tugboat. Maggie, near Jake, caught Hugh's eye and shook her head.

Seaweed waved from the tug's port gunwale, which just broke the water's surface. Barnacles and oysters gripped the flowing weeds. Randy idled over to Jake. "Seventy feet of rusted hull, held together by holes," he said.

Who invited him? He was right, of course: the "Baltic Herring" was steel Swiss cheese, but his saying so made Jake want to raise it for himself. He left their floating huddle and set out looking for Sally.

As Jake continued downstream, toward Narragansett Bay and toward the wind, he came upon Sally and Glone looking up at the sailing ship, with its gaudy paint job, blue and yellow, and a fierce-faced wooden damsel for the figurehead. Glone told them that it was a facsimile of the HMS *Bounty*, which had been given to the city of Fall River after having been built for a film. The ship towered above them, grotesquely tall, thick with pigment. They waved to the tourists wandering around the decks, and Jake was sure that if they had thrown him a coin or a bauble he would have torqued overboard to dive for it; the disparity of size had turned them into small naked natives paddling up to white man's seagoing glory.

Sally came toward Jake. "Well," she said, "it's perfectly clear."

"What is?"

"I would have mutinied, too: there are no portholes at all except in the captain's quarters in the stern, and he has real windows. I'd go berserk if you kept me in a hold without air or light."

Glone stroked over in the mandolin, "Exactly what I was thinking," she said.

Since the two women were in agreement, it seemed safe to introduce them. Sally looked stunned by the sudden incarnation of Jake's mother.

"Ah, Sally," Glone said. "Aren't you two. . . ?"

"Not really," Sally said.

"It's not clear," Jake said at the same time.

⌣·

Glone still wanted to see where the waters actually fell into the river, the waters that used to drive the textile machinery in the mills of the city. Sally and Maggie and Jake followed her away from the HMS *Bounty* just as all the others were paddling up to it. In the next cove floated immense hulks rising out of the water like gray cities of war—the gigantic battleship, the SS *Massachusetts*, and moored at an angle to it a submarine, the SS *Lionfish*. The triangular space between these ships formed a quiet pond, sheltered from the wind and the choppy waves, but to paddle there felt daunting and out of scale.

Hovering on the embankment above them a round carousel sparkled with lights and glass. From their boats they could see the wooden horses inside it turning to a dim breathy music. Glone called to them and they followed her to where two soot-colored swans floated along a small canal.

"Well," she said, "this is obviously it." She pointed to the circular tunnel opening at the end of the canal. A dark entrance over a stony bed, the water too low there for them to enter.

Glone exulted. "I can't tell you how glad I am to have seen this," she said. It seemed as though she felt that by finding this municipal culvert, something had been explained to her, something about history or the workings of the city. But for Jake it was just pointing out the locus of yet another mystery, and the idea of that watery tunnel under the city left him feeling somehow puzzled and burdened and immensely lonely.

Jake let the others go on without him; his mother wanted to go ashore and see the carousel from inside. He nudged his kayak against the shore of the canal and sat there drinking coffee from his metal thermos. The pair of brown swans sidled over for a handout, but he told them it was only coffee and they wouldn't like it. It is useless to talk to swans, they are mean creatures wrapped up in their own lives and thoughts, stopping only to dive-bomb you if you get too close to their nest.

What wreckage love causes. Grenville's truck and all Jake's gardens gone up in smoke because of love or wanting or claims to entitlement. Jake thought he was more deserving—by reason of closeness and seniority and sheer vast desire—of Maggie's physical affections than was Grenville, the interloper. And Sally had felt even more betrayed when she found Gillian rolling around in Jake's arms in the garden. But this was trying to put a set of almost rational thoughts into that wordless muscle, the heart. That animal engine. Jake marveled that Maggie had stopped herself from ruining anything the way Sally and he had; Maggie, who had a life so full of things she could destroy. He knew it was presumptuous, but if he could get out of this black and dripping mood, he wanted to warn her to do nothing unforgivable. He wanted to protect her from the harm of her desire, keep her from the carnage of her own longing. He knew she wouldn't listen. People never listened. He would just have to watch out for her and make sure she didn't pull harm down on herself the way he had.

Jake wondered if Sally had killed his perennial beds. If she had done it, then he could take that as a sign of love, or a sign of love twisted into jealousy—he knew all about that cold fever. Would he have to hate her for it? Not if she hadn't ruined the earth beneath. Not if he could grow things again. Jake still felt that somehow Grenville had been involved in it also, but in his present upheaval, he couldn't figure out the connection between them.

The dun swans were bumping against Jake's boat, stabbing at his elbows with their beaks. He could smell their swamp breath. He paddled in choppy strokes trying to swat them away as he made his way to shore. He pulled his boat out and overturned it beside the brightly colored craft of his tribe.

⌣·

Upstairs in the carousel building the merry-go-round was turning, full of kids and grown-ups, all looking off into that private near-distance of motion-induced dreams. Lightbulbs outlining the edges of the carousel's frame heated the large room and seemed to be in some way responsible for the loudness of the steam calliope music, breathy and piercing. It was an Old World polka, leaden and jumpy from a tradition of too many plum dumplings beside the ham hocks and cabbage.

Jake, too, must have been dreaming, watching the thickly enameled flanks of horses rising and falling and turning out of his path, for he didn't notice that several of the riders were waving at him, until Maggie laughed at him, "Jake, Jake, why don't you ride with us?"

The music wheezed and slowed; the horses rose and fell; the platform rotated and slowed and stopped. Jake went over to Maggie's horse, a palomino with flaring nostrils and banded legs. Glone was astride a black charger just beside Maggie. Sally, who was riding a camel beside Randy on the other side of the platform, had dismounted and was walking over to Jake through the forest of brass poles and painted animals.

The music took up again; Jake hadn't bought a ticket, so he started to leave the platform. Then he turned back to talk to Sally before it was too late. He put a hand on her arm and bent over to say into her ear, "Listen, I'm desperate to see you. Do you think you could come over tomorrow? I have to take my mother up to Boston, to the airport, but I'll be back home by five at the latest. Please come."

Then he stepped off, and leaned against the outside wall feeling lighter. He watched as they all went on their curvy periodic path. Above the horses, on the rim of the canopy, between gaily painted scenes of Old World life, mirrors reflected the cove outside, the battleship, the submarine, the gray-green river and arching above it all, the herringbone sky.

Chapter Twenty-Five

THE DAY AFTER THEIR EXCURSION to Fall River, Jake drove his mother to Boston to put her on the plane. His Nissan did not appreciate long drives, so he had borrowed Maggie's Volvo, and had given her his sweet ugly truck in exchange, in case she wanted to go anywhere. During the summer visit of her family there were always more desires than vehicles.

In the car, Glone was excited and talkative. She wanted to know whether Jake would really visit Alexandria. She kept looking behind them, as though she thought someone would try to stop her from reaching the airport. Jake helped her check in, and then they went to the bar for a quick drink.

"Are you frightened?" He raised his Sam Adams to her as he spoke; he was shocked that he had dared ask her.

"There are two things that really frighten me," she said. "The thought of finding your father here in the airport. And the thought of staying with him for the rest of my life and rotting back there in Newport."

"And Egypt doesn't frighten you?"

"Good Lord, no. It might not work out; it might turn out to be intolerable, living there, for me. We might lose interest in each other, Ahmad and I. Grow to hate each other. But we will not bore each other to death."

Then it was time to walk her to the gate.

"There is one thing," she said.

"Tell."

"I would like to write you letters, if it wouldn't be an imposition."

"Not at all."

"There's not really anyone else I feel like writing to," she said. "Your siblings think I'm demented; my friends are aghast."

"I never get letters," Jake said. "I don't know if I'll write back."

"Doesn't matter. You'll write me when you have something to say."

Jake put her bag and purse on the conveyor belt of the X ray. Then he took her in his arms and hugged her tall thin bones. He let her go through the metal detector without him, and stood watching as she walked down the corridor.

Jake was back in Cranford by six in the evening. He showered after his drive home and was just pulling on his jeans when he heard the horn of his own truck, several loud bleats, then a slur of gravel in the drive-way. By the time he got outside, Grenville was running around to the passenger side of the Nissan. Maggie lay slumped along the seat.

"Hugh's away for the day," Grenville blurted. "Maggie said you would know what to do. She said you knew about this kind of thing." He stopped to catch his breath. "We were swimming. Oh, Christ. Stung."

Jake didn't understand what Grenville was saying. He felt stupid and out of it as though Grenville and Maggie were in cahoots, acting out a charade that he was supposed to guess. "Stung," he repeated dumbly.

"Portuguese man-of-war."

"Oh, Christ."

They supported Maggie between them and walked her up the front steps and into the house. She was wrapped in two towels. Her face still had color and she didn't seem feverish or shivering. Jake didn't tell them that man-of-war venom can paralyze you, stop you from breathing, throw you into shock. Maggie had once known this, too; she and Jake had studied the subject together as children. Fright-ened and attracted by the iridescence of the bluish sails they had learned that a single man-of-war is not one animal but many—a hive containing reproductive-beings; sail-beings in charge of the inflated colored bladder with its transparent sail; and finally tentacle-beings that feed beneath the float. It is these feeding polyps whose fifty-foot-long tentacles are armed with poison cells, triggered to shoot their toxin on contact.

⌣•

Grenville and Maggie had gone for an afternoon swim, first dozing on the beach and then going into the water. Floating in the jade-colored waves Maggie had turned to him and said, "Is it seaweed?" And then, before Grenville could ask her what she meant, "Shit. Fire. I'm on fire. Oh, God." Grenville saw, beside her, the glistening sail-bladder of the man-of-war. She flailed as he scrambled over to her, and half swimming, half running, pulled her through the breakers until they stumbled up the beach. Maggie threw herself onto her towel, rolling herself in it to try to damp the pain. She said she felt smothered. Her lungs were pumping.

Grenville wrapped his towel over hers, then lifted her onto his shoulders and carried her to the parking lot and put her into the truck. Maggie told him to take her to Jake's house. "Jake will know," she said.

⌣•

"Hold her up," Jake said. "I have to get something." He ran to the kitchen to get rubber gloves, putting them on as he returned, explaining that stingers could stay alive, even when the rest was dead or missing.

Jake unwrapped the two damp towels from Maggie, rolled them up and threw them into the corner where no one would step on them. Maggie's naked back was laced with clear threadlike tentacles. The skin under them had turned red.

"We've got to get your suit off, Mags, OK?" Jake didn't wait for her to reply. It would be a clumsy business, taking a damp nylon bathing suit off the woman you love, using rubber gloves, in front of another man, whom she loves. Jake had just gotten his yellow rubber fingers under the thin blue straps and was sliding them down her shoulders when Grenville put a hand on his arm.

"I'm not sure that's necessary," Grenville said.

"What's not necessary?"

Jake wanted to hiss at him, Who the hell do you think you are? Look what you've done to her. But he needed Grenville's help.

"If the stingers are still alive, why aren't they going to be triggered when you pull the suit from her skin?"

Jake looked at Grenville. There he was, tall and lean and sweating and scared to hell. His beard was still matted with sand and salt from his afternoon lolling about the beach with Maggie. His faded red T-shirt showed a dark heart of sweat forming in the middle of it. Grenville was a sly troublesome old satyr, but he was still thinking, and he was also correct. It hurt to have to agree with him.

"Right," Jake said. "There's something to be said for that."

"Shouldn't we call a doctor?" Grenville said.

"It's Apthorp. He's on vacation."

"We could try my wife."

Jake had forgotten that Denise Grenville was a doctor.

"Keep her upright," Jake said, handing Maggie to Grenville. "She may get wobbly." He had to leave her there, in Grenville's arms, while he got a load of towels from the closet. He laid them out on the wooden bathroom floor, until they formed a mat that they could lay Maggie down on. Her breathing was noisy. She heaved her whole chest each time she inhaled. They helped her stretch out.

"Oh, no," Jake said. "I just remembered." He wasn't very good at all this. He had read about it, but never done it before. "We'll have to get her up again." Jake turned to her. "Maggie, do you think you can swallow some pills? It's important."

Maggie nodded. Jake found a bottle of antihistamines in the medicine cabinet, and gave her two of them and a glass of water. She grimaced and took them, still wheezing. As she was still awake, he decided to give her some aspirin as well.

"Look, do you know what you're doing?" Grenville said.

"OK. Give your wife a call if you like," Jake said to him. "It's probably about time," he added quietly.

"You know, it's awkward, if I call," Grenville said. "I think it would be quicker if you called her and got her to come here—then I can do all the explaining afterwards." He paused and added, "Or I can try." He told Jake his wife's phone number. "Her name is Denise."

"Right," Jake said. "I'll be right back. Watch her and if she stops breathing, give me a yell and start mouth-to-mouth." Jake hated to leave him with Maggie, and to give him that excuse to put his mouth to hers. He knew he shouldn't be thinking that. They were in a serious business now, not the usual lechery, and whose mouth was where was not the question.

Jake called Denise Grenville and told her; she asked him what he had done for Maggie and then said he was on the right track. "Watch her breathing," she said. "Watch for shock."

"How will I know?"

She told him. "Keep it up," she said. "You're doing fine. I'll be there in half an hour."

Then Jake went to the kitchen and found the new bottle of Glenlivet that his mother had given him.

"Are you sure it's the moment for a drink?" Grenville was pale now. His shirt was damp all down the back as well. He was kneeling beside Maggie. "Shouldn't we get these tentacles off of her?" He started to pluck at one of them.

Jake knocked Grenville's arm away from her. "Jesus. Don't touch."

Jake opened the bottle and poured the Scotch whisky all over Maggie's back to neutralize the poison that had already been discharged.

"Keep breathing, Maggie, OK?" Jake said.

Maggie shuddered from the chill of alcohol on her skin. "Christ," she slurred. "You know, I don't really feel so great."

Jake kept dousing her. "The doctor's coming, Mags. Just hang in there." He bent down and touched her cheek with his fingers. Then he kissed her. On the cheek. Her color was still OK. She wasn't cold or hot.

Denise had said that aside from shock, bronchial spasm and paralysis were the dangers, that the venom worked like curare, that it was almost as strong as cobra venom, but that luckily tentacles were not as efficient as fangs. Jake wanted to stay with Maggie, kissing her, holding her, watching her breathe. Instead he told Grenville to stay with her and ran to the kitchen again.

When Jake came back, Grenville said, "I didn't think they came this far north."

"Who?"

"The jellyfish. Men-of-war."

"They're not jellyfish. They're siphonophores."

"Right. Whatever. I still didn't think they lived around here."

"They don't; storms blow them here." The previous November Jake had found seven dead ones on the beach, like slightly deflated purplish party balloons, like lures. They are just as dangerous when they're dead.

Maggie raised her head like a turtle and was looking at the bathtub spigots. "It's so bright," she said. "All that silver shimmering. It's pulsing at me, you know?"

"Hang on," Jake said. "I know."

"Too much glinting," she said. Then she laid her head down, and slept.

"Watch her breathing," Jake said, "I have to mix this." He emptied half a bag of sea salt into a bowl in the sink.

"I hate to ask this, old man," Grenville said. "But what the hell are you doing?"

Jake opened a box of baking soda and shook it out until he had a handful, which he put in the bowl, then ran a dribble of water to mix the salt and soda into a paste. He didn't know if what he was doing was right. He no longer remembered whether he had dreamt it or read about it, or whether their grandfather, Ezekiel Beecher, had told him about it. But when he had asked Denise, she had told him to go ahead. "I'll get there before it dries," she had said. What if Denise didn't know about these things either? Jake wasn't sure what kind of doctor she was. He couldn't remember if she was a general practitioner or a shrink.

Jake had to straddle Maggie to get the paste on properly, so he kneeled there, with his blue bowl in his arms, flinging globs of white paste onto her back. She moaned a bit each time the salt and soda hit her. He was no longer sure he could save her, and he must have been moaning, too, as he didn't hear the front door open.

"Jesus, Jake. Is that Maggie?"

Jake had been expecting Denise, and didn't recognize Sally's voice at first. He had forgotten that he had begged her, on yesterday's carousel, to come and see him today. She looked as though she had come straight from the car salesroom: she was all groomed, summer frock.

"Hey, guys, why are you doing that? Is this a game? Stuart? Somebody tell me what's happening."

"Hello, Sal," said Grenville. He explained the situation to her while Jake dropped the remaining blobs of salt-and-soda paste onto Maggie's back, and while he slowly realized that Grenville's tone to Sally was not only friendly but familiar. Cranford was a small town, but he didn't think that accounted for it. Jake would get Sally and Grenville to tell him how they knew each other, later. For now, he just wanted to keep Maggie from harm until Denise got here.

Maggie's back was covered with white paste. Jake lingered there, straddling her, feeling possessive and protective until his thighs ached. Maggie was asleep, now, and her breathing sounded normal.

Jake told Sally that Denise Grenville, Grenville's wife, was coming in a few minutes. Sally looked at Grenville, then at Jake, then at Maggie. Her face had silenced. She tried to keep from showing surprise, but her pupils went all dark. So Grenville had slept with her. The bastard. He apparently hadn't told her he was married.

"She's a doctor, Denise Grenville," Jake said. "Apthorp is off on his fishing trip and I don't know who's covering for him."

Sally picked up her bag from the floor and walked out of the room. Jake caught up with her outside the front door and grabbed her wrist, smearing it with white paste. "Sal," he said. "Don't go."

Sally looked at him. At first he couldn't make out her expression, but then it seemed as though she was daring him to say something.

Jake gave her an awkward hug, trying to keep his hands from her dress so as not to mess it. "Please stay," he said.

"I didn't know he was married," Sally said.

"Yes, I could see you didn't. He's a strange fellow," Jake said.

"Yes," she said. She didn't try to move away, so Jake held her wrist.

"Perhaps he's a bit of a bastard," he said. "But I guess I'm not one to talk."

"Well," she said, as though she was considering the ranking of bastards.

"Sal," Jake said. "Would you stay and have supper with me? He'll be gone by then." It was impossible to keep a sense of urgency out of his voice. His need for her croaked out at her, like a crow, harsh and black with flapping wings.

"What?" she said. "What is it?" She looked at him as though frightened of what he would say.

"I have so much I want to tell you. And ask you."

"Here's the thing," she said, looking down at the gravel where she was tracing a design with her foot. She had on blond sandals, but her skin was dark with summer. Jake watched her foot, she watched the gravel. "The thing is," she said, "I'd rather not be here when his wife comes. There's no real need for me to meet her. I can tell you about it all, later. I'll go pick up something to cook for dinner; I'll change my clothes; and by the time I come back—they'll be gone, won't they?"

"Sal?" Jake still held her.

"What is it?"

"I have a long story for you."

"We'll have time," she said, giving him such a luminous smile that he wanted to touch her arms, her hair; he wanted to kneel on the gravel and hug her legs, but his hands were all caked with white soda paste, and he had already braceleted her wrist with salt.

"Oh, Sal," he said. "Drive slowly."

~.

Grenville said he would go out to Jake's vegetable garden when he heard his wife's car in the driveway. "I'll let her deal with Maggie first," he said.

Jake wasn't sure whether that was wise or cowardly. He knew he would have done the same thing.

Denise was gaminlike, deft in her movements. Her black hair was cut very short, and she tilted her head to one side as she listened to Jake. Then she crouched down beside Maggie, who was still stretched out on the towels on the bathroom floor. While Denise touched, listened, prodded—and then as she injected Maggie with Demerol and more antihistamines—Jake was so relieved that it felt as though his shoulders were unlocking themselves from his back. He felt a sudden stark fury at Grenville. At himself.

"This is Margaret Gifford," Denise said, turning to Jake. "We know each other."

Jake had forgotten that they had met. "Yes," he said. "She's my cousin."

Denise took a tongue depressor from her bag and started to scrape the white paste from Maggie's back. "We're going to need some towels, and a sink full of hot water," she said.

Jake brought her what was left of his towel supply: three small white swimming-pool towels from a Newport country club, dating from some old childish escapade. Oh, God, if he could scrape away his own stupidities, all of them, would there be anything left but the chalky scaffold of bones?

Jake ran the hot water until the sink steamed, then plunged a towel in, wrung it out, folded it once to keep the heat in. "Shall I do it, or do you want to?" Jake asked.

"Why don't you go ahead. Give her warning, though. Even though she looks asleep, it's quite a shock to be hit with a hundred and twenty degrees."

"Maggie. I'm going to put a hot towel on you. It's to kill any remaining poison. Really hot, OK?"

Maggie grunted. Jake slapped the towel on her back.

"Hey!" Maggie lifted her head. "Don't do that."

"I have to, love." He took off the old towel and slapped on the new one that he had waiting in the steaming sink. Then he rinsed the first one, ran more water to heat it up, flopped it down on her.

Maggie yelled again. "Why?" she cried. "Why are you doing this?" Tears ran down her cheeks.

"Just a couple more," said Denise. "Can you take it," she asked Maggie, "if it's just a few more?"

Maggie groaned.

Then it was all done.

Denise asked Jake if Maggie could sleep there at his house. "Of course," Jake said. "I'll let her family know."

She said they should take Maggie's bathing suit off, and asked Jake if he had some clean pajama bottoms.

"Actually," he began. He shrugged.

"Oh," she said. "Sorry. Shorts then?"

Jake went to the bedroom and got a clean pair of boxers. Together he and Denise rolled down Maggie's dark blue suit, now encrusted with salt, soda, and the denatured tentacles clinging like transparent spaghetti. Jake blotted her with the one remaining dry towel. Her back was streaked with reddish welts. The rest of her was tanned except for her pale buttocks. Putting his undershorts onto his cousin Maggie's nude sleeping body was one of the most puzzling things he had ever done—until he carried her into his bedroom and laid her, facedown, on his own bed. Emergency and absurdity had banished, for the moment, desire. Here was Maggie, in his bed. Oh, Maggie. Why is life so strange?

Jake pulled the sheet up over Maggie's shoulders. He knelt beside her and said, "Call me if you need anything, OK?" He kissed her.

Denise was waiting at the doorway. She touched Jake's arm. "It's all right, you know. She'll be fine. She'll be sore in the morning, but fine."

Jake told Denise how grateful he was to her as they went into the kitchen. "I would offer you a beer," he said. Then he paused, and added, "But there's something much more crucial."

"Oh?"

He could have sworn Denise already knew what he was about to say. She pulled her striped jersey down at the front and tucked it into her black jeans. She ran her hand over her jet hair. It was so short-cropped that Jake briefly wondered what it would feel like to ruffle it. He put his hand in his pocket.

"Your husband," Jake began, wondering how to announce it.

She looked startled.

"Stuart. He's waiting for you in the garden."

⌣·

Denise went out the kitchen door slowly, as though she didn't quite believe what Jake had told her. As she left she grabbed a dish towel and took it with her, whether for offense or security, Jake wasn't sure. The act was lovable in itself, that grabbing of the blue-striped linen, without asking him. A sudden need, taken care of. The empty whisky bottle was there on the counter, but she took a piece of cloth.

Jake had been planning to call the farm and let Maggie's family know where she was and what had happened. Hugh was off sailing and wouldn't be back until the evening, but Jake did want to tell the others. He put off the call, though, to wait until Denise and Grenville had spoken in the garden.

Grenville stood with his back to Jake's house, watching an osprey tracing an invisible current of warm air over the river.

"Stu," Denise said. "Is that you?"

Grenville turned around. His face and beard were wet. He covered them with his hands for a moment, hiding himself from her gaze, wiping his tears.

"Is that you?" he echoed her question.

Denise answered with a nod.

Grenville held out his arms to her, but she didn't move, unsure.

"I was waiting for you out here," he said. "And it all began to hit me. As though I'd fallen to earth. And it was too much for me. Sorry. This is so dumb." He blotted his face and beard with his shirtsleeve.

"I know Magaret Gifford," she said.

He looked up at her, startled. Denise paced back and forth. She ran her hand over the tomato plants, brushing them like a breeze. She touched the beans and the peppers, and finally back to the tomatoes.

"What are you looking for?"

"I don't know. Sorry. It's hard to know what to say or what to ask." She told him of Maggie's visit to her.

"Why ever did she do that?" he asked.

Denise shook her head. "You know, when you left, I wondered if I'd done something to make you unable to stand me. But I couldn't think what."

"I know," Grenville said. "I know. As soon as I realized I had no explanations, I couldn't come back. Leaving you was too grave. And too senseless. I don't know if I'm fit to be with you anymore. Or with anybody. I know what I'm capable of and it's too hideous."

"It's as though you'd gone missing in action," she gestured. "Without any war. There wasn't any war, was there?" she looked up. "Between us, I mean?"

Grenville shook his head. "Not between us." He lowered his head.

Denise raised both hands. "Are you," she moved her hands as though to elicit from herself the words. "Are you back now?"

"Back to you?" Grenville pointed. "Back to my senses?"

She meant both.

"I think I'm back to my senses."

Then, it was as if she didn't dare ask him to come back to her.

Grenville looked down at the earth. Now he was asking, "How could you want me? How could you take me back?"

She smiled.

He turned as if to leave, then turned back to her, digging the toe of his sneaker into the dirt of Jake's kitchen garden, gouging a hole. "Oh, don't you see: there would be such eternal bitterness. I've done something to you so grievous that it could never be buried between us. It would grow and flower and fester." He stopped here, unable to go on. They should have been starting something but he wasn't letting it happen.

Then Grenville spoke again, more softly, thoughtful. "It would be the most important thing between us. It would be the story that we tell each other most often about ourselves. There may always be this imbalance of harm." He paused and then took up again. "You will become the angel and I will stay the scoundrel. I will be dependent on your mercy. I don't know if we can ever find balance again."

As his contrariness gave way to simple pure uncertainty of the future, Denise saw that change, and looked up suddenly. She didn't smile. She was biting her lip, but she held out her hands to him.

⌣·

Later, Denise and Grenville came into the house to say good-bye to Jake. They were blotchy-faced and held themselves straight, as though stunned, even while they kept hold of each other.

⌣·

Maggie's tribe came to visit. In twos and threes they peeked in on her as she slept in Jake's bedroom, while the rest of them congregated in the kitchen. Connie made a pitcher of lemonade and found some crackers and cheese. They spoke in whispers. When Hugh joined them, Jake went up to him and hugged him. "I'm so glad she's going to be OK," Jake said.

"Thank you for everything," Hugh said.

"No, no," said Jake. "Not at all. I should have taken better care of her. I should have been watching."

Hugh looked at him sharply, but embraced him again.

Jake knew that his words were ambiguous, that he was implying that he was the one who had been swimming with Maggie. Hugh did not know about Grenville's existence yet, and Jake did not wish to explain how deeply knotted into everyone's life Grenville had been.

Chapter Twenty-Six

"OH, SALLY. OH, GOD." Jake held Sally's hands across the kitchen table. Night had fallen. Cicadas combed the dark. Spring peepers straddled the trees. Katydids *kekked* their three-word sentences. Candles burned in the windows. Jake had cleaned up the Portuguese battlefield in the bathroom and then showered. Sally had grilled striped bass, zucchini, corn. She had brought four bottles of wine from Tony's vineyard. She and Jake were working now on the fragrant white dessert wine.

Maggie was still asleep in Jake's room; she had not awakened since Denise and Jake put her to bed. How perverse was human desire. For years, Jake had been moaning to the genie to bring Maggie to his bed. Now that she was there, his focus had shifted. The events of the summer had swamped him, and he felt that only Sally could bring him calm. He also needed her to save him from thinking of crawling into bed with Maggie, and to save him from himself. Jake had spent most of his adult life in a forest of obsession, where he traveled as though blind, led only by longing. Now he wanted to construct new gardens, slowly and in the light. He wondered if Sally still wanted to marry him. He was no longer young, he was neither kempt nor salaried, and he still had the drone of Maggie in the background of his heart. But he could promise gardens, though none were in evidence at the moment, except for the vegetable plot.

Sally got up and blew out the candles.

This startled Jake. He pushed back his chair and rushed to her. "Oh. Why? You're not leaving?"

"What?"

"You're not blowing them out because you're going?"

"No. I just wanted to sit in the dark."

"I was hoping that you would stay longer."

"How long?"

"I don't want to be alone."

"You wouldn't be alone: you've got Maggie."

"That's not what I mean. Where are you? I mean, could you stay for a very long time?"

"I could."

"Why did you blow the candles out?"

"We'll be able to hear the night noises better."

Jake groped in the sudden dark and then collided with Sally near the sink; there he hugged her and held onto her. Her hair smelled of charcoal smoke. He led her out onto the porch where they sat side by side.

"Sally," he said. "Oh, Sal. Oh."

"What is it?" she asked. She put her hand on his and he brought it to his lips.

"What you thought of as horrible was the least of it."

"You mean you and Gillian fucking in our garden?"

"I mean that." Jake paused. "Yes. Not even fucking; it was crazed rutting. It was nothing. I'm sorry that you saw it and that I hurt you." He did not say that seeing her standing there with her picnic basket, he and Gillian had been startled out of their lust. He did not want to excuse himself by telling this lesser truth, for he knew that the greater truth was that only Sally's chance appearance at that moment had stopped him.

"If Gillian is the least of it, what's the worst of it, then?"

"That I've been wasting our time. All these months and years we could have been doing things with each other, you and I."

"Things?"

"Gardens. Children."

"Oh." She drew away.

"I thought that's what you wanted."

"It's not that."

"What then?"

"I went to Grenville after I saw you with her."

"I guessed that you had. How did you even know about him?"

"Gillian, Tony. This is a very small town, you know."

"I know. Where?"

"Where what? Where did I sleep with him?"

"Yes."

"In the boat shed. But that's not all."

Jake stopped her there. He didn't want to know anything else. He no longer wanted to know for sure if it was Sally who killed his gardens, or Grenville, or both of them. "I deserved whatever it was," he said. "I love you."

She leaned into his shoulder. "Do you mean that?"

"I do."

Then Jake asked Sally if she would stay up all night with him, that night. He wanted to mark some passage, to bear witness to the difference of this night and its strangeness. Maggie had his bed, and that felt right, and although there was the bed in the guest room that his mother had used, they were not to be guests in their own house. They would drink wine and keep watch, listening for animals in the night.

⤙•

That was the end of the events of that summer except for one thing that happened two weeks later.

Sally and Jake had awakened before dawn and decided to bring a thermos of coffee down to the marsh. The tide was in, so they sat on one of the boulders under the scrub oak. They watched as first light bloomed in the sky and brought the land of the promontory into existence and made it hard. Sky and water were streaked with yellow and gold and they couldn't stop watching as they held each other. Then a dark piece of the shore detached itself: silhouetted against the reflections on the water was a woman standing in the back of a flat-bottomed wooden punt, poling with a single long oar. It was Maggie, and she didn't see them, but continued sculling until she got out to the middle of the river. Then she shipped her oar, crouched and moved to the middle of the boat where she retrieved something that could only have been a gasoline can. She unscrewed the top, filled it with river water, recapped it, and let it fall into the river where it sank.

Jake and Sally had been intent on watching Maggie and it wasn't until they saw her look back at the shore that they followed her gaze. Part of the black-green land was as though it had been ignited from the sunrise. Maggie's boathouse was in flames.

They left their coffee things on the rock and rushed along the edge of the marsh toward the blaze. When they got as close as they dared, Sally said, "Tell me there's no one inside." Tongues of fire licked the edges of the diamond-shaped window in the loft.

"Grenville is gone," Jake said. "All the children and their children have gone. On the day after Labor Day, Tony and I took all our boats home. Nothing but ghosts."

The smoke rose straight up into the windless dawn sky. A flaming roof beam fell to the ground with a shower of sparks. Sally gripped Jake's arm and they stood there watching the burning to make sure that it was complete.

⌣·

Tree swallows dart and swoop over the sea of tasseled corn. The tops of the stalks are golden purplish brown. Jake watches and listens. He recognizes, now, that there are different dialects of love and that he must learn to distinguish between them. With Sally in his house, everything is calm and he can breathe easily no matter what the hour is. His only wish is for this peace to continue.

For Jake the notion of getting married and living happily ever after has changed. He sees that when we marry, we are really asking, Do you take this panic-stricken man and all his demons? and, Do you take this woman, and all of hers? He will have to rewrite the ceremony to include the demons.

He used to think that with age we lose the capacity for the proud and daring assumption that we can mesh our interlocking gears with those of someone else. But now he considers his mother. Glone is still in Alexandria; she writes him letters on crisp blue paper, exhorting him to visit, congratulating him on his engagement.

The wonder is that we believe in buoyancy enough to ever dare leap into any of these dark pools. It is a branching thing—love— meandering, looping off, coming together again, with more hidden channels and tributaries than we can ever know.

About the Author

GRACE DANE MAZUR is the author of a collection of stories, *Silk,* which was a *New York Times* notable book of the year. Before becoming a writer, she was a postdoctoral research biologist at Harvard University, studying the microarchitecture of silkworms. She teaches creative writing at Harvard and lives in Cambridge and in Westport, Massachusetts, with her husband, the mathematician Barry Mazur.

Trespass has been set in Adobe Caslon, a font drawn by Carol Twombly in 1989, and based on faces cut by William Caslon in London in the 1730s. His work is the typographic epitome of the English Baroque and is remarkably well preserved. Caslon published thorough specimens, and a large collection of his punches is now in the St. Bridge Printing Library, London.

Book design by Wendy Holdman
Composition by Stanton Publication Services, St. Paul, Minnesota
Manufacturing by Friesens on acid-free paper.

Graywolf Press is a not-for-profit, independent press. The books we publish include poetry, literary fiction, essays, and cultural criticism. We are less interested in best-sellers than in talented writers who display a freshness of voice coupled with a distinct vision. We believe these are the very qualities essential to shape a vital and diverse culture.

Thankfully, many of our readers feel the same way. They have shown this through their desire to buy books by Graywolf writers; they have told us this themselves through their e-mail notes and at author events; and they have reinforced their commitment by contributing financial support, in small amounts and in large amounts, and joining the "Friends of Graywolf."

If you enjoyed this book and wish to learn more about Graywolf Press, we invite you to ask your bookseller or librarian about further Graywolf titles; or to contact us for a free catalog; or to visit our award-winning web site that features information about our forthcoming books.

We would also like to invite you to consider joining the hundreds of individuals who are already "Friends of Graywolf" by contributing to our membership program. Individual donations of any size are significant to us: they tell us that you believe that the kind of publishing we do *matters*. Our web site gives you many more details about the benefits you will enjoy as a "Friend of Graywolf"; but if you do not have online access, we urge you to contact us for a copy of our membership brochure.

www.graywolfpress.org

Graywolf Press
2402 University Avenue, Suite 203
Saint Paul, MN 55114
Phone: (651) 641-0077
Fax: (651) 641-0036
E-mail: wolves@graywolfpress.org

Other Graywolf novels you might enjoy:

Heart-Side Up by Barbara Dimmick

War Memorials by Clint McCown

The Ghost of Bridgetown by Debra Spark

Loverboy by Victoria Redel

And Give You Peace by Jessica Treadway

Ana Imagined by Perrin Ireland